DEADLY POSSESSION

M. K. Danielson

ISBN: 9798374744347

Published by M. K. Danielson
To contact the publisher email: MKEEDanielson@gmail.com

Cover design by: GetCovers

CONTENTS

PROLOGUE

Bud Rogers didn't consider himself a criminal, but he had friends who were.

He sat in an old swivel chair, his spindly, five-and-a-half foot frame resting almost horizontally. He had his feet propped up comfortably on an old wooden desk and his hands behind his head. His fingers were laced through his light brown, shoulder length hair. His small brown eyes and skinny lips gave him a smug appearance even though his heart was pumping furiously.

With his chin pressed into his chest he watched the changing expression of his friend Jimmy T through the valley formed by his blue jeans and sneakers.

They were in the large office of Jed's Tavern, a solid old building with a wild reputation that Jimmy T had nurtured since buying the place several years before. The walls were covered with posters of scantily clad women. Boxes of liquor were stacked up beneath the lone window which framed western New York's early October countryside -- a multitude of dairy farms peppered across a gently rolling landscape whose trees had just begun to change from green to orange, red and yellow.

The water in Jimmy T's private toilet never quit running and Bud could hear it during the moment of silence they experienced. He tried to ignore it as he watched Jimmy T stroked his shaggy beard. It had alternating streaks of brown and silver that clashed with his psychedelic tee shirt.

Jimmy T took a deep breath, ran his hands through the gray hair above his ears, then grabbed his pony tail and stared at his old desk for a few seconds. Bud wasn't sure what would happen next, but he tried to keep his cocky expression as Jimmy T folded his hands on the desk and said in a raspy, calculated voice, "Tell me how you know."

Bud was no longer comfortable in his position, but he didn't want to squirm around and appear scared. He began talking while still looking at Jimmy T through the frame of his expensive sneakers.

"A couple weeks ago I was hanging out with the crowd." He motioned with his eyes toward the door behind him to indicate that he meant the regular crowd at Jed's. "After a long night of beer drinking I decided to head on home, but when I got outside I could see a sheriff's cruiser sitting just up the road. I know it's only a little ways to the county line, but I didn't want to chance leaving just then. I need my license to drive for my brother you know?"

Jimmy T was well aware that Bud drove a concrete mixer for his older brother Chris. He nodded impatiently, prompting Bud to continue.

"Well anyway, I decided to throw in a chew and wait it out, you know, let some other poor bastard deal with the fuzz." Bud waited for some kind of reaction, but Jimmy T just nodded some more, waiting for him to get on with it.

Bud still wasn't sure what was going to happen, but it was too late to turn back. "After a few minutes I felt the need to unload some of the beer I'd been drinking, but I didn't feel like going back inside so I decided to just go out behind the building."

He nodded toward the back wall. Jimmy T stared at him.

"Well -- " He shifted around in his chair, despite his resolve not to. "While I was pissing, I noticed the air conditioner that usually sat in your office window was on top of the garbage heap in the dumpster, and I could hear you talking because your window was still open."

Jimmy T's eyes grew wide. He looked away and glanced at

the open window. After several seconds he turned his attention back to Bud. He gave him an icy stare but remained silent.

Bud took a deep breath, but realized he was just stalling so he said, "I assumed you were on the phone because I couldn't hear anybody else. You were talking about the goddamn border guards at the Peace Bridge and thousands of dollars and how you were always having trouble finding a reliable carrier. It didn't take a rocket scientist to figure out that you were talking about smuggling drugs into Canada."

There, it was out. Bud felt relieved for a second, but then Jimmy T's hand swiped his feet off the desk so hard and fast he thought he might fly out of the chair. Instead he just spun around like a top until Jimmy T caught him around his neck and pulled him back onto the desk. Bud felt the legs of the chair tip back, and he worried that if Jimmy T pulled him any further the chair would tip over and the arm around his neck would snap it like a twig.

That didn't quite happen. Bud just balanced there and wondered if there was any way he could get out of what he'd gotten himself into. The plaster ceiling disappeared as Jimmy T's face came into view, upside down and inches away. Bud could see little crow's feet forming around his green eyes. Little bits of spit mixed with the smell of stale beer on his face.

Jimmy T spoke slowly and deliberately. "I'm going to give you one chance to answer this question." The grip around Bud's neck tightened and he felt Jimmy T's right hand grab his jaw. "I want to know who else knows, and I want to know right fucking now."

Bud had expected Jimmy T to be pleased when he told him of his plan, but he realized if he didn't give the correct answer, things might not get that far. He didn't think Jimmy T would actually kill him, but he never expected to wind up in such an untenable position either. He was having trouble breathing but he managed to squeak out a word that sounded like nobody.

The death grip tightened and Bud thought he might pass out. Fortunately, his answer was true. He really hadn't told anybody else, and was glad of it.

Jimmy T looked right into Bud's eyes and asked, "Are you absolutely fucking sure?"

Bud could barely draw in enough air to stay conscious. He nodded his eyeballs up and down and hoped Jimmy T would take it as a yes.

He closed his eyes and concentrated on drawing another breath, wondering if Jimmy T was ever going to let him go. After a few seconds -- although it seemed longer to Bud -- he did. There was a small thud as Bud's chair returned to its natural position. He sucked in great gulps of air and watched with wonder as Jimmy T walked out of the office without looking back. He left the door open and Bud could hear the jukebox out by the bar playing The Who.

After a minute his breathing smoothed out and Jimmy T returned with two bottles of beer. Bud watched as he closed the door and moved around behind the big desk. The pissed off look Bud had seen when they were up close was gone. In its place was a very businesslike front, not smiling but not hostile either.

Jimmy T set one of the beers in front of Bud, took a big swallow from his own bottle and said, "So, what exactly was it you had in mind?"

Bud considered his words carefully, not wanting to upset Jimmy T again. Finally he began. "I could tell from your phone conversation that you have trouble getting people to carry your -- " He hesitated, not sure exactly what kind of drugs they were talking about. " -- dope across the border. I imagine that's because it's probably damned near impossible for them not to panic when it gets right down to crunch time. Is that right?"

Jimmy T nodded and said, "Yeah, that's about it. But don't tell me you want to give it a try, I know damn well you don't have what it takes. You've got to have cold steel balls in order to fool the border guards."

Bud shook his head. "No, no. I'm talking about getting a carrier who knows nothing about the dope. If you had somebody who was totally oblivious to the fact that he was carrying a load of drugs, you wouldn't have to worry about him wimping out at the last minute and tipping his hand."

Jimmy T cocked his head and looked skeptical. "I take it you have someone in mind?"

Bud sat up straight and said proudly, "Phil Waters."

Jimmy T considered Bud's answer while he took a few sips from his beer. Finally he said, "Phil goes to all those rodeos in Canada, that's not a bad idea. But how do we retrieve the stuff on the other side?"

Bud smiled. "Over the years I've asked Phil dozens of questions about what its like going to those rodeos, I've thought from time to time that I might like to try bull riding." He let out a small laugh while Jimmy T looked unimpressed. "Anyway, it seems that every rodeo has a special parking area for the contestants, usually an area where they can camp out if they want to. If you knew somebody in Canada who was into the rodeo scene -- you know, somebody who wouldn't look out of place or attract attention by always being there -- he could retrieve the stuff in the middle of the night while everybody was sleeping or off at the dance."

"The dance?" Jimmy T raised his eyebrows.

"Yeah. According to Phil, no matter what town they're in, there's always a country band playing or a pig roast or a carnival or something going on in conjunction with the rodeo. On Saturday night all the contestants usually go check it out, you know, to get a look at the local chicks and whatever."

Jimmy T swished beer around his mouth while he thought it over. Then he said, "So you're telling me that all we've got to do is plant the stuff somewhere over here, let Phil drive it across the border, and then have somebody who doesn't look suspicious recover it on the other side." He took another long pull on his beer, wiped his mouth and smiled. "That just might work."

"It's foolproof," Bud said. "As long as you've got good connections on the other side."

"Let me worry about that. What concerns you is how you're going to plant the stuff on Phil's pickup."

Bud stiffened. "Me? No, no, no. I don't want to have anything to do with planting a bunch of drugs. I just thought you could pay me for giving you such a great -- "

"Shut up. You will be the one and that's it."

"Why? I don't -- "

"Because I said so. And because you're going to make a lot more money that way. Isn't that what you really want, to make a lot of money like your brother?"

That stung Bud more than he showed. Ever since Bud's parents had died in a car accident, his brother Chris had taken his share of their inheritance and made a small fortune. It seemed like everything Chris touched turned to gold, and although Bud had a house and was doing okay for a twenty-five year old, he usually bristled whenever people reminded him that Chris was doing much better.

"How much are we talking about?" Bud said, suddenly interested.

"For every kilo of coke that is safely recovered on the other side, you'll get one thousand dollars just for planting it."

Bud was shocked. He tried to hide it by taking a drink of beer, but he couldn't believe what he'd just heard. He had no idea Jimmy T was dealing in such volume. *Good God,* he thought. *Kilos of coke!*

He did some quick math. He knew a kilo was a little over two pounds, but since he didn't really know the price of an ounce, or even a gram, he wasn't sure how much a kilo was worth. All he knew was that it was a lot. He also knew how much work it took to earn a thousand dollars driving a concrete mixer with his brother still paying 1970s wages well into the 1980s, and decided he'd be doing all right if he took Jimmy T's offer.

Jimmy T was rolling, moving forward, asking questions two and three at a time. "Where would you like to plant it, in Phil's driveway? When does he usually leave?"

"He usually leaves right after he gets out of work on Friday. And no, I would not like to plant the stuff in his driveway. He still lives on the farm with his parents and there would always be somebody around who knows me. If something should go wrong I don't want anybody associating me with him as anything more than an acquaintance. You know how it is in this small town, everybody knows what everybody's doing."

Jimmy T thought for a few seconds and said, "He works at the Fletcher Corporation, right?"

Bud nodded.

"That's a huge company with a gigantic parking lot. If I got you a security badge you could get in there and plant the stuff. You could take time off, right? I mean, you work for your brother, he'll let you skip a Friday every once in a while?"

"Yeah, I suppose but -- "

"Good, now all you have to do is run into Phil often enough to know when and where each rodeo is. That shouldn't be too hard, he comes in here at least two nights a week to play pool. I'll see that you get the packages the day before he leaves."

Things were moving much too fast for Bud. He wanted to talk things over a little more, but Jimmy T kept moving forward.

"When's the next rodeo, next weekend?"

"Yeah," Bud said. "But don't you think -- "

"I'll have to get to work, but we can pull it off. Get next Friday off. I'll get you a security pass for the Fletcher parking lot and get the stuff to you on Thursday night. Okay?"

Bud tried to back up. He needed time to think so he said, "Wait a minute. I never said I'd do it. I just came up with the idea. I don't want to have anything to do -- "

"Listen." Anger showed in Jimmy T's eyes again. "I can't afford to have you running around freely with the knowledge you have. You will be the one who plants the package, that way if you ever have thoughts about squealing on me you'll have to hang yourself too. I'm paying you good money and you will come through, end of discussion."

Bud gave it one last try. "I'm not going to squeal on you. I just don't want to get so deeply involved that I can't get out."

Jimmy T leaned forward and looked Bud straight in the eyes. An unsavory smile appeared on his face as he said, "You already are."

CHAPTER 1

Six Months Later

Jeffrey "Bud" Rogers pulled his blue four-by-four off route 490 at the exit commonly referred to as the "Fletcher" exit -- just about everyone who used it worked at the Fletcher Corporation -- and waited for the light to change. He watched with wonder as an endless stream of traffic passed from the west.

Finally, after several minutes, the light turned green. *About damned time,* Bud thought. *How the hell can these people do this every day?* He let the truck ease forward, squinting at the early morning sun. He was glad winter was finally gone.

Bud looked at his watch. It was six-forty, right in the middle of Fletcher's morning rush hour. As he inched along with the line of cars he lost himself in a song on the radio and wondered whether his ears would last longer than the six speakers that surrounded him.

He turned the volume down as he neared the entrance and checked to make sure his identification tag was fully visible to the guard. "Damn," he said. "All the decent tunes come on when you gotta go to work."

He rolled down the window and held up his badge as he glided past the guard shack. The round-faced guard looked at it with a glazed expression that told Bud he'd seen so many of them he couldn't care less. That irked Bud a little, but only because he knew Jimmy T had paid a good buck for it. Jimmy T claimed that Bud's tag was the real thing, not just a cheap imitation.

Somewhere in the bowels of a Fletcher data bank was the name Jeffrey Rogers -- with access to building #5 and all Fletcher parking lots located in the Fletcher Road complex. If anybody actually wanted to find out more, they probably would discover that Mr. Rogers had never set foot inside building #5, nor did he ever intend to.

Bud couldn't see himself sitting in a sterile building full of sterile people making sterile electronic components for automobiles, computers, tanks, missiles, and God only knew what else. Even the Fletcher Corporation's location on the outskirts of Rochester was too close to the city for Bud. He lived in western New York's farm country, a good thirty miles from both Rochester and Buffalo, and would rather spend the day driving a truck across the rural countryside delivering concrete.

Most days anyway. Certain Fridays were set aside for this other enterprise.

"Bingo," Bud said to no one as he spotted his target. In a sea of suburbanite transportation, a red Chevy pickup with a gray cap on the back wasn't hard to find.

As he pulled into a spot near the pickup, he glanced at the license plate, "CHAMP 87" was all he needed to see. He recognized it as Phil Waters', his neighbor who was the Southern Ontario Riders Association's bull riding champion the previous year. Phil was also trying to be the current year's champ, which meant that he'd be riding in Lindsay, Ontario during the upcoming weekend. The particulars of that week's episode were unimportant to Bud. All he cared about was that at three-thirty that afternoon, Phil was going to get out of work and head straight for Canada.

Bud and Phil had known each other for years. They both lived in a small town called Picton, which was nothing more than a collection of farms and houses clustered around the intersection of routes 98 and 35, about eight miles south of Batavia.

Picton was situated south of another small town, Alexander, and just north of the village of Attica. The three small towns were so closely situated, separated only on paper by the Genesee and Wyoming County boundaries, that the residents thought of the area as a single town which they fondly referred to as "County Line."

Like Phil, many of County Line's residents commuted to work in Buffalo and Rochester. Those who didn't usually filled their shopping needs with a short drive to the smaller city of Batavia.

So there Bud sat, running mission number eight, with at least six more to look forward to before November. Phil always parked near the back of the lot. It was a longer walk but there were fewer cars to compete with at quitting time so Phil could get out quicker and get on the road. Bud could usually find a spot on the far side of Phil's pickup facing away from the guard shack. He had to admit, planting the dope in the mammoth Fletcher parking lot worked superbly. With so many cars around he just blended in and nobody looked twice.

Bud shut the engine off and sat still with the window up and the radio turned down. The lot would be deserted in just a few minutes as everybody hurried inside to punch their time cards. He sat with a folder open across his lap, appearing to anyone who might walk too near that he was studying something. The last thing Bud wanted was to be unoccupied when somebody came by and wanted to talk to a coworker during the long walk to the building.

After a while, he looked up from his lap. He checked the rearview mirrors slowly, not wanting to draw attention and also not wanting to startle himself should he be surprised to see somebody. Satisfied that he was alone, he reached under the seat and pulled out two packages, each containing two kilos of fine Colombian coke. Ever since the first two trial runs Jimmy T had decided it was safe enough to risk losing four kilos instead of two.

He looked around one more time to see if anybody was around, then took the coke and four bungee cords out of the truck. He quickly slid under Phil's pickup and felt the warmth of the solar heated asphalt through his flannel shirt. He slid the packages up along the frame. They fit perfectly, Bud had told Jimmy T what he needed as far as size and shape was concerned after the first run. He hooked the bungee cords to the frame and then wrapped them around each package, hooked them again to the frame, and slid back out from under the truck. He thought about the fact that the bungee cords never came back and was glad that Jimmy T's connections never left any loose ends.

Bud started up his truck and backed out into the lane. All the parking lots were connected at the Fletcher Road complex so Bud turned and headed for the roadway that separated the offices from the manufacturing section. He drove through a maze of modern, metallic-gray, two-story buildings and merged with the traffic coming and going from the offices. He kept going to the north end of the complex, not wanting the same guard to see him twice within the hour, and exited on the opposite side from which he'd entered.

Three minutes later Bud was on 490 heading back to County Line with all six speakers blaring. He drove home enjoying the picturesque countryside with its alternating fields and forests bathed in the greenness of spring. He sang along with the radio at the top of his lungs and thought about the four thousand dollars he would receive as soon as Jimmy T's Canadian connection recovered the goods.

Making money had never been so easy.

CHAPTER 2

The Picton Diner was busier than usual, each of its ten tables were in use. Toni Birch figured it was the nice spring weather that was bringing people in. After a surprise snowstorm that had brought a fresh six inches of snow and then three weeks of rain in April, just about everybody was ready for some sunshine. Toni hoped that Patty Sinclair, her replacement for the evening shift, would show up on time so she could leave.

She thought about the skirt she'd seen in Batavia the day before. She couldn't wait to get her paycheck and go get it. For two months she'd been playing an acoustic gig at Jed's Tavern every other Friday night with her guitar and a rented sound system. The locals seemed to love it. Friday nights had been slow until Jimmy T started having live music. Toni was glad the place wasn't too big, Jed's seemed to thrive on solos and duets. Bigger bands didn't fit in there as well.

Although she liked to think the people all came for her music, she figured a miniskirt wouldn't hurt. Toni was a short girl, but she always thought she had nice legs. She was practical enough to know that half the people who showed up were regulars and would be there whether there was live music or not, but there was no doubt that she was responsible for the other half.

"Are you going stand there all day, or go out there and serve table six?" George asked.

George Lewis, owner of the Picton Diner and Toni's boss, was a big man. His wavy brown hair and wide shoulders towered above her, starkly contrasting her dirty blonde hair and blue eyes. Toni had to tip her head back to look at him. George had a square jaw, and when he wasn't smiling people who didn't know him thought he looked ornery, but the warm sparkle in his brown eyes told her that everything was fine.

"Oh, sorry," Toni said. She'd been staring out the kitchen window, mesmerized by the brightness of everything. "I guess I got lost for a minute."

George shrugged.

Toni had found out, in time, that despite his grumpy appearance and sarcastic attitude, George was really a caring person. There were very few people, if any, in County Line who didn't like George. He was a widower, about forty five but not really out of shape despite his size, and fairly handsome.

Toni had thought more than once that he would have been a prize catch in his younger days. Since losing his wife, however, George didn't go out with women very often. He could usually be seen hanging out at the Silver Nickel most nights until closing, although he'd always go to Jed's to hear his top waitress play and sing.

The phrase "like a father to me" never occurred to Toni, but George had kept a watchful eye over her since her late teens when her stepfather kicked her out of the house after she'd rejected his advances. Toni thought of George like a big brother and she loved him in a platonic way.

When she'd told him about her Friday night deal with Jimmy T and asked for a schedule change to get every other Saturday off (she didn't want to have to come in at six-thirty after playing at Jed's until closing), George granted her request. Toni had been a great waitress for almost four years, often working extra hours when some of the other help didn't show up or got sick. Twice she had even filled in as cook when George had the flu and couldn't get out of bed.

"I expect a copy of your first CD," was all he'd said.

"And free tickets to Carnegie Hall," Toni had joked.

She looked out through the order window to see who was at table six. Tommy Chandler was sitting there reading the paper. Tommy was twenty five years old, two years older than Toni. His angular frame supported well defined muscles and his straight back held his head and neck high above his shoulders. A well trimmed mustache matched his short, dark brown hair, and he had two dark eyes that turned Toni's knees to jelly.

She reminded herself that he had a girlfriend, but they were always fighting so Toni figured there was always hope. Still, she could never bring herself to steal another woman's man. As far as she was concerned cheating was for losers, even if they weren't married, and anybody who would cheat wasn't worth having. If people didn't want to be together they ought to at least have the decency to be honest with each other.

She checked her reflection in the cooler door, then grabbed a menu and walked between the rows of tables with their red and white checkered coverings. Tommy always made her feel uneasy so Toni tried an old trick she liked to use whenever she was on stage. As she neared the table, she pictured Tommy sitting there wearing nothing but a pair of black socks. It worked well and caused a natural, devilish smile to appear.

"Late lunch or early supper?" she said.

Tommy looked up from the newspaper he was reading and said, "I don't know, what would you call a cheeseburger with fries at quarter to three in the afternoon?" He smiled a little.

"Well it depends on what you had last."

"Oh yeah, I guess it does. I had a bagel so I suppose technically this is an early supper."

Toni noticed that his eyes gave her the once over as he spoke. She assumed her best French accent and said, "Would you like a bottle of wine with that?"

Tommy laughed. Everybody knew the Diner didn't have a liquor license. "Just a Pepsi."

"Coming right up." She turned and walked away, filled the Pepsi, ordered the food and went back to Tommy's table.

Toni had known Tommy's girlfriend since kindergarten so she figured she was obligated to ask, "How's Lisa?"

"Wouldn't know. We haven't spoken in about a week."

"Oh, bummer," Toni didn't hide the fact that the news uplifted her.

"Not really," Tommy said. "We should have broken up a long time ago. I'm kind of glad it's finally over, I haven't had an argument in six days."

"Well you have to do what's right for you." The conversation was getting more personal than Toni had expected.

"Yeah, I suppose."

"Are you boys running DUI roadblocks tonight?" Tommy was a deputy sheriff, so she tried to get him to talk about his job and forget about Lisa.

"I'm not, I've got tonight and tomorrow night off." Then Tommy brightened up and said, "Is this your night at Jed's?"

"Yeah," she said with a wide grin. "Nine o'clock sharp."

"Well maybe I'll see you there."

"I hope so."

An elderly couple walked in the door. "I'll be back with that burger when it's up." Toni smiled and walked toward their table.

She also noticed, in the reflection of one of the diner's large windows, that Tommy watched her as she did.

CHAPTER 3

Phil Waters had been riding in rodeos since his early teens. When he graduated from high school, he got an associates degree in computer science at Genesee Community College. While he loved the sport and competition, he didn't realistically think he'd ever be able make a living as a rodeo cowboy. So he figured he'd better find a way to make a living, and then join the large number of people who just rode on weekends.

When he was hired at the Fletcher Corporation, Phil was delighted. He had a good paying job with weekends off, retirement, and just as important for a young man with a hazardous hobby, full medical benefits.

With two days off per week being the norm, however, Phil found it was difficult to make enough trips to be competitive in any of the American associations. It just wasn't possible to cover the distances from one rodeo to the next without having a Friday or a Monday (sometimes both) off. Instead, he opted for the Southern Ontario Riders Association, with their one rodeo per weekend and close proximity to western New York fitting his schedule to a tee.

Except for the driving rock music coming from inside his pickup, he was the typical rodeo cowboy; long and lanky, short brown hair under a white straw hat, and a clean-shaven, lean face.

He sat in his truck on the side of the New York State

Thruway, surrounded by the rustic buildings of the City of Buffalo. He looked back occasionally at the officer writing him a ticket. Phil had been so wound up after getting out of work and anxious to get to the party in Lindsay that he never saw the New York State trooper sitting in the median. This was going to be his first ticket in four years.

He watched in the mirror as the tall, olive-skinned trooper made his way along the side of his truck, staying mindful of the heavy traffic. He wondered how much it was going to cost. He didn't suppose the fines were any smaller in Erie County than they were anywhere else.

The officer towered over Phil's window. He looked down through mirrored sunglasses and said, "I know the speed limit's been raised to sixty-five in some areas, but this isn't one of them. However, our supercomputer says you're squeaky clean so if you promise to slow down when you drive through here I'll let you slide."

"Hey, thanks!" Phil was clearly surprised.

The officer handed Phil his drivers license and said, "Have a nice day."

Phil pulled back out onto the Thruway and drove the last five miles to the border, happy with himself for having kept a clean record over the years.

He crossed the Niagara River at the International Peace Bridge and waited in line. Traffic was backed up with the Friday afternoon rush of weekend travelers. There were several rows of inspection booths, Phil drove to the furthest one where the line was always the shortest.

After the number of cars ahead of him were cleared, he turned off the rock 'n roll and drove onto the tilted platform that helped the inspectors look inside each vehicle. The customs man was a wrinkled old veteran that Phil had seen several times before. His no nonsense approach told Phil that he'd been working the border for years, and Phil knew from experience that the man wanted straight answers to his questions.

"What's your citizenship?" the man said.

"United States," Phil replied.

"And where are you off to this weekend?"

"Going to a rodeo in Lindsay."

"How long will you be staying in Canada?"

"Until Sunday night."

"Are you bringing anything with you other than clothes and personal items?"

"I've got one case of beer and one carton of cigarettes for a friend of mine."

That was the exact amount Phil could take into Canada without having to pay duty. The customs man said, "Good luck."

"Thank you," Phil said. He drove into Canada, thinking about how easy it was and wondering why the two countries needed a border at all.

CHAPTER 4

Bud walked across the yard between the barn and his house. He was raising a litter of piglets and had just finished feeding them. He could still hear the buzzing of the corn shredder in his ears even though he'd shut it off several minutes earlier.

The evening air was chilly but Bud didn't mind. He let the cool, fresh air fill his lungs as he opened the back door and went inside.

He lived in an old, two-story farmhouse that he and Chris had inherited when their parents died in a car crash while on vacation in Texas. The walls and floors were solid, and the natural finish on the woodwork complimented its early American style.

Bud took a shower and thought forward to hearing Toni Birch play at Jed's. He really liked Toni and was thinking of asking her out.

As he dressed himself, he heard someone come in the front door. That didn't surprise him, he had friends who stopped in frequently and he never locked his doors. County Line had never been a high crime area. Bud's parents grew up never locking their doors and now that Bud lived in their house alone, he just never got in the habit.

He came out of the bedroom to see Jimmy T sitting on his couch. He had his feet up on the coffee table and Bud noticed that he'd helped himself to a beer. In fact, Jimmy T appeared to have made himself at home except for the cold, empty fireplace.

Bud looked at the fringed leather jacket and wondered if Jimmy T would ever grow out of the sixties. It didn't seem likely and Bud found himself wondering if Jimmy T wanted something in particular or if he'd just stopped in for a beer.

"Well?" Jimmy T said in his throaty voice. He looked at his half empty beer, then tipped it back and drained off some more.

Bud assumed he was inquiring about the drug run. "Smooth as silk," he said. "No problems whatsoever."

Jimmy T took another gulp, wiped his mouth with the back of his hand and said, "I've got to hand it to you. Your little scheme works like a charm." He swilled down the rest of the beer and let out a tremendous belch.

"You want another?" Bud said.

"Nope. I've got to get over to the bar. Hopefully it'll be busy tonight. You coming out?"

"Yeah, I'm on my way there as soon as I finish getting dressed."

Jimmy T got up from the couch, set the empty bottle on the coffee table and headed toward the door. He said, "If you're nice to me maybe I'll buy you one. I'll have your money on Wednesday." Then he walked out.

Bud put on a pair of sneakers and a light leather jacket and went out to his truck. That was the first time Jimmy T had ever stopped in to ask how things had gone and it weighed on his mind. He hoped there weren't any problems. Things had been going smoothly and that's how Bud liked it.

He checked traffic and pulled out onto route 98 heading south toward Attica. After about a hundred yards he realized that he was actually going north.

"Bonehead," he said under the thunder of the stereo.

He made a quick left on Hutchins Road and did a U-turn. After waiting for a mini van, he turned and headed north on 98 again.

"What the fuck is going on here?" he said. "I don't believe I just turned left again."

Maybe you did and maybe you didn't, someone said. Bud wondered briefly if it was on the radio. He turned the volume down to about three-quarters.

Why don't you turn it down all the way so you can hear something besides that Godawful noise? the voice said clearly in a dissonant, high-handed tone.

Bud slammed on the brakes and stopped right in the middle of the road. This time he turned the radio off. "What the hell?" he said. "Don't tell me I'm losing it, I'm only twenty-five."

If you want to see twenty-six you'd better get out of the road.

Bud screamed frantically for several seconds, but something told him he probably should get out of the middle of the road. He pulled the truck over to the shoulder and stopped in front of a small ranch house. He sat there quietly, wondering what was happening.

Sorry about that little left turn right turn thing, the voice said. *I just can't help myself sometimes.*

Bud screamed again.

We're not going to get anywhere if you just keep screaming.

"Fuck you." Bud said. "This is not happening and you are not real!"

I assure you, I am quite real. Now won't you calm down so we can get to know each other?

"Fuck You! I don't want to know you. I don't believe in you and that is that. Good-bye!" Bud checked his mirror and pulled out onto the road, attempting to make a U-turn. He hit the accelerator and went straight ahead, unable to turn the wheel.

"What the fuck?" he screamed.

Perhaps we should go back to your house and discuss this, the children in that front yard are staring at you.

Bud looked out his passenger side window. There were three kids that looked to be about twelve years old watching him. "Fuck off!" he yelled. He whipped them the bird. The three kids whipped the bird back with both hands each and started laughing. They were yelling something but Bud couldn't make it out.

He turned his head back and pounded it on the steering wheel. After about thirty seconds of self abuse he quit, but only because a pair of headlights coming from the other direction brought him back to his senses.

For a few minutes he just sat there, impervious to the three kids who were trying to gain some more thoughtful gestures. He started thinking maybe it was all in his head.

Don't you find that painful, Bud?

He leaned his tender forehead on the steering wheel. "Good God, this guy even knows my name. Who are you? What do you want?"

I know, I know, a thousand questions. But first, don't you think you should get off the side of the road? People are going to start wondering about you.

"I don't give a flying fuck about anybody right now except me -- and you, whoever the hell you are." Bud realized he was talking to the voice out loud. He decided he would keep it up, the sound of his own voice was the only comforting thing around.

Bud, I wish you would stop using that "F" word so much, It's very rude.

"I give up," he said, shaking his head. "I've been possessed by a demon with good manners. Fuck you."

Instantly Bud was driving again. The formerly impossible U-turn was suddenly happening and bud was powerless to stop it.

He turned across both lanes and onto the other shoulder right in front of a Mack truck. Bud thought for a second that the chrome bulldog on the front of the truck was going to replace the ache in his forehead with something a little more permanent.

"Jesus Christ. Are you trying to get us killed?" Bud screamed. He realized, nervously, that he'd just said "us" instead of "me."

I'm just trying to show you who's in charge around here. And I doubt that I could be killed by anything as inconsequential as a truck.

"Well, who am I to argue?" Bud found himself finally heading south and said, "Where are we going?"

We are going back to your house to iron out a few details and solidify our relationship.

"It seems to me that I'm at your mercy, what's to iron out?"

I don't like to force a body into motion, it takes a lot of energy, which is something I strive to preserve.

"Well, whatever your name is, I'm having a little trouble accepting all of this. This stuff only happens in books and movies."

My name is Jasper Czymiak, and I can assure you that all of this is quite real.

Bud turned the truck into his driveway. The whole thing seemed preposterous and had him feeling strangely humorous despite his fear.

"Well, Jasper -- " he hesitated, contemplating the results of what he was about to say.

Five, one to hold the light bulb and four to turn the ladder.

"So, you can read my thoughts?" Bud said as he stopped the truck.

Indeed, and you'll have to do better than that if you want to impress me, I've heard them all.

"Yeah, I'll bet you wrote the book on Polack jokes didn't you Mr. Shimmy-ack?"

You can just call me Jasper. I think we're close enough for first names, don't you?

"Not necessarily. In fact, I don't know Jack shit about you and I don't think I -- Ouch! What the hell are you doing?" Suddenly Bud had the feeling that somebody was inside his head banging on the back of his skull with a pointed hammer. "Ouch! Don't do that, please. Ouch!"

You will learn, one way or another, to cooperate with me and to submit to my wishes. I do not like your foul mouth, but do not despair, for I prefer to get along with people and I can be very generous as well as persuasive.

"You mean every time I swear my head is going feel like that?" Bud said.

Every time you do anything I tell you not to do, or vice-versa, your head is going to feel like that.

"So we're back to square one, I'm at your mercy."

Well, technically yes, but it doesn't have to be so difficult. You have been chosen and there isn't much you can do about it, but it is up to you how hard or easily things progress.

"Chosen for what?" Bud said.

Never mind about that for now. You've already got a lot to absorb. I'll be leaving you for a while, but I won't be completely out of your life. I'm going to give you an example of my generosity and hopefully the next time we meet you will have a slightly better attitude towards our relationship.

"Well, you're the boss, although I'm not sure I like the way you use that word 'relationship,' you sound like most of the women in County Line."

A compliment I'm sure. Jasper said. He was instantly gone.

"Was that laughter?" Bud said, still talking out loud. He could feel the absence of Jasper as soon as he left. A healthy, refreshing feeling washed over him and mixed strangely with his fear.

He stayed in the driveway for several minutes trying to digest what had happened. He sat motionless with his hands on the steering wheel and his eyes staring straight ahead.

Staring without seeing.

CHAPTER 5

Toni noticed that Jed's wasn't too crowded, but at least there weren't any empty seats. She looked across the room from her perch on the stage. The long bar ran away from her against the wall on the right. The row of seats contained a host of customers in various stages of Friday night revelry. There was a small dance floor directly in front of her, with a scattering of tables beyond. At the far end of the building, in the left-hand corner, was the pool table and jukebox. The walls, stained a dingy yellow from years of exposure to cigarette smoke, were spread over with numerous mirrors and lights, each one enamored with its own catchy slogan.

The stage was made of plywood and two-by-fours and rose to the staggering height of one foot. Toni thought it made her seem almost as tall as everybody else. She was dressed in her new, navy-blue miniskirt and a white button-down blouse with a V neck. As always, whenever she performed, she'd kicked off her shoes in order to be comfortable and eliminate distractions.

She felt a familiar rush of adrenaline turn her stomach into a big knot. She remembered her public speaking teacher in high school had once said that what seemed to be a nuisance was actually a blessing in disguise. The adrenaline helped one's performance by heightening her sense of awareness -- or something like that. Toni wondered why anything that was so good for you had to be so damned unpleasant.

She strapped on her guitar, checked the microphone for the

fifteenth time, and looked around the room. She was pleased to see George sitting in the back. There were several people she didn't recognize. She thought the word must be getting out to come to Jed's every other Friday night.

"Good evening," she started. "First off, I'd like to thank you all for being here, I hope I can make it an enjoyable evening for you."

A round of applause went up as some of the regulars shouted out their favorite songs. "I'd like to dedicate this first song to the wild and crazy people of County Line." She began to play. The Friday night crowd, made up mostly of people who had stopped in for a cold one after work and hadn't left yet, went into a tizzy and made so much noise that Toni considered turning up the volume and starting over.

When she addressed the crowd again she could see Bud Rogers and his brother Chris doing shots at the far end of the bar. She sang a popular country song about drinking tequila and the crowd got so wild that Toni had to concentrate on the lyrics just to keep from laughing. She laughed anyway but at least she didn't botch the lyrics.

She watched as a group of girls lined up and tipped their heads back so Jimmy T could feed them a round of upside down shots. Bud and Chris Rogers were high fiving just about everybody they ran into as they circled the bar, singing along with Toni at the top of their lungs. Tanya Lambert, the regular bartender, was dancing on the bar, leaving Jimmy T alone to handle the customers. Her long, red hair swished back and forth while all the men eyed her large breasts. Even George grabbed a young woman and did a little two-step on his way to the bathroom.

Toni was pleasantly surprised by the crowd's reaction. She continued playing with a smile fixed on her face.

*****

Jed's calmed down after a while. Bud was fantasizing about

how it would be living with Toni. It was a scene he'd played out before. He would be lying in bed on the verge of sleep when Toni would come home after a night of playing at Jed's. Bud envisioned her coming into his bedroom and taking her clothes off. As she crawled under the covers, he would act like he just woke up and take her into his arms.

"You ready for another one?" his brother said. "Or are you just going to sit there and stare at your beer?"

Bud looked up. Chris' hair was shorter than his, and he was taller and broader in the shoulders than Bud, but their facial features were almost identical.

"Set 'em up!"

Jimmy T brought over two beers. "These are on me."

"You're a good man," Bud said. Chris said, "Thanks," at the same time.

"Don't tell anybody, you might ruin my reputation."

They drank in silence for a while, Bud stared at the stage. After a while he said, through a haze of tequila and beer, "I'm crazy about that little girl."

"Well, go get her," Chris said.

"Shit," Bud replied. Suddenly he was reminded of his encounter with Jasper on the way over. It seemed so distant that Bud wondered if he'd imagined the whole thing. "Shit," he said again, as if to reaffirm the fact that there was no little guy inside his head with a pointed hammer.

"That's the spirit," Chris said. "Just sit at the far end of the bar, tell your shot glass how you really feel, and all your dreams will come true."

The two had been through it enough times before, with one woman or another, to know there was no sense in arguing. Chris was happily married and claimed to be the expert, while Bud maintained that since Chris' wife, Cindy had all but dragged him to the alter, and since she was the only woman he'd ever had, Chris didn't know squat about how to go about getting a girl. Bud had to admit, though, sitting at the far end of the bar and staring into his beer wasn't going to get it done.

"Yeah, I know all that, but we've known each other since grade school, and I'm certain she's not interested in me."

"Ten-Four Buddy Boy, you should know as well as anybody," Chris said, "Maybe you need another shot to straighten yourself out."

"Set 'em up," he blurted.

*****

Toni was happy with the way things had gone so far. She was just about ready to take her first break when she saw Tommy Chandler come in with his girlfriend Lisa Bahn. They saw her looking their way and smiled and waved.

Lisa had long brown hair that she wore beneath a little pork pie hat, which, although Toni hated to admit it, was extremely cute. She let out a sigh, then smiled and waved back.

She thought about how her day had turned. She was totally deflated from the high she'd been on for the past hour. The last thing Toni wanted just then, however, was to take a break and have to mingle with the crowd.

She knew it was no way to act, but she couldn't help it. She decided to give the crowd something new and see how they reacted.

"I'd like to play a song for you I wrote a while back," she said. "It's kind of a downer, but I think you'll like it. It goes like this -- "

She played her song and worried that it might dampen the crowd's mood. But the song had a catchy beat despite the lonely lyrics, and as Toni looked around she was pleased to see that most of the people were listening attentively. She never considered herself to be arrogant, but she was pragmatic enough to know that part of the reason she wrote songs and played in public was to experience the exaltation that resulted when she gave a good performance. There was a certain degree of satisfaction that resulted when she knew the crowd was paying attention to her. And the extra money was nice too, of course.

When she reached the end of the song the whole place gave

her a big round of applause. Toni said, "Thank you. I named that song *Last Call,* I hope you liked it. I'm going to take a little break now. I need a beer."

She made her way across the floor, avoiding Tommy and Lisa. After a number of compliments, followed by an equal amount of thanks on her part, she made it to the bar and got a beer.

To hell with Tommy Chandler, she thought, even though she didn't mean it. She was feeling good again.

*****

Bud tried to work his way closer to Toni when she took a break, but there always seemed to be somebody talking to her. After unsuccessfully trying to get her attention, he finally gave up and went back to the other end of the bar. Once there, he turned his attention to his beer. Chris had already gone home so Bud sat in silence.

When his beer was nearly empty he tried to order another but had difficulty getting Tanya's attention because Jed's had filled up considerably. He decided, in the interim, that he didn't really need another one anyway. He grabbed his jacket and headed for the door. Just before he got there, he heard:

"Don't tell me my singing's that bad."

Bud looked up and saw Toni walking past him. "No, not at all." He had a hundred things he wanted to say to her, but he'd been caught off guard and his mind drew a blank. Before he could think of anything to say, Toni smiled and turned away. She started talking to Johnny Davis, a regular customer at Jed's.

Bud walked, a little unsteadily, out into the parking lot. Once the cool air hit him he felt the need to relieve himself so he walked around back to take care of it. As he stood there, he thought about Jimmy T, Phil Waters and the Canadian connection. In a day or two, four thousand dollars would find it's way into Bud's pockets. That picked up his spirits considerably and he thought about going back inside for another beer.

He heard Toni's voice on the sound system just then, and figured that by the time she took another break he wouldn't be able to walk or talk or even see straight. It never occurred to him that he could sit in the bar without drinking. He decided he should go home and hoped he could avoid the police on the way.

If he'd been at the Silver Nickel instead of Jed's, Bud could have taken a series of tractor paths through the farm fields and come out on route 98 right next to his house. Jed's was in the Village of Attica, however, so Bud had to take route 98 in order to get out of town. He drove the two miles to his house hoping there wouldn't be any sobriety checkpoints, and also watching closely for deer. There were always deer crossing the roads at night and the last thing Bud needed was to smash up his truck on the way home.

He made the trip without any trouble. He sat in silence in the driveway for a few minutes and considered the days events. The incident with Jasper seemed distant. His inability to talk to Toni Birch did not.

CHAPTER 6

Toni sat at the bar finishing her last beer and thinking about the night's performance. She started daydreaming about how wonderful it would feel to be on a giant stage in a big stadium with tens of thousands of people yelling and cheering. She wished she could say: "Thank you, thank you. I'd like to do one last song for you before The Grateful Dead comes out. It's the title track off my first album and it's called, Last Call."

The crowd would go wild, dancing under the hot July sun, reaching their arms up as the water from the fire hoses rains down on them, trying to keep them cool. Toni laughed out loud at the thought of all those deadheads trying to light up their waterlogged joints.

"What's so funny down there?" the bartender said. Tanya was thirty-five years old, divorced with three boys and a radiant smile that never failed to lift the spirits of those around her. She was busy washing glasses. The bar was empty except for Toni, Tanya, Jimmy T, and the two young men that had rented Toni their sound system.

"Oh nothing," Toni said. "I was just thinking about my future."

"Well I'm glad you've got a sense of humor about the whole thing," Tanya said. She had a habit of always flipping her long, red hair back over her shoulders. "Most people get scared when they think about the future."

"It was just a daydream that turned funny all of a sudden.

Nothing to worry about. Besides, if you can't at least laugh at yourself in your dreams, you might as well give up living." She finished the rest of her beer.

"I suppose," Tanya said, frowning a little. After a moment she was back to her normal, cheery self and added, "You want another beer?"

"No, I better not. Don't want to get you or Jimmy T into any trouble for serving after hours."

"I'll never tell, and Jimmy T just left out the back door."

Toni looked around. The sound system boys were just leaving with the last piece of equipment, and for a moment Toni considered having one more beer while Tanya closed up. What she really felt like doing, though, was going for a moonlight drive up into the hills. She wondered if there was an all night party and a bonfire up at Bald Eagle point.

"Thanks anyway," she said. "But I guess I'd better be going. That is, if you don't mind being here alone to close up."

"No problem," Tanya assured her. "There's nothing to worry about in this town anyway unless you heard of a recent escape from the prison."

"Well, okay," Toni said. "I suppose you're right about that, nothing exciting ever happens around here."

"You gave them a good show tonight though, girl."

"Well thank you," Toni said. She was truly flattered by Tanya's compliment. "Thank you very much." She picked up her guitar and headed for the door. She was thankful for the rental boys and was glad she didn't have to worry about all that equipment. She turned back as she left and said, "See you later."

Toni left the parking lot and headed east toward the state lands and Bald Eagle point. About a mile out of town she got a sudden urge to swing by the old loop and see if the high school kids still partied out there on weekends.

The loop was a section of a narrow road that climbed Seneca hill. It didn't really go anyplace except up to the top and then back down the other side towards Picton. Toni supposed maybe there used to be a house on top or something years ago. On the way up there was a large pond that the road followed all the way around until it came back to where it started only about twenty feet higher. On the higher side there was a wide shoulder where Toni and dozens of other high school kids had built campfires, drank beer and made out over the years.

Toni figured that from the time she was seventeen until she was nineteen or so, she must have gone there twenty or thirty times on warm nights just to hang out with the gang. There was always something happening there, people breaking up, people going steady, people puking their drunken guts out or just plain having fun.

It was the place where she had fallen in love with the idea of playing guitar after seeing a couple of the older boys from Attica there playing together one night. It was also a great place to meet new people since all the kids from Picton went to school in Alexander. It was only a few miles from the school in Alexander to the one in Attica, and that created a strange sort of separation in an otherwise tight community. Quite often the young adults were amazed at how close together they had grown up without really knowing each other as kids.

Toni remembered the loop was a place where young people went and never worried about getting busted. In fact, in all the times that Toni had been up to the loop, she only remembered seeing a police car once, and it had just driven by without even stopping.

She was thinking about how times had changed and wondered if there would be anybody up there at all as she drove up the hill. She remembered the first time she'd gone up there. It was very much like this night -- not too warm but definitely the nicest night of the year so far. She and three other girls had heard of the loop from some friends at school and decided to check it out one night. When they got up there they were surprised to see a large bonfire and fifteen or twenty people.

This night, however, Toni saw only two cars on the side of the road, both with steamed up windows. She drove past, looking out across the pond and the lights of Attica down below.

She continued up the winding road, past the TV tower and on down the other side of the hill into Picton.

The Loop road, as everybody called it, merged with route 98 heading north, so Toni kept going that way. As she passed the Picton Diner, she looked forward to being able to sleep in and not having to get up early and go to work.

When she reached the intersection of 98 and 35, she thought she would turn left and head for Slot Road. The moon and stars were shining brightly and Toni started thinking there might be a new song forming in her head.

As she attempted to slow down and turn her little car onto Slot Road, Toni discovered that she was unable to do anything but go straight on through the intersection. She began to panic when she tried to move her foot from the accelerator to the brake and couldn't. She tried to turn the wheel but her arms seemed to have a mind of their own.

When, after about a half-mile, Toni suddenly found herself turning into Bud Rogers' driveway against her will, she was terrified.

*****

Bud woke up when the headlights shined on the side of his house. He looked at his clock, it was after three in the morning. Bud had plenty of friends who sometimes stopped in to see if he wanted to party all night. Other times it would be somebody who shouldn't be driving in the first place, had finally come to his senses, and decided that Bud's couch was a good place to sleep. Bud's door was always open, but he didn't feel much like having a party. He hoped whoever it was would just crash on the sofa and be quiet.

The car outside shut off and Bud was glad to hear only one car door slam. At least it wasn't a whole carload. He tried to imagine who it might be, but the pool of names he had to pick from was too large.

He noticed that it was a bit chilly in his bedroom. He pulled the covers up over his head and thought about how great it would be to have a woman there to warm him up.

As he listened to the front door close, Bud wondered again who it was and whether or not he was going to try to wake him up to share a beer. He could hear the footsteps cross the living room and head for the hallway. He hoped maybe it was just somebody stopping to use his bathroom.

He listened as the footsteps passed the bathroom and kept coming down the hall. He expected to hear a familiar voice any second.

Instead of hearing a voice, Bud was surprised to hear his bedroom door open.

"Jesus Christ," he said. "You sure got a lot of balls." He strained to see who it was in the ray of moonlight that shone through the window. What he saw left him speechless, as well as uncertain as to whether or not he was really awake.

Toni Birch stood at the end of Bud's bed, staring at him with a look in her eyes that Bud had seen many times in his fantasies. "Holy shit," he whispered as Toni took off her denim jacket and started unbuttoning her blouse. As she unleashed her breasts, he thought about taking her erect nipples into his mouth and smiled.

When Toni dropped her miniskirt and panties, Bud thought for sure he was going to explode right then and there. The object of his fantasies was standing in front of him, completely nude, looking like she was ready to make his one big dream come true. He lay there, still a little unbelieving, unable to do anything but stare at her beautiful body.

Toni reached down and grabbed the covers. She peeled them off as a devilish smile crossed her lips. She grabbed Bud's underwear and ripped them off with a quick, powerful tug. Instantly his member was hidden inside her mouth and he was lost in a flood of ecstasy. He exploded and let out a loud moan, unable to contain his pleasure for more than a minute.

Bud remained hard and after a few playful strokes Toni mounted him. He was amazed at the intensity with which she rode him. She went up and down, front to back, and even turned around and faced the other way for a while. This time around Bud felt like he could last forever. When she turned to face him again he could see that she was lost in her own pleasure. Her hands gripped his shoulders and she threw her head back as she breathed heavily through tightly clenched teeth. Bud reached up and pinched her nipples, softly at first, then harder. Toni let out a cry, then leaned forward and started breathing in short, high pitched squeals as Bud matched her rhythm.

She climaxed again and again, then settled into a hard, fast pace and Bud's passion grew savagely. He reached down, grabbed her buttocks, and pulled himself deep inside as he came amid the tangle of sweating arms and legs.

When it was over, silently, Toni curled up next to Bud and breathed warmly onto his neck. He was awash in feelings and emotions. He couldn't seem to sort anything out so he contented himself to lay there and try to take it all in. He found himself wondering if there was any significance to the fact that the two hadn't said a word to each other since they'd seen each other at Jed's several hours earlier.

He decided it didn't matter and wondered how long it would be until they made love like that again. Bud looked down at the top of Toni's head cradled in his arm and thought he was just about as on top of the world as anybody could get.

CHAPTER 7

The first rays of sunshine came through the window and Toni woke with a start. At first she couldn't remember anything and her mind struggled to figure out where she was.

Her first impression was that she must have gotten really bombed the night before and done some wild and impulsive things which she couldn't recall. She didn't feel the least bit hung over, however. In fact she felt strong and healthy -- and well used.

Toni looked around the bedroom, wondering whose it was and how she got there. It was sparsely decorated. The walls were paneled with a light birch grain. Other than the double bed there was just a tall oak dresser by the hardwood door and a color photograph of an elderly couple on the wall. The curtains on the lone window had a paisley design that tastefully matched the bedspread.

She forced herself to think about the previous night. She remembered sitting at the bar with Tanya. Then she remembered going for a drive.

"Oh my God," she said. She sat up straight, eyes wide, looking around frantically as the memory of the previous night came to her. She wondered where Bud was and how she was going to get out of there without dealing with him.

She recalled how scared she'd become when she found herself unable to control herself in the car. And she remembered being terrified when something made her steer her car into Bud's driveway.

Toni tried to recall what happened after that but she drew a blank. She knew what had happened, was absolutely sure of it in fact, but she couldn't remember it happening. It was as though she was watching a movie up to that point and then the power went out.

She could hear water running in the shower, and beneath that she could hear Bud singing. Toni realized if she stayed there a little longer he would probably be glad to fill her in on the night's missing details.

The thought didn't appeal to her. Getting the hell out of there did.

She was up and moving instantly. She threw on her skirt and blouse, grabbed her underwear, jacket and shoes and ran down the hall. She could hear Bud singing loud and clear as she passed the bathroom.

The early morning air was cold but Toni let it penetrate her, welcoming the clean, fresh feeling it gave her. As she hobbled across the gravel driveway, thinking maybe she should have taken the time to put her shoes on, she looked at her small car sitting there and was reminded of a scary movie. She pictured herself sitting in a car that wouldn't start while Bud came out of the house and attacked her.

She found little comfort in telling herself that Bud would probably be quite friendly if she gave him the chance. After the night's terrifying experience, facing Bud Rogers was the last thing Toni wanted to do. She opened the door, threw her underwear and shoes onto the passenger seat, and jumped in behind the wheel.

A sigh of relief escaped her when she saw the keys still in the ignition, having to search for them would have been agonizing. When she turned the key there was one horrible moment when she thought the little car wasn't going to start. After a few spins the engine coughed to life, however, and Toni felt better.

She revved the engine a little before putting the car in gear, still afraid it might stall. It shot forward so fast that Toni had to swerve to keep from hitting Bud's truck. She found herself driving through the lawn, hoping it wasn't too soft after the late spring. The back tires spun a little but she kept her foot on the accelerator until she was back on the driveway and out by the road. While she waited for a milk truck to pass, she looked in the rearview mirror at the damage she'd caused to Bud's front yard. It wasn't too bad and she figured he could fix it in no time.

Toni worried about how she'd lost control of her body and mind, and she wondered if the same thing had happened to Bud. It was the strangest feeling. She knew she wasn't bombed when she left Jed's, or even when she inexplicably lost control of herself. It wasn't like somebody slipped her a Mickey and she passed out. Too many strange things had happened before the memory lapse that didn't make sense.

As she drove down route 98, Toni decided she couldn't hold Bud responsible for what had happened -- it was her who arrived at his house after all. She'd known Bud for a long time, and although they were never really close, she figured that someday she'd level with him and explain exactly what had happened. Not right away though, at that moment Toni wanted to get as far away from Bud as possible.

She drove to her apartment and took a long, hot bath. She stayed in the tub for a long time, turning the hot water on time and time again, letting the perfumed water cleanse her mind and body. Trying, at least.

After an hour and a half of soaking, Toni got out and dried herself off. The temperature outside was rising so she opened all the windows in her efficiency apartment and let the fresh air sweep the staleness from the room as she got dressed.

It looked like it was going to be a beautiful day so Toni put on a pair of white denim shorts and a purple tee shirt that matched her sneakers. There were friends she could call, but Toni felt like being alone. So she put her guitar and a roast beef sandwich in the car and started driving south on route 98.

At first she wasn't headed anyplace special, but after a

spontaneous left turn had her heading toward Warsaw, she decided to keep going that way until she reached Letchworth State Park. It was a forty minute drive and she doubted anybody from County Line would be there. She felt a need to distance herself from Bud Rogers and County Line altogether.

CHAPTER 8

Saturday afternoon was a pleasant day until Tommy Chandler burned the chicken. He and Lisa had decided to fire up the gas grill and have a cookout. A week apart had the two of them feeling glad to be together again, and spending the day without anybody else around was just what the doctor ordered.

After spending most of the morning in bed getting reacquainted they finally got up, took showers and dressed in shorts and tee shirts. Tommy rented a ranch style log cabin that had a large front porch. The sun was shining so brightly they felt they had to go out there and sit. By noon they decided they were hungry so Tommy went to the hardware store in Attica and filled the propane tank for the grill while Lisa took a wire brush to the rack.

He busied himself cooking the chicken as Lisa prepared some vegetables and made a Caesar salad in the kitchen. He had run the cable feed out the living room window and hooked up a portable TV. It was, after all, Saturday afternoon and Tommy wasn't about to miss the Grand National race.

Lisa didn't care one bit about auto racing and wondered how anybody could just sit and watch a bunch of cars go around in circles. Tommy had offered to take her to the races numerous times so she could feel the excitement and maybe change her mind, but Lisa was convinced it was a waste of time. It had been the source of many of their arguments in the past.

There was no arguing that day, however, just a lot of playful grabbing and touching. When Lisa came out to bring Tommy a beer, she noticed the TV but didn't say a word. Tommy thanked her for the beer and grabbed at her behind as she ran back into the house laughing.

He'd been cooking the chicken for almost an hour over a low flame. His stomach was growling at the beer he'd fed it for brunch. He turned the flame up and basted the chicken one more time, hoping to get a nice crispy coating on each piece.

He was flipping each piece for the last time while watching TV when the two cars in the lead spun each other out and created a spectacular wreck. All the cars behind them scrambled to avoid the first two as well as each other. About twelve of them weren't so lucky and they plowed into the inside wall, the outside wall, and a few ran right into one another.

When Tommy saw all the smoke on the TV he forgot about the chicken. He went over and stood staring at the mess of wrecked cars. One car was on fire and the safety crew was struggling to get it extinguished. Another car had flipped over and slid across the infield. It was up against the wall, trapping the driver for a few minutes while the crew punched out the passenger side window.

Tommy was totally absorbed when Lisa came out with the salad and vegetables. "Hey babe," he said. "Check this out, one car is on fire and another guy can't get out 'cause he's upside down and against the wall."

Lisa was staring at the last two pieces of chicken that Tommy hadn't flipped. A cloud of smoke rose in front of her as she looked at the television set unbelievingly. "You asshole," she said. "Look what you've done to the chicken you fucking dick."

Lisa could be very abusive and that cut through Tommy like a knife. He cringed at the thought of another argument with her. He turned around and looked at the chicken, then at Lisa. Her hair hung down over her face and Tommy could only think of how it made her look like a witch.

"Well don't just stand there," he said. As he moved over to

turn the gas off he bumped into Lisa.

She dropped the salad and screamed, "Lookout numbnuts, are you trying to kill me?"

"No I'm just trying to save the chicken, or do you think we should stand here and watch it burn for a while longer?"

"What the hell's the difference, you can't take yourself away from your circle-jerking race cars for five minutes."

Tommy looked at the chicken. There were only two burned pieces and there was still plenty of others for each of them to eat. He couldn't believe Lisa was making such a fuss, but then he realized that's how she always acted and that was the reason they were always fighting. "Okay," he said, much calmer, trying to save the day. "Let's just forget about it. We've still got the vegetables and most of the chicken is fine."

"Forget about it? Forget about it?" Lisa was obviously not contented. "How can I forget about it? You ruin our meal because you can't live without your precious race cars for one day of your life, then you damned near run me over and ruin the salad besides."

"For crying out loud," he said, his voice rising. Lisa was getting to him. "It's only two pieces, the rest is fine. Why do you have to get so upset about every little thing? Why can't we just forget about it and -- "

"Fuck you!" Lisa screamed. "I hate you."

"Well let me get your car keys you fucking bitch." Tommy was normally very easy going but Lisa had a way of raising his anger to abnormal heights. "You can take your uptight ass and get right the fuck out of my life."

He went into the house to look for Lisa's keys. He found them on the kitchen table and when he came back into the living room he threw them at her as hard as he could. Lisa was just coming into the house to get her purse and she ducked just in time. The keys hit the front door window and a crack appeared from one corner to the other. "Just get the fuck out," he said and walked back into the kitchen.

As he listened to Lisa's car start and pull out of the driveway,

Tommy filled a cooler with beer. He took it out to the front porch, ignoring the propounderance of salad that stared up at him. He rolled the gas grill over next to the TV, got a chair and sat down. He popped the top off a fresh beer, grabbed a piece of perfectly cooked chicken, put his feet up on the cooler and watched the race.

*****

Toni sat on the man-made rock wall, looking down over the gorge carved by the Genesee River. Her guitar rested on her knee. The open case lay next to her with some coins and a handful of loose bills scattered across the bottom. She'd spent most of the afternoon soaking up the sun, playing her guitar and entertaining whoever happened to come by.

The sunlight was fading behind her and Toni tried to imagine herself as the huge shadow that climbed the rock wall on the far side of the gorge. She thought about what kind of song that would make as she watched the mighty shadow envelop a small pine tree.

Just then a hawk glided out of the sunshine and into the shadow. Toni stared at the hawk and realized that it was much more powerful than the shadow was. The hawk turned and ascended and was once again back in the sunlight. *The shadow is not powerful at all,* she thought. *The shadow is as helpless as a newborn baby. The shadow has no more control over it's actions than the little pine tree that it just overtook.*

Toni found herself feeling a little sorry for the shadow.

She reached up and ran her fingers through her hair. As her eyes caught the motion across the way she realized she could see part of her own shadow along with the larger one. She sat and thought about that for a few minutes. She was already a part of the mighty shadow, and there was nothing she could do to keep herself or the hawk from becoming totally assimilated.

Toni decided it would be too difficult to write a song about time, life, space and all the continuums of the universe.

She shrugged and decided to play an old favorite before the disappearing sun made it too chilly to stay any longer.

The park was deserted but Toni didn't mind, she loved to play by herself. In fact, she often tried to explain to people that playing music didn't always have to be for somebody else's benefit, it was very rewarding to just play and sing all alone once in a while.

"This one's for you, Mr. Shadow," she said out loud and then started playing. When she sang the chorus for the last time she heard a man's voice join in behind her.

Toni was a bit startled and a little afraid because it was almost dark and the park was just about empty. She almost stopped singing and turned around to see who it was, but then decided that any guy who knew the words to a Joni Mitchell song couldn't be all bad. Besides, he had a nice voice and it sounded familiar.

When they finished, the man started clapping and Toni turned around to see Tommy Chandler smiling and applauding. He was wearing a dress shirt, blue jeans and a NASCAR windbreaker. He had a daisy clenched between his teeth and Toni couldn't help but laugh.

"Yikes," she said. "You scared me."

Tommy held up his hand, spit out the daisy and said, "Police ma'am, don't be alarmed."

Toni asked, still laughing, "How did you manage to sneak up on me like that?"

"It's my job ma'am, if I tell you I have to kill you."

"And what are you doing all the way out here in Letchworth Park?"

"Well, I was hot on the trail of this bank robber you see, when I heard an angel's voice singing to me from up the path. I was unable to resist the beckoning."

"Oh sure." Toni blushed, feeling adulated. "You're in Livingston County now and out of your jurisdiction, not to mention forty miles from home. Now why don't you tell me what brings you all the way out here by yourself."

"I will, right after you tell me what you're doing out here all by yourself." Tommy took a seat on the rock wall next to her.

Toni thought about the previous night and decided there was no way she was going to tell Tommy about that. She decided to tell half the truth. "I felt like getting away from everybody I knew for a while, so I threw my guitar into the car and wound up here. What's your story?"

"Not so fast," Tommy said as he raised a hand. "You weren't thinking about staying here were you?" He leaned out over the edge of the gorge and looked at the river three hundred feet below.

"Get back here." Toni reached out and grabbed his collar. She pulled him back into his seat and said, "Of course not. I was just enjoying myself so much that I hated to leave. Now tell me, what are you doing way out here?"

Tommy took a deep breath, stared out across the gorge and said, "I had another fight with Lisa and decided to go for a drive. It was either that or sit on the porch and get bombed out of my gourd, so I started driving and wound up here."

"I'm sorry," Toni said, even though she wasn't.

"Oh hell, don't be sorry. Me and Lisa having a fight is nothing new to anybody. I think we really did it this time though. It's finally over." After a minute he said, "Aren't you getting cold in just that shirt?"

Toni looked down at her bare arms. "Yeah," she said. "I guess I am. Good thing I've got a jacket in the car."

Tommy carried her guitar as they walked down the footpath. Toni listened quietly as he told her all about the fight with Lisa, about the racing accident and the burned chicken. He looked at her when he finished.

"So, who won the race?" she said.

"Don't tell me you're into racing?"

"Well, not like some of you gearheads, but I like to watch the big races once in a while."

"No kidding, how did you get interested?"

"Remember when I was going out with Dave Taggert a

couple years ago?"

Tommy nodded. "Yeah."

"He got some tickets for a race down in Watkins Glen that year. We went down for the day and I got hooked. That thunder from all those big engines just reaches out and grabs you."

Tommy nodded and put the guitar in the back of Toni's car. Then said, "Would you like to stop in Warsaw and get something to eat?"

Toni was a little surprised. She thought about the previous night and hesitated.

Tommy noticed her frown and said, "Just a cheeseburger or something." He held up both hands up and smiled.

His smile put her at ease. She finally grinned and said, "Okay."

"Great. Meet you at the Town Pub, last one there is a rotten egg." He turned and jogged towards his own car.

"Well Toni," she said to herself out loud. "It's what you wanted." She climbed in behind the seat and started her car.

She followed the winding road through a tunnel carved out of giant, shadowy oak trees, to the nearest park exit. She couldn't stop thinking about her encounter with Bud the night before. She wondered what had come over her and why she couldn't remember anything.

CHAPTER 9

Bud looked at the remains of his traditional Saturday night snack: Cheese, pepperoni, crackers, and a six-pack of beer. He had polished off the pepperoni stick over a half-hour earlier and was concentrating on the rest of the cheddar cheese and the Ritz crackers.

Bud loved to sit at home on Saturday nights. Most of the people in County Line went out after work on Friday, so Saturdays were usually much slower.

As the credits rolled up the TV screen, Bud threw a couple logs on the fire in the fireplace. He had been watching an old western movie on one of the late-night channels, and figured he might as well stay up late and sleep in on Sunday morning. Besides, there was no sense in going to sleep at this point because there was always a chance that one of his friends would stop in after the bars closed and wake him up anyway.

He thought about what had happened with Toni for the hundredth time. The way she came in without speaking and then the way she sneaked out had left Bud completely baffled. He didn't know if he should try calling her or what.

Once he got a strong flame burning again, Bud sat down in his large overstuffed chair and put his feet up on his favorite footstool. He reached into the Igloo cooler by the chair and grabbed a fresh bottle. With the beer in his left hand, the remote control in his right, as well as the TV screen in front of him, everything seemed right. He flipped through the channels and saw an old low-budget science fiction show.

After a moment of laughter, he changed the channels again. This time he saw a comedian doing a standup routine with a wooden dummy. Bud started laughing and there was no stopping him.

Then he heard: *What's so funny Bud?*

He stopped laughing, hoping he hadn't really heard what he thought he'd heard. Images of the past twenty-four hours flashed before him. He had a vision of the three kids whipping him the bird, and his brother Chris doing a shot of tequila down at Jed's. His mind was racing from one thought to another.

Finally, he settled down and sat still, his eyes darted around nervously as if he could see what it was that had his heart pumping so furiously. He turned the volume down on the TV. No sooner had he muted the sound when he heard:

Thank you.

"Oh no," he said. "Not you again."

Now Bud, Jasper said. *Is that any way to greet anybody? I thought we were friends. I thought you'd be glad to hear from me.*

Bud remained silent. The memory of the little guy in his head with the hammer repressed his urge to say what he really thought of their friendship.

What's the matter, Bud? Cat got your tongue?

"No," he said. "It's just, I mean, you know, you caught me by surprise."

Yes, well, I do have a tendency to sneak up on people. It's just my nature. I'd wear a bell around my neck if I could.

"What exactly are you anyway?" Bud said. He figured that was harmless enough but braced himself for the pain just in case. When there was none, he added, "And why do you have to pick on me, aren't there some other spirits having a party somewhere tonight?"

Oh, we have so much to discuss, but I suppose it's only fair for me to spell it all out for you. Let me see, where shall I begin? After a moment he said, *Why don't you make yourself comfortable? We have a lot to do tonight.*

Bud got up, put another log on the fire and grabbed a blanket that was draped over the back of the couch. On his way back to the chair he grabbed a bottle of bourbon out of a cabinet in case he needed to dull his senses. He was afraid of what he was about to hear.

He wrapped himself up in the blanket, turned the TV off and took a big swig of whiskey before saying, "Okay Jasper, let her rip."

As you know, my name is Jasper Czymiak. I was born in nineteen hundred and forty-nine in Buffalo, New York, the only child of two Polish immigrants, survivors of two World Wars and the horrible influenza pandemic. My parents died in a house fire when I was eleven years old, and I was raised in an orphanage run by a Catholic priest.

At the age of eighteen, I joined the United States Army to try to stop the spread of communism in Southeast Asia. One night during the summer of nineteen hundred and sixty-seven, near the Cambodian border, I was wounded by an RPG. Do you know what that is?

"No," Bud said. He took another swig of whiskey.

That's a rocket propelled grenade, and it landed near my bunker. My upper face was ripped almost completely off. I couldn't see. I couldn't talk. My nose was mostly gone. As I lay there, left for dead by the overrunning North Vietnamese Army, I prayed to God to please let me die.

I guess God was still mad at me for all the mean tricks I used to pull on the nuns at the orphanage. I was left lying in the jungle for the insects and rodents. I assume that I was paralyzed as well, because I couldn't move. I could only lay on the ground and listen to the sounds of the jungle. Imagine how that must have felt.

Bud didn't think that he could ever come close to imagining that, but he closed his eyes and tried anyway.

Sometime during that first night, I was confronted by a man who introduced himself as William. He communicated with me through some sort of telepathy, the same way I communicate with you. William said he could take away my suffering and give me some sort of eternal life. He said he was a vampire who lived in Cambodia, and that he was over seven hundred years old. Do you believe in vampires Bud?

Bud thought for a while before answering. "I will say that your presence here has opened my mind to a wide range of what I believe is conceivable. Either that or I've gone completely bonkers, in which case it doesn't matter."

Good enough. I'm sure that by the end of the night you'll be a true believer anyway.

Bud took another swallow of whiskey, not liking the sound of that.

Anyway, in my condition, I accepted William's offer. Had I been thinking clearly, I would have asked this William to just kill me and let me be. Unfortunately, I was in no position to bargain, helpless as I was and in excruciating pain.

William went to work right away. He started sucking the blood out of my wrist. I could not see or feel that part of my body, so I took him at his word. He explained that he would only take a portion of my blood that first night, and that he would be back each of the next two nights. The next night to suck more of my blood, and a final night so that I could take blood from him, after which I would become a vampire like himself. He placed my limp body in the remains of the bunker, and then he left.

I spent the next day in a deep sleep, without pain thankfully, waking only when William returned to suck more of my blood. After the second night, I found that I could rise out of my body and travel through the sky at will. William assured me that after completing the final transfer, I would be able to take my body with me and move and see and hear like I had never before imagined. I was very anxious to complete the process. On the last night however, when I was to take blood from William, he failed to return. I waited and waited, wondering, and unable to do anything.

On the final day of my former life, my apparently lifeless body was unceremoniously dumped into a hole in the ground and just as unceremoniously covered up as the North Vietnamese Army cleaned up our fire base they had overrun previously. As I began to suffocate,

I rose from my human body for the final time. Although I'm sure it was still barely alive at the time, I never returned.

Bud was listening intently, absolutely amazed and more scared than ever. "What happened to William?" he said.

I found out later, from a friend of mine, that during the day before the night he was supposed to return, William was killed with a stake through his heart by one of Southeast Asia's finest vampire hunters. Did you know there are people in your world who devote their entire lives to finding and killing vampires?

Bud shrugged and said, "I suppose it goes with the territory. You can't have one without the other."

That's true, Jasper said. *The only thing is, this particular vampire hunter's timing really screwed things up for me. I was never allowed to fulfill the transfer of undead blood, and so I wasn't able to take my body with me. I traveled the earth aimlessly for days until I came upon another vampire, this one living in Australia. His name was Angus, and he helped me learn how to use my powers and to understand what I had become. Unfortunately, he said that since William was the one who had taken my blood, he was the only one with whom my transformation could be completed. And since my human body was dead, there was nothing that could be done.*

I must say, however, that without Angus, I would probably have gone crazy trying to understand my newly discovered existence. He was indeed a blessing. You see, vampires generally do not consort with each other very much, they get on each others nerves.

"You mean there are others like you?" Bud said.

Not exactly, all the others have a body of their own with which to perform their necessary acts of survival. I, on the other hand, am effectively a vampire without a body, and the only one of my kind.

"Well, if you don't have a body, then you don't need to suck blood to survive," Bud said. He hoped it was true.

I'm afraid I do though, Bud. I have to use other peoples bodies to suck blood. I don't know exactly what happens to all the blood, but there is a metamorphosis of some sort that takes place. It gives me what I need to live.

"Whoa," Bud said. "Are you saying you can turn a bunch of

matter into some sort of energy? Because if you can do that, you sure as hell -- " he flinched automatically. "Ouch, sorry. You sure don't need plain old human blood to survive."

It's not a case of protein and minerals that we're talking about, Bud. It's the life-force that is carried within. Not things like DNA and plasma, but the part that makes you alive. The part that makes it impossible, even with all the technology in your world, to define life.

I can't explain it myself, we have mysteries of life in my world too, although to my knowledge there are no others like me. The beings that exist here were all born here so they don't know what it's like to be three-dimensional. To them it would seem strange and foreign. But for me it's different. I was once human, so I constantly long for human things even with my extraordinary powers. That doesn't mean that we're not without questions. I can't define the universe for you. The only sure thing is that I must have human blood periodically or I will die.

"But you said a while ago that you would prefer to be dead." Bud felt a sickening horror mounting inside his gut. He started to take another shot from the bottle, but then he feared it might come right back up, so he put the cap back on and set it down.

I suppose the word "dying" isn't entirely accurate. A vampire does not die from starvation, but he does become overwhelmed with need. It's a sensation that grows steadily with the passing of time, and if not satiated periodically it becomes unbearable. It is a fate worse than death.

Bud was sure that there would be a muddle of snack food on the floor any second. He threw the blanket off, no longer cold -- sweating even, and leaned forward, expecting a flood of whiskey, beer, cheese and crackers to come forth. The sick feeling only stayed in his guts, however, and his body refused to purge itself.

After a while, as the realization of what he was to be used for set in, Bud said, "But why did you have to pick me? Of all the people on earth, why me?" He was almost in tears.

Well, Bud, I travel the world in search of people who are evil -- people I think deserve a taste of what it is they convey toward others.

Bud was almost pleading. "Hey, I know I'm no saint, but there must be plenty of people worse than me you could pick. I mean -- "

That is true, but I like to save the worst people, the ones who are far beyond any hope of rehabilitation, to be used as victims. I also like to get to know those whom I decide are to help me, so I pick people who speak English.

"But why me?" Bud said. "I never hurt anybody."

Well there I was, just traveling around looking for somebody who I thought deserved a chance to help me with my quest for nourishment, when I found you loading four kilos of cocaine into your truck. I entered your mind to read your thoughts and was astonished at what I found. I said to myself, "Here's a man who would let one of the nicest guys in the world go to prison for most of his life just to gain a few thousand dollars for himself." The next thing you know I'm introducing myself, and here we are.

Bud was incensed. "How dare you play God with me? What gives you the right? Who the hell do you -- ouch." His anger quickly reverted to fear. The guy with the hammer was once again knocking on the back of his skull, a little harder this time. "I'm sorry," he said. "Please stop. Please."

As far as you are concerned, I am God. Jasper's voice had acquired a violent edge. *You will do well to remember that everything we do together is not open for debate. The sooner you realize that you are helpless in this matter, the sooner we can finish our business together.*

"And just how much business do we have together?" Bud hoped he wasn't overstepping his bounds. He winced instinctively.

I haven't decided yet. I'll let you know.

"And when you leave, what will become of me? Will I be as you are? Will my sucking of blood condemn me to an undead eternity?"

No, not at all. When I am gone you will be as you always were, physically.

Bud didn't need Jasper to tell him that he would never be the same mentally.

Listen Bud, it's not as bad as you're thinking. Jasper said. His condescending tone had returned. *The victims are carefully selected and they only die. Since I must go through you, they do not become bloodsuckers themselves. And besides, you won't remember a thing afterwards, just like Toni Birch doesn't remember that wonderful episode of lovemaking last night.*

Bud snapped to attention at the mention of Toni and said, "You were responsible for that?"

Did you really think she would come to you all by herself like that?

"Well, I didn't really know what to think about the whole thing. I've been thinking about it all day and most of the night trying to figure it out.

Really, Bud, don't you remember at our parting yesterday when I said, "I'm going to give you an example of my generosity and hopefully the next time we meet you will have a slightly better attitude towards our relationship?" And wasn't that what you wanted more than anything else?

Bud nodded.

Well there you go. I'm an unman of my word.

Bud didn't know if that was true or not, and in his fantasies Toni would show up of her own free will. So Bud felt some guilt there, but arguing with Jasper wasn't much fun. He sat quietly for a minute, thinking about everything. Then a thought occurred to him and he asked, "Why don't you find somebody in a coma or something and just take his body for your own?"

It has to do with William's failure to return on that final night. I was never able to complete the transfer of his undead physical existence. Therefore, I can only fully embody people for relatively short periods of time. I exist in a different realm than you now.

"I don't get it," Bud said.

Let me try to explain. Take the coffee table there next to you. It seems solid right?

"Right."

Now think of it on an atomic level. You've seen illustrations of how atoms are structured, a nucleus with orbiting electrons?

"Sure."

Good. Now, when you look at a picture of an atom it appears to have plenty of open space between the electrons and the nucleus, but when you make a coffee table out of googles of them it seems solid as a rock, understand?

"Of course. I mean, I understand it as well as anybody." Bud shrugged.

Well think of me as the space between the electrons and the nucleus. I refer to it as being one-dimensional, although that is hardly accurate. I'm different on an atomic level and therefore cannot occupy humans for extended periods of time without causing damage to their atomic structure. My own body was the only one which could have handled such an existence since it was being prepared by the ill-fated William.

I have no depth when I'm in my natural state. That means I'm not bound by the normal laws of existence you would normally associate with humans and vampires. For example, in my natural state I don't have to avoid sunlight because sunlight is a three-dimensional force and won't affect me when I'm one-dimensional. I also don't have to worry about things like wooden stakes and garlic and all that stuff that vampires don't like unless I encounter them while I'm inside a body.

Even if there was a way to assume a body full-time, I doubt that I'd be interested any more. I've become used to existing as I do. It also gives me the freedom to be different people, speaking of which, you were wonderful last night.

Bud closed his eyes and tried to absorb everything he'd just heard. And although he had already known all along, he asked, "So I was making love to you last night?"

Actually, I was making love to you. But don't worry, the moment I fully overtook that woman's body, she lost all consciousness and won't ever remember anything.

"Well that explains why she left without saying good-bye," Bud said. He suddenly found the whole thing hilarious despite his overwhelming fear. "You weren't too bad yourself."

Why thank you. And now I think it's time we started thinking about taking care of business.

Bud closed his eyes and said, "What do I have to do?"

CHAPTER 10

The Town Pub in Warsaw was an old brick building with exposed wood beams in the interior. It was a long, narrow room with a bar and pool table up front and several dining tables in the back. The walls were covered with rough-cut pine. Country music played in the background as the lone TV behind the bar silently showed an old western.

Toni and Tommy were seated in a booth along the back wall, talking about whatever came to mind. A large, black-and-white portrait of a local, long gone Civil War hero stood guard on the wall next to them. Their double order of stuffed mushrooms and loaded fries was also long gone, but the conversation kept flowing so the two had stayed for a couple drinks. After a long afternoon and evening of partying, most of the people who were there when they showed up had left. The rest were finally calming down.

"That was a whale of a birthday party they had in here tonight," Tommy said. "I almost felt like we were intruding."

"I don't think anybody even noticed us when we came in." Toni shook her head.

"Good point. I thought it was sort of dying out right about the time we showed up, but then that guy with the straw hat started dancing on the pool table and all hell broke loose."

An ice cube bounced across their table. Toni jumped back. "Oh no, not again." They both laughed as the remaining handful of birthday well-wishers broke into another ice cube war. It was the fourth one since the two of them had sat down three hours earlier.

Somebody whipped a piece of ice from his drink at Shirley, the rotund bartender who had also been Toni and Tommy's waitress. Shirley retaliated with a whole scoop full from the ice maker. That resulted in three young men, and a girl that Toni figured couldn't possibly be over twenty-one, attacking Shirley from all sides.

One of the young men, the big one with a beard they called "Oso," got a little too close and Shirley squirted him in the face with a steady stream of club soda from that nozzle thing that supplies a bartender with all the different mixers at the touch of a button.

Oso let out a surprised scream and wiped his face with his hands, his beard glistened in the dim light. He vaulted over the bar and tackled Shirley while yelling out, "Chicken pile!" The rest of the gang converged on the two behind the bar, oblivious to the days accumulation of dirt and spilled drinks.

Toni looked at Tommy with a warm smile and said, "I've had a great time talking to you tonight." Then, looking over at the partiers she said, "But I think it's time to get out of here."

Tommy just nodded, as though he was thinking exactly the same thing. As they grabbed their jackets and headed for the door they kept their distance from the others just to be safe.

Outside, they walked down Main St. toward their cars. Both sides of the village's busiest street were lined with century-old, two- and three-story brick buildings. At the north end of the main drag was a war monument with a small traffic circle around it. Just past that, a sheriff's patrol car came out from behind the new jailhouse, also a brick building, and drove towards the couple. Tommy recognized the driver and waved to his Wyoming County counterpart.

When the car had passed he turned to Toni and said, "I know that to most people this would sound like a lot of bull because we just broke up today, but I'm sure it's over between me and Lisa. In fact, it's been over for a while, we just didn't know it or want to believe it. Anyway, I'd really like to get together with you again. I enjoy your company."

Toni had been hoping for something like this, but she really wasn't sure what she would say if the time came. Her mind was bombarded with thoughts about Bud Rogers and Lisa Bahn. She'd been anxious and confused for most of the day, but she knew that deep down she was attracted to Tommy. She put her hands in her jacket pockets, looked him in the eyes and said, "'kay." It surprised her that half the word stuck in her throat. Tommy smiled and Toni found that attraction working it's way up.

"If you're not busy tomorrow," he said. "Some of the guys I work with are having a race party in Batavia. There should be several couples there. It starts at one o'clock if you'd like to go."

Toni thought for a moment and said, "I've got to work at the diner at six tomorrow night, but the race should be over in plenty of time for that, so I guess I'll say yes."

"Great," Tommy said. Then he added, with mock sincerity, "You're not a Ford fan are you?"

Toni laughed. "Not hardly."

"Good, for a minute there I thought we might have to call the whole thing off."

Not hardly, she almost repeated.

Tommy stuck out his hand and Toni gave him hers. "I'll pick you up at twelve-thirty," he said.

"Don't be late, I hate to miss the start."

There was a brief moment when Toni thought he might lean forward and kiss her, but then he just gave her hand a gentle squeeze.

"Me too." Tommy turned and walked towards his car, saying over his shoulder, "Be careful going home, will you?"

"You got it." Toni climbed into her car, looked at herself in the mirror and smiled as she started it up.

CHAPTER 11

"You know," Bud said. "I really shouldn't be driving considering all the beer and whiskey I had tonight."

Don't worry about a thing, I'm right here to take over if anything goes wrong, and you wouldn't believe how quick my reflexes are.

Then why didn't you get out of the way of that RPG back in Nam, Bud thought, instantly wishing he hadn't.

I heard that, Jasper said. *I was a mere mortal back then, just as you are. Or have you forgotten already?*

"If I'm so normal, then how come I'm driving down a cow path with my lights off at two-thirty in the morning?"

Just think of yourself as helping a friend in need.

Bud started to think of several contrary opinions, but the little guy with the hammer kept his thoughts as innocent as a newborn baby. After a minute he asked, "Why do we have to do this so close to home anyway? I mean, everybody who hangs out at the Silver Nickel knows me. In fact, everybody knows everybody here in County Line. The chances of us, I mean me, being seen by somebody who recognizes me are pretty darned good."

Time is of the essence, it's been too long since my last meal. I'm good for about a week, then during the next few days my hunger grows furiously. Besides, our first victim deserves everything he gets.

"Who is our first victim anyway?" Bud realized for the first time that it was probably going to be someone he knew.

George Lewis.

"What? George Lewis of the Picton Diner?"

Yes. Do you disapprove?

"Well no, not if you're going to hit me with that hammer thing. But why George, he just might be the nicest guy on the face of the earth?

That's what all you mortals think. What would you say if I told you that George Lewis killed his wife?

"I'd say you're full of sh--, I mean, no way. George wrote the book on nice guys."

Well Buddy boy, you just stick with me and you'll find out lots of things you never knew.

"You're the boss." Bud shrugged. "I still find that hard to believe though. George Lewis killed his wife. I thought she fell off the route 35 bridge and went through the ice."

Actually, she was pushed. And while we're on the subject, did you know that George once raped and killed a twelve year old girl in Vietnam?

"No way." Bud wondered if it was true or if Jasper was just making it up to ease his misgivings about what they were about to do.

Believe it Bud. I may be something you consider truly evil, and even though I can't help being what I am, I am not a liar or a killer of innocent people.

"Well, if you say so. Besides, I'm in no position to argue."

Good answer. Pull off into this field, it's just over the hill from where we want to be.

The Silver Nickel was located on route 238, about three-quarters of a mile from the village of Attica, and just over the Genesee County line. It had a large gravel parking lot behind the building, and there was a crude roadway that ran into a hayfield farther back. It was mostly a tractor path that ran through to the Waters' farm, and since it was over a mile to the next road, the roadway itself turned into a complex series of access roads to all of the different fields. They had been used for years and were rock solid, so when the snow was gone, many of the locals used them to get from one point to another.

The path behind the Nickel was one of their favorites. Many of the patrons could get almost all the way home without ever driving on the highway. Bud and Jasper were coming in from the back side. It was a route Bud had used many times over the years.

He pulled his truck off the roadway, into the edge of the hayfield where Jasper had indicated. He knew from experience that it was just over two hundred yards, over a slight hill, to a small patch of woods and then to the parking lot of the Nickel.

"I don't want to tell you your business, Jasper, but it's almost three AM and the bar's been closed for about an hour. What makes you think George is anywhere near here?"

He'll be here. About three nights a week George leaves with the rest of the crowd at closing time. Instead of going home he parks his car just inside the edge of that patch of woods. When the parking lot clears out, he returns to help the bartender clean up.

"See, I told you George was a nice guy. But why would he hide his car just to stick around and help Mindy clean up the bar?"

Because when they finish cleaning the bar, George and Mindy like to get it on.

"Get out of town!" Bud couldn't believe it. Small towns like County Line didn't hold secrets for very long. "What would she want with an old fart like George Lewis? She's not even half his age."

While I am privy to a lot of information that escapes you, Bud, do not expect me to be able to tell you what it is that makes women do the things they do.

"Yeah, I hear you there. What's the plan?"

We walk over to George's car and wait for him.

*****

Bud sat on a fallen tree about twenty feet from George's car. His camouflage clothing hid him very well, even with the almost full moon casting eerie shadows over the entire scene. It was a chilly evening, but Bud's camo clothes were made for hunting deer in the late fall so he was plenty warm. He took out a can of chewing tobacco and put a pinch between his cheek and gum. He hoped a little nicotine would calm him. His heart was racing and his stomach kept trying to climb up into his throat. He sat motionless and tried not to think of what he was about to do. He tried to picture George doing the things that Jasper had said. It was certainly hard to believe.

Jasper had left him temporarily, and Bud at least felt easier about letting his mind wander. The thought of getting out of there lasted about one second. He didn't know of any place he could he go. Getting away from Jasper wasn't like folding on a bad poker hand. Besides, although he was scared out of his mind, he had to admit it was a lot more exciting than watching TV all night.

He felt Jasper enter him a split second before he heard:

Be quiet now, Bud, dinner's on the way. Jasper sounded excited. *And for crying out loud, get that garbage out of your mouth, we've got some bloodsucking to do.*

Bud spit out the tobacco wad and wished he was anyplace except where he was. *Jasper, is there going be much of a fight?* He said in his mind rather than talking out loud. He didn't want George to hear him. *I'd just as soon not leave too much sign of a struggle?*

No, don't worry. Once I fully embody you, we will be just as powerful as any other vampire. Once he looks into your eyes he will be unable to resist. And he will look into your eyes, mere mortals caught out in the open are no match for the power of the undead. In fact, there will be very little blood, if any. I promise not to spill a drop. Now be still, he's coming.

Bud felt his mouth water. Horror struck him as he felt two of his teeth grow slowly into fangs. He sat there, his body shaking, hoping to God that what Jasper had said about him not remembering anything would be true. He could hear George walking along the edge of the woods and he waited anxiously for the moment when Jasper would take him over and he would black out.

*****

When Bud came back, he was looking down at the lifeless form of George Lewis, a man he had known all his life. Bud had eaten countless meals in his diner, and George had been his coach when he played little league baseball. He was still trying to picture George doing the things Jasper had accused him of when Jasper said:

Thank you, Bud. You did a wonderful job.

Bud had been joking somewhat before, but he didn't feel much like it anymore. He just stood there looking down at what used to be George Lewis. Finally he said, "What do we do now?"

Well I don't know about you, but after a big meal I like to take a nap. In fact, I'll be leaving you for a few days, but I'll be back to check on you.

"Don't you dare leave me out here all alone you son-of-a--" Bud didn't dare finish, the memory of extreme pain was still quite vivid. "Come on Jasper," he pleaded. "Stick around, I don't want to be alone with this -- " He struggled for a moment before saying, "I don't want to be alone in the woods with a dead body."

But Bud, I can't help you. Besides, you've been recruited to help me, remember? Not the other way around.

"But what am I supposed to do?"

If I were you, I'd get rid of the body. The longer it takes to find it, the longer it will be before they start looking for the killer.

"Yeah, but -- "

Farewell my friend, I'll return, Jasper said. Then he was gone.

Bud felt that same healthy feeling wash over him. It was a stark contrast to the sick feeling that had accompanied him for most of the night. He looked down at the body again, took off one of the thin gloves which Jasper had recommended he wear, and wiped his forehead. He was sweating like a pig.

After a while, he realized he couldn't just leave the body there. Somebody working the Waters farm would be sure to spot it within a day or two. He considered leaving the car because he figured people would be looking for George by the next day and Bud didn't think it would matter where they found his car as long as they couldn't trace it to him.

Bud looked around for a moment and decided there was no way he was going to haul George's enormous body all the way back to his truck. He closed his eyes for a few seconds, wishing the scene before him would go away. Of course it didn't, so Bud put his glove back on and went to work.

He opened the door to the back seat of George's car, then dragged him the fifteen feet or so from where he lay. *Man, this guys heavy*, he thought. Bud had shot several deer in his life and he figured the biggest one weighed about a hundred and eighty pounds, not counting the pile of guts he always left behind for the wildlife. He guessed that George weighed in at more than two-fifty.

Bud hoisted what was left of George up into the back seat of his own car. He closed the door and got in the driver's seat. He was glad the keys were in it, it gave him one less thing to deal with. He turned the ignition switch and let out a sigh of relief when the car started even though it was practically brand new. He didn't want to think of what would happen if it didn't.

He drove down the roadway, past his own vehicle. Bud figured he would go to the railroad tracks, take the access road along them until he reached Johnson's woods. It was at least a half-mile through the woods to route 35. He planned to drag George's body as far out into those woods as he could and hope the coyotes, foxes and raccoons would spread him out piece by piece. He decided he'd take George's clothes and all his ID and burn it, that way there wouldn't be any trace of George left once the wildlife disposed of him. He looked back at the dead body, amazed at how white it was. "Sorry George," he said. "It's the best I can do under the circumstances."

He wondered if it was true.

As Bud drove, he worried about how long it would take him to dispose of George, get the car to George's house -- he figured that would be the least suspicious place for it -- and get back to his truck. He knew he had to get it done before the sun came up. He didn't want anybody to see him driving around in George's car, or even walking around in the middle of the night for that matter.

He reached the railroad tracks and turned down the road that paralleled them. There's nothing like a good set of tracks to give a person access to otherwise remote places. He drove on, hoping his plan would work. After a while he looked down at his clothes, then checked himself in the rearview mirror. "I'll be damned," he said out loud. He had developed a habit of doing that since meeting Jasper. "Jasper was right, not a drop of blood anywhere."

CHAPTER 12

The morning sun fought against the heavy curtains. Toni lay snuggled up in her bed, safely shielded from the relentless, blinding rays that tried to divorce her from a pleasant dream.

The telephone on the night stand succeeded where the sun failed. Toni struggled for a moment, temporarily lost between sleepy dreams and reality. The second ring put the dream to rest for good. She looked at the clock, then closed her eyes and sighed. It was just before seven, and the only person who ever called that early was George.

She had fleeting images of the previous night's meeting with Tommy, and she remembered their agreement to go watch the race with his friends. She knew the phone was ringing because somebody hadn't shown up at the diner, and she knew that George wouldn't have called her unless he absolutely needed her to come in. Before she could try thinking of a way to help George and still see Tommy, the phone rang a third time.

For one guilty moment Toni considered letting it ring until the answering machine picked up, pretending not to be home. She could never do that, though. George had been her best friend for several years. He'd gone well out of his way to look after Toni during her late teens. As she grew older she came to realize that George had, in a very subtle way, steered her away from the life of drugs and dependency for which she was undoubtedly headed.

George's approach had been very delicate. Rather than try to intimidate Toni, causing her rebellious nature to further alienate her from the few remaining people who cared, George became Toni's friend. He then went on to treat her as his equal, never portraying himself as better than her or anyone else, while encouraging her to do the same. As their friendship grew, George would try to show Toni, through examples of his own life as well as others, how the decisions people make can affect their entire lives.

She thought about his subtle references to statistics on single parents, and to the high percentage of inmates over in Attica who were there because of drugs, and the many other little things George was always nonchalantly pointing out. The more Toni grew up, the more she came to appreciate what George had done for her. He'd helped her to feel good about herself again, and she learned to value things like responsibility and prudence.

As these feelings came to her, the phone rang a fourth time. Toni picked it up without any more hesitation. George was that important.

"Hello," she said.

She was surprised to hear Patty Sinclair's squeaky, mouse-like voice say, "Toni, I went to work this morning and George wasn't there. The place is all locked up just like when we closed last night."

Toni was shocked. She'd never known George not to show up unless he was just too sick, but if that had been the case he would have called her to fill in. She couldn't think of anything to say right away.

Patty obviously didn't like the silence much. She also must have known that George's behavior was out of character. In a shaky voice she said, "Toni?"

Toni finally said, "Look, I'm sure there's a reason. George hasn't taken a vacation in who knows how long, maybe he just decided he needed a day off and went fishing or something. Did you try calling him?"

"Yeah. I didn't know what else to do so I went home and tried calling him." Patty's voice became even softer. "When I didn't get any answer I figured I should call you. I know it's early, you're not mad at me are you?"

Toni almost laughed. Sometimes Patty could be such a wimp. "No, I'm not mad. I just don't know what to say. I can't imagine where George might be, but maybe he's just going to be late." She thought of the dream she'd been having and wondered if there was any way she could get back to sleep and continue it. "Why don't you give him a half-hour or so then try again."

Patty hesitated, then finally squeaked, "Okay. Okay I'll do that. But what if something's wrong?"

"George is a big boy, Patty. I'm sure he'll be all right."

"Okay, I'm sorry Toni."

Toni couldn't help but laugh. "Don't worry about it Patty. Everything is going to be fine. I'll talk to you later."

"Okay. Sorry."

Toni shook her head and hung up. She closed her eyes and burrowed into her blankets, convinced that she could get back to sleep. Unfortunately, the conversation with Patty kept repeating itself in her mind. She had told Patty everything was going to be fine. The thing was, the more she thought about it, the less likely that seemed. It really was out of character for George not to show up or at least call. And if he wasn't home, then he must be someplace else. That meant it was more than just a case of George oversleeping.

Toni buried her head under her pillow in one final attempt to let it all go, but it was no use, she could no more go to sleep than she could sprout wings. She reached for the phone and tried George's number. When she got the answering machine she couldn't help leaving a nasty sounding message.

"George, it's Toni. It's seven o'clock Sunday morning. Where the hell are you?" She still believed there would be a logical explanation for everything, and she wasn't worried about George taking offense to the message. She had never spoken a cross word to him in her life, and the two often communicated in mock anger. It was an integral part of their friendship.

Unable to sleep, but still certain that George would show up sometime, Toni decided to call Patty back. She had a spare key and although it had been a while since she'd filled in for George as cook, she thought it seemed like the right thing to do.

She called Patty and arranged to meet at the diner at eight o'clock. Then she crawled out of bed, bidding a final farewell to her sweet dream and thinking of how George was going to owe her one.

Just before she got into the shower, Toni remembered her date with Tommy. They hadn't exchanged numbers, and like most police officers, Tommy's was unlisted. She thought about dialing 911 and asking the dispatcher for deputy Chandler's phone number, but she didn't think it would go over very well, nor did she think they would give it to her.

Oh well, she thought. *It's the thought that counts. If Tommy is the man I think he is, he'll understand how important George is to me.*

*****

Bud woke up feeling sensational. He couldn't remember the last time he'd slept so soundly. His ordeal with Jasper the night before seemed like a distant memory. It was almost as if it had been a dream, or maybe a movie Bud had seen.

He made his way toward the bathroom in his old farmhouse. He walked down the hall, his bare feet skipping along the hardwood floor like those of a kid on his way home from school.

Except for the towel over his shoulder he was nude. There was no reason for him not to be, he lived alone in the country, it just never seemed right before. Growing up in the house with his parents and brother, he'd become accustomed to having other people around, so he always stayed in the habit of wearing something.

It just seemed right on that particular morning for Bud to walk around naked, he felt so alive. He knew, of course, that his euphoria was the result of Jasper's besiegement and their subsequent collaboration on the previous night's activities, but he felt so good it didn't matter. He got the water going good and hot, took a long shower during which he serenaded the porcelain and woodwork at the top of his lungs, then wrapped the big towel around himself and went out onto the front porch.

He sat down in a plastic lawn chair, put his feet up on the railing, and let the sun shine down on him. It was the beginning of a beautiful day, even though it was still chilly. Bud didn't seem to notice. He clamped his hands behind his head and howled at the sun like a lonely coyote might howl at the moon. Then he laughed at himself.

He let his mind wander. He thought about the way Toni Birch had come to him on Friday night. His business with Jasper might turn out to be a lot of fun. He thought of the four thousand dollars that was on it's way to him in a day or two, and of how someday he would be able to quit working for his brother and be his own boss, even though he had no idea what business that might be in.

It was true that Jasper claimed to detest Bud's involvement in the smuggling scheme, and that was undoubtedly the reason Jasper had chosen Bud to be his puppet, but as good as Bud felt it didn't seem like it was going to be a problem.

He stood up, aiming to go back inside to get some breakfast. Just as he turned to go through the front door, a car went by.

George!

For a moment Bud thought it was George Lewis' car, but of course that was unlikely. He thought about how he'd dragged George's body out into Johnson's woods and told himself he'd been mistaken. Route 98 was a busy road, and it was just somebody driving by in a car like George's. He shook his head and went inside.

As he crossed through the living room he glanced over at the baseball on the mantle above the fireplace. He didn't need to see the writing on it to know what it said:

[Bud Rogers -- no hitter, May 28, 1976 -- Congratulations,

Coach Lewis]

Bud was almost to the kitchen when it hit him. The elation was gone instantly. He stopped, looked back at the baseball, and almost fell to the floor as the strength went out of him. He made his way back to his couch. Tears filled his eyes as he thought about how he had helped murder one of the finest people on the face of the earth.

He grabbed a pillow and held it over his face, ashamed of the sobs that spilled out of him. He pictured the day in his mind. His little-league teammates were all jumping up and down, his mother and father were already bragging, and his coach, George Lewis, had come over and handed Bud the ball that made the last out.

"Here, this is for you," George had said. "It'll give you something to tell your grandchildren."

Bud wondered if his mother and father would be so proud of him now. He leaned over and wept, his face buried in the couch, muffling his wailing sobs.

* * * * *

At about twelve-fifteen, as Tommy was driving down route 98 to pick up Toni, he saw her car parked at the diner. Assuming that somebody hadn't shown up and that she had to work, he stopped in, although a little discouraged that she hadn't bothered to tell him. When he walked in and saw Toni behind the grill, he realized that it must have been George who hadn't shown up. When Toni saw him she immediately waved him into the kitchen so they could talk. The diner was filling up with people who were just getting out of church and Tommy could sense her urgency to explain.

He remained silent while Toni told him what had happened. He was still a little dismayed at her failure to at least call him, although she was obviously very busy. As she finished telling her story, Tommy considered mentioning this to her, but before he could speak, she said, "And you haven't given me your number and like most cops it's unlisted."

He felt like a heel, and he was grateful that he hadn't spoken too soon so he wouldn't have to get his foot out of his mouth. "I understand," he said. "Let me give it to you now so we won't have this problem again."

As he wrote his number on the back of an order slip, he said, "I know you're very busy right now but I really want to get together and spend some time with you after things calm down a bit."

Toni smiled in spite of it all, and said, "Me too."

Tommy thought for a moment, then said, "I took the afternoon off to be with you." He realized immediately how selfish that sounded and put both hands up and smiled. "What I'm trying to say is, even though I'm not on duty, I could poke around and see if I can find out anything, unless someone's already filed a formal complaint, in which case I'd have to stay away from the case."

"Thanks," Toni said. "George doesn't have any family so I guess I'd have to be the one to do that. Do you think I should?"

"Well, do you have any idea at all where he might be? I mean, is there any reason to suspect that something's seriously wrong?"

"I don't know, it's just not like George. I can't understand it, but I also can't picture anybody doing him harm. You know what I mean," Toni said, more a statement than a question.

Tommy nodded. "I saw his car is in his driveway, I can at least swing by and make sure he's not home."

Toni smiled at him and said, "I'd appreciate it. And I guess if nobody's heard from him by tonight maybe I should file a formal complaint or whatever. Do I have to wait twenty-four hours?"

"No, that's just in the movies. Don't be afraid, especially if you suspect anything. Anything at all."

"That's just it. I don't suspect anything. It just bothers me that he hasn't called anybody."

Tommy put his hand on Toni's shoulder and said, "Just hang in there, I'm sure everything will turn out fine."

They nodded and smiled at each other as Tommy turned and left. He walked out to his car. When he turned to get in he was happy to see Toni still watching him out the window. He waved. She smiled and waved back.

*****

"How did you do?" Phil Waters' mother asked. She had sharp features and short, gray hair. Steady exercise had kept her figure well defined even in her early fifties. She wasn't nearly as tall as Phil, but she looked down at him through a pair of round glasses as he sat in the spacious kitchen in their farmhouse.

A cup of hot cocoa sat on the hardwood table in front of him. He was surrounded by yellow, painted cupboards and hundreds of black and white cows on the wallpaper.

"I came in third, got two hundred and eighty bucks," Phil said. "And no broken bones," he added quickly, knowing what his mother's next question would be. She always waited up for him to come home and Phil was grateful, it helped him unwind from his fast-paced weekend.

He rubbed his right side absentmindedly. He may not have broken any bones, but his ribs were definitely a little tender, the result of his particular bull giving him a kick during his dismount.

"Are you sure you didn't break your ribs?" she said.

"No, it's just a little tender."

"This is no time for heroes, you know. Your father got kicked in the ribs by a cow once when you were just a little boy and was too proud to tell anybody, he just kept right on working -- "

"Until you caught him spitting up blood and made him go to the doctor and saved his life," Phil said.

His mother looked at him sternly. "I don't know why you can't just play softball for fun like the rest of the kids your age. Why do you have to spend your weekends driving all over God's creation just to jump on wild animals? It can't be the money, two hundred and eighty dollars won't even make a monthly payment on that truck of yours. You probably spent more than that on gas and beer. Not to mention all the miles you put on."

Phil rolled his eyes and took a deep breath. His mother said the same thing every time he came home so he knew there was no sense in arguing. Besides, she wasn't exactly wrong. He stared at the table and rubbed his ribs.

"Well I'm glad you got third place," she said. She glared at Phil, watching closely as he massaged his right side.

Thinking that he'd had enough of that particular subject, Phil decided to change the course of their conversation. He asked his standard Sunday night question. "Did I miss anything exciting this weekend?"

Nothing exciting ever happened in County Line, but Phil's mother could gossip with the best of them. He was prepared for something like: "The police had to break up a fight at Jed's Tavern," or "Your father won another bowling tournament."

His mother surprised him when she said, "George Lewis has disappeared without so much as a trace."

"Disappeared?"

"Vanished, right off the face of the earth. Nobody has a clue where he is. His car is in the driveway. That little Birch girl ran the diner today and then went to the sheriff's office to get them officially involved. You know she's a wonderful girl. I don't know why you don't ask her out. Maybe she could keep you home once in a while."

Phil couldn't argue with that, but he had to say something. "She's going out with Dave Taggert."

"She hasn't gone out with Dave Taggert in over a year and you know it," his mother said. She shook her head, put her hands on her hips and added, "I don't think you like girls. I think all this weekend roughhousing has softened your brain. She's a wonderful girl. Why don't you ask her out?"

Phil didn't really have an answer for that. He'd thought about it a time or two, but he was a little shy and always gone on the weekends so he never seemed to get around to it. He decided to change the subject again. He got up, a little too quickly for his ribs but he managed to keep from letting it show. He headed down the hall towards his mother's sewing room and asked, "How's my suit coming?"

His mother followed him into the small room. It was littered with numerous articles of homemade clothing in various stages of development. Phil held up the upper half of a bigfoot costume, the right arm had been freshly mended.

"It's fine," his mother said. "But I can't believe you're going to go out and try that stunt again. You almost hung yourself on that old fence the last time. Why do you want to start a silly rumor anyway? Can't you just play basketball or something? What is it with you? Didn't I raise you to be a good boy?"

Phil smiled and said, "I just want to give you and your card-playing buddies something to chat about. Are you sure nobody said anything about seeing me last time?"

"I haven't heard a word." She crossed her arms and said with a frown, "Why don't you forget about this silly scheme? No wonder girls won't go out with you, you're nuts."

Phil couldn't help laughing as he slipped the top half of the suit on. "I can't wait to give it another try." He looked toward the door.

"Don't you even think about going out there tonight," his mother said. "It's raining and you're in no condition." She drove the point home by poking Phil in his already tender ribs.

He jumped back and looked at her incredulously, but he got the point and knew she was right. He took the suit off and said, "Soon."

Phil's mother turned and walked out. He laughed as she walked down the hall going on about girls and wild animals and kids growing up crazier every generation.

"Soon," he said again.

CHAPTER 13

When Tommy didn't see or hear from Toni, he decided to call her after he left work on Monday. He realized it was eleven o'clock, but he couldn't help himself. He was surprised when she answered on the first ring.

"Hello?"

"Hi Toni, it's me Tommy. I hope it's not too late."

"No, not at all. In fact, I just walked in the door."

"I suppose you've got to get up in a few hours to open up, I just wanted to say hello."

"Actually, I've decided not to open for breakfast. It's just not worth it during the week, and it makes for an awfully long day. I don't have to be there until eleven. Has Mr. -- um, Griswell found anything out?" Ronald Griswell was the investigator assigned to George's case.

"Not much. There just aren't any leads. I think he spent most of the day trying to figure out who saw him last, but I was out on the road so I really don't know."

"I wish George would at least call somebody and let us know where he is. I'm having a terrible time sleeping."

"I know. It must be really hard on you. I'll tell you what, I could grab a six-pack and give you a famous Chandler back rub."

A long silence followed. Tommy became very anxious. Finally he said, "Toni?"

"Yeah, I'm still here. It's just that I wasn't prepared for that, you know?"

"Yeah, I know. I'm sorry. But in all honesty, I wasn't trying to move too fast or anything like that, it's just that I think about you all the time and I'd love to be able to spend some time with you."

There was more silence. "Listen," Tommy said. "I don't want you to think I'm pressuring you or anything, but you can ask anybody who knows me and they'll tell you that my word is as good as gold. If I say I'm just coming over to have a couple of beers, then that's all I mean. We can forget the back rub if it makes you uncomfortable. I just want a chance to gain your trust."

"Okay," she finally said. "I suppose I am being a little too timid, and I know you're a good guy, and I have to admit that I think about you a lot too. But give me a chance to jump in the shower, I smell like a greasy spoon."

"You got it. I'll see you in a little bit."

* * * * *

Bud rolled over in bed for the hundredth time. He looked at the digital clock, it's red numbers mocked him. He couldn't sleep. His head was an endless stream of scenes from the previous three days.

He rolled over again so he wouldn't have to look at the clock. He'd spent the day feeling like he was just going through the motions. He drove his concrete mixer, delivered several loads, went home, fed his pigs, watched TV and went to bed. He was in some serious trouble and had absolutely no idea what to do about it.

He closed his eyes, but knew it was pointless. He resigned himself to the fact that he wasn't going to be able to sleep, so he jumped out of bed and put on some jeans and a golf shirt. He grabbed his leather jacket and went outside into the rain. He didn't usually go out on Mondays but he figured Jed's would be open.

After narrowly avoiding a collision with a pair of deer on

route 98, Bud arrived at the edge of town. The village of Attica came into view as he drove around a large bend in the road. Suddenly the streets were all lit up, contrasting the dark, rain soaked surface of the short rural section of road on the drive from Picton. A supermarket, gas station and motel gave way to a double string of quaint, two-story houses just past the Wyoming County Line.

Just before the first of two traffic lights in the village, the chain of houses blended back into a collection of small businesses. Bud drove past the Attica Deli, another gas station, a hardware store and a car wash before turning into Jed's parking lot on the right.

He went inside, surprised to see how many people were there. Unfortunately, Jimmy T wasn't around so there was no way Bud was going to get his four-thousand dollars. He felt a little deflated even though Jimmy T had said he'd have the money on Wednesday. Bud wondered if there was anything left that could cheer him up.

Tanya came down to his end of the bar, her radiant smile perked him up a little. He wasn't surprised. She'd brought a beer with her so Bud didn't have to order. He thanked her and watched her walk away. He wished he could go back in time, back to the day he'd gotten himself involved with Jimmy T's smuggling operation. He relived that day in his mind over and over.

Suddenly he became aware that he wasn't paying attention to what was going on around him. He told himself to straighten up or people would start thinking there was something wrong with him. Then he almost laughed out loud at himself for thinking that there wasn't. He thought of how strange he would look sitting at the bar by himself and laughing and that really got him going. He had to concentrate for a few seconds to keep from bursting.

Before long a vision of George popped into his head and quelled his desire to laugh. He looked around and saw Phil Waters playing pool. Bud decided he might as well go over and take him on. At least he could find out when the next rodeo was for Jimmy T. He walked across the room, both glad that he had something to occupy him and also wishing that he didn't have to do it.

And this is only Monday, he thought. *It's going to be a long week.*

*****

Toni answered the door and let Tommy in. He produced a six-pack and a bag of pretzels. There was an awkward moment, then Tommy smiled and put his arms out. His smile had a way of making Toni melt. She put her arms around him and gave him a hug. Tommy had a way of making her feel comfortable.

She took the beer and put it in the refrigerator, saving two for themselves. They sat on the couch with the TV on, but they really didn't watch it much. They talked about George and racing and whatever came to mind, each taking turns. They drank beer, ate pretzels, and laughed a lot. The conversation seemed to flow naturally from both of them and Toni found herself totally at ease. She kept looking at Tommy, thinking how perfect he was.

After a while Tommy said, "So when did you decide that you wanted to play guitar?"

Toni noticed that his beer was empty. She grabbed the bottle and skipped across the small space that separated the living room from the kitchen. "I guess it was on one of my first visits up to the Loop," she called from behind the refrigerator door. "You know, there was always somebody playing a song on a guitar and I thought it was kind of cool."

She came back with two fresh brews and plopped down next to Tommy, a lot closer than she'd been before. "Last two," she said.

Tommy smiled and took his beer from her. They looked at each other for a while, then Tommy said, "Yeah, I remember those days. The Loop was the best."

After another pause Toni said, "When did you decide to

become a cop?" They were doing a lot more staring and a lot less talking. Tommy was saying something about his grandfather but Toni wasn't listening anymore. She thought about how Tommy was just coming off a relationship, and she even thought of Bud Rogers for a fleeting moment, but she ignored it all. Being with Tommy just felt right.

She leaned forward and kissed him warmly on the lips. To her surprise, Tommy backed away. She looked into his eyes, trying to tell him it was okay, that she really meant it.

Tommy looked back, but his eyes were a little hard. He set his beer on the end table and took Toni by the shoulders. Then he said, "I've got to admit that I really like you, but lets just be sure. You know that I've just broken up with Lisa, and I know that you're worried about George and you're probably all mixed up inside, so if you want to wait until we're sure, I'll understand.

Toni stared into his eyes from a couple inches away. He was serious. He was being a perfect gentleman and doing the right thing. His posture only reaffirmed her belief that he was the right guy for her. She smiled and said, "It feels right, Tommy." She nodded as she stared into his eyes. "Don't you feel it? It feels more right than anything."

She saw his eyes soften a little, and he said, "It does feel good. I just want to make sure."

Toni kissed him again and said, "I'm sure." Then after a moment she said, "I'm sure. I don't care what we should be thinking, I only know that it feels right." She kissed Tommy again and this time he responded. Slowly at first, then with mounting passion.

They were at each other, touching, kissing, exploring. After a while he took a breath and said, "Yeah."

CHAPTER 14

After two days of rain had dampened his spirits, Phil decided it was time to have some fun. County Line was small town USA and he was tired of the same old things happening. Except for the notorious prison riot in Attica back when Phil was only a small child -- which was certainly nothing to celebrate, the only exciting thing to happen in the area was an alleged UFO sighting in the mid-seventies. Phil thought the town needed a good scandal, something everyone could enjoy.

He remembered reading about a man in Perry, another small town about thirty miles from County Line on the shore of Silver Lake, who created a fake sea serpent back in the eighteen hundreds. It seems the man had devised some sort of underwater roller coaster that looked like a sea monster surfacing out in the lake. The town had come unglued until his scheme was finally exposed. The part that intrigued Phil, though, was the fact that the local residents still celebrated the event many years later.

Phil had been talking for years about pulling the bigfoot stunt, and one day he decided it was time. He persuaded his mother to sew together the hairy suit, saddled up Sally, his chestnut mare, and headed out through the fields.

This was Phil's second outing. His first one, a week earlier, hadn't generated much of a reaction, but he hoped when enough people started seeing a tall, two-legged, hairy creature, the rumors would begin.

Like most people who lived in Picton, Phil's hangouts were just over the county line in Attica. Since most of the local patrols were county sheriffs, he decided to make this second sighting on the north side of the village, in Genesee County. He had friends who were deputies in both Genesee and Wyoming County and he didn't want to leave anybody out. Everybody knew everybody anyway, the county line was nothing more than a sign on the side of the road, except where the law was concerned.

Phil thought about that. *Make sure it's good clean fun. Make sure that there's only one car coming, I don't want to cause an accident.*

The full moon created long shadows as he walked Sally along the side of the railroad tracks between routes 238 and 35. When he reached the area known as Johnson's woods, he hitched her to a pine tree just out of sight from the tracks. He had told his father exactly where he'd be so he could know where to look if Phil failed to come home. Anything could happen in the woods at night, and even hunters who went out in the middle of the day liked to tell somebody where they were going.

Phil could have driven his truck along the tracks to the same place he parked his horse, but it would be sure to be spotted by anybody taking a shortcut to the Silver Nickel. Instead, he chose the old-fashioned, four-legged means of transportation. If anybody noticed his pickup in the area during the same time frame as the purported sighting, the jig would be up before it started.

After following an old logging road for a half-mile through the woods, Phil approached route 35 at the same spot he'd seen a dead deer earlier in the day. He waited just over the edge of the embankment, going over his mental checklist one final time. *Be sure the driver gets a good look, back away from the deer, then jump the guardrail and run into the woods. Follow the old logging road. Make sure there aren't any clouds around when I pick a car so the full moon can light the getaway. Run deep enough into the woods so they won't be able to see where I stop, then get behind a tree and rest. When the car has left -- if it stops at all -- get the suit off and get back home.*

Phil climbed up the embankment and waited by the guardrail. Route 35 wasn't busy so he had to wait a while for a car. Finally, he saw a pair headlights coming over the second of two hills that separated him from the little town of Picton. When the lights disappeared behind the next hill, Phil jumped the guardrail and hunched down over the remains of the dead deer.

The lights reappeared at the top of the next hill, shining brightly on Phil. He waited until he figured the driver was close enough to see what he was, then he looked right into the lights as though he were startled. Hoping to appear confused, Phil looked down at his presumed dinner again, then he stood and faced the oncoming car to make sure the driver got a good look at him.

With the car only about a hundred and fifty yards away and slowing down, Phil leaped over the guardrail and ran down the embankment. He crossed the fifty yards of open field and ran back up a slight hill towards the woods, the full moon lighting his way.

As he reached the edge of the woods, Phil heard the car stop and two doors slam. He found it difficult to run because he was laughing hysterically, but he kept on. The edge of the woods was thinner than the deeper section. He turned there and ran parallel to the road for a ways in order to get to the old logging road. It had grown over through the years but was still much thinner than the rest of the woods.

While he was going in that direction, he couldn't help but turn to see if he could recognize the vehicle. It was hard to be sure, but he thought it looked like Johnny Davis' flatbed truck. *Perfect,* Phil thought. *I know Johnny will be down at Jed's later. He practically lives there.* He turned up the old logging road and sprinted another hundred yards until he was just over the top of a little knoll. He stopped behind a big tree, catching his breath and looking back too see if the truck was still there.

It was.

Phil figured he must be at least a quarter-mile away from the road. He didn't think he should be able to hear voices. He looked back at the way he had come, and there by the edge of the woods was a man who appeared to be Johnny Davis. He was jogging with a flashlight along the general path Phil had taken. There was another man trailing him and carrying a rifle.

"He turned right about here," Phil heard Johnny say. He looked in horror as the two turned and started running towards him.

He didn't think he would have much trouble outrunning Johnny, but he didn't know who the guy with the rifle was. He turned and ran as fast as he could. He cringed when he heard one of the guys behind him say, "There he goes."

After another two hundred yards, he decided to leave the old logging road and turn into the thicker part of the woods. He saw an enormous tree that had fallen and he headed for it. Just as he got there a cloud covered the moon and darkness swept through the forest. Phil heaved himself over the fallen tree and lay there, trying to be quiet.

He could hear the other two coming through the woods. Still behind the tree, he took off his headpiece. The cool air hit him and he sucked it in greedily. He was breathing so loud he was afraid the others might hear him.

Phil sat up and listened to his pursuers as they approached his position. He was about to give himself up rather than get shot when he heard Johnny say, "I guess he's gone, too bad the damn batteries in this flashlight are dead. He's be easy trackin' in this soft ground."

Phil struggled to contain his laughter as he heard the two walk away. He'd been sweating heavily and couldn't wait to get out of the rank and suffocating bigfoot suit. As he sat there, making sure the two guys were gone, Phil noticed that it wasn't just him that stank. He leaned forward and sniffed, then grimaced. There was no mistaking the stench of rotting flesh. Phil had grown up on a large dairy farm and smelled plenty of dead animals in his life.

He sat still for another five minutes, wondering what it was that smelled so foul. Even a small animal like a woodchuck could be pretty ripe after a couple days, Phil had the feeling it was something bigger.

He listened quietly. When he heard Johnny's truck leave, he unzipped his left leg piece and pulled a miniature flashlight out of his sock. He turned it on and shined it around. When the beam rested on a clean-picked ribcage, Phil thought the animal was large enough to be a deer. When he moved the light a little further he realized that he'd just discovered County Line's mysteriously missing person.

Phil stood in the light of the moon. He closed his eyes and tried to convince himself that he hadn't really discovered the remains of George Lewis. Unfortunately, it wasn't working. He tried telling himself it could be somebody else, but it was pointless. He knew perfectly well that what was left of the human being before him was the last earthly remains of George M. Lewis, owner of the Picton Diner and founder of the County Line Youth Athletic Association.

"Damn," Phil said out loud. Things like that just didn't happen in County Line. He thought back to when his mother had first told him of George's disappearance. Like just about everyone else, Phil had just dismissed it. George was a big boy, he'd be all right. Now he stood deep in the woods over a rotting corpse in the middle of a Wednesday night thinking about how wrong they all were.

His reflections had temporarily softened some of the reality of what was happening. A slight wind shift brought it all back with crystal clarity. He realized that he had to get out of the woods and call the police.

Phil thought about what the sheriff's reaction would be when he told him what he'd found. Before the cop walked all the way out there in the middle of the night, he'd surely ask at least once, "Are you sure its a human body?"

Phil shined the miniature flashlight around the scene. He moved it slowly along the ground. There were the remains of two legs, just bones with a little rotting meat left on them, a ribcage, two arms, both hands, and a skull with some maggots still crawling in and out.

As Phil stared at the decomposing body, wondering at the morbid thoughts that forced their way into his mind, a tidal wave of infirmity worked it's way up from his toes, turning his knees to jelly. He'd seen lots of dead animals on the farm, but this was different. He looked away, but much too late.

*****

Another ten minutes or so and I'll go fill this sucker up with gas and check out for the night, Tommy thought at just after ten o'clock. He'd been on duty since three o'clock in the afternoon. Nothing exciting had happened, it hardly ever did. He had written two speeding tickets earlier but that was all.

He was sitting in a well hidden, abandoned driveway on a rural stretch of route 20 in Bethany, trying to take a nap. The radio was playing an old Eagles tune. The car was dark inside, except for the digital clock and the digital readout of the speed of the last truck that had gone by about ten minutes before at sixty-seven miles per hour. The speed limit still being fifty-five in that area, Tommy had thought about writing him a ticket, but then decided he'd rather just get done on time. He figured he'd rather spend time with Toni than with some truck driver.

He put the cruiser in gear and drove out onto route 20, dreamily thinking ahead to getting off duty and going see his new girlfriend. He looked at the clock and calculated his drive back to Batavia, he wanted to be off duty by eleven.

He'd driven less than a mile when the dispatcher's voice came over the radio. "Genesee to one-thirty-one."

Oh great, what do these idiots want now, he wondered. *Probably some old lady's cat up a tree again.* "One-thirty-one, go ahead."

"The good news is that one-oh-two won't be coming in tonight, so you've got four hours overtime if you want it," the voice said.

"I don't," Tommy said curtly. "What's the bad news?"

"The bad news is that you're going to get it anyway. We've got a call from Phil Waters at two-three-three-niner Slot Rd. in Picton. He says he's discovered the remains of a human body out in the woods, and you're the only available officer at this time to check it out."

Tommy felt like somebody had dropped a bomb in his guts. He'd been on calls of a similar nature before. Usually it was some kids playing in the woods who had found some deer bones or something and then their mother would call the police. This was different. Tommy knew Phil Waters well enough to know he wouldn't be mistaken.

He thought about Toni. George Lewis was missing and Phil Waters just found a body. *Poor girl, this is really going to hurt.*

CHAPTER 15

Bud had been going to Jed's more often than usual since Jasper had caused him to kill George. Wednesday made it three nights in a row. He sat at the end of the bar trying not to talk too much, but people kept dragging him into their conversations.

It all started just as Bud came out of Jimmy T's office four thousand dollars richer. He decided he might as well have a couple cold ones before he left, even though he was supposed to be at work at six in the morning. Besides, he was afraid walking into the bar, heading straight for Jimmy T's office, and then leaving without at least having one drink might look a bit odd.

He had just sat down alongside four or five of Jed's regulars when Johnny Davis and his brother Mick came in. Johnny was tall and lean with shaggy black hair. He always had dirt under his fingernails and usually wore a grease-stained, hooded sweatshirt. His brother Mick was shorter and stockier, always clean-cut with a handlebar mustache and dark, piercing eyes.

Johnny seemed especially wound up and quickly grabbed everyone's attention by yelling, "You ain't going to believe it, me and Mick just chased a fucking bigfoot through the woods off route 35!"

Johnny was always loud and he was usually telling a story about something, but the whole bar looked at him dubiously. Seeing a bigfoot in western New York was a little too far out even for him.

Realizing that nobody was going to reply, Johnny kept going. "I'm serious, a real fucking bigfoot." Each time he said the word "bigfoot," his voice rose almost to a squeak. "It was gnawing on a dead deer on the side of the road until we came along and it ran like hell. Ain't that right Mick?"

"Absolutely," Mick said. "I ain't never seen nothing like it. It was like a real bigfoot man." Mick's voice rose even higher than Johnny's when he spoke. Since he was the total opposite of his brother, usually quiet and never saying more than two words at a time, the gang at the bar started believing maybe the two really had seen something out on route 35.

Finally, Tanya tossed her mane of red hair back over her shoulders. She put her hands on her hips and said from behind the bar, "Come on you guys, there aren't any bigfoots, or bigfeet, or whatever around here. Maybe it was a bear or something."

Bears were sighted in County Line on the rare occasion that one wandered up from the Southern Tier or northern Pennsylvania. It seemed a bit more reasonable and everyone grunted and nodded in agreement.

"Bear my ass!" Johnny replied. "The son-of-a-bitch was at least six feet tall and ran on two legs faster than me or Mick. What kind of bear did you ever see that could do that?"

The bantering went back and forth like that for almost an hour. Someone would offer a possible explanation and the Davis boys would curse and swear that what they saw was the real thing.

After the initial curiosity had worn off, Bud realized the two were talking about running through the woods in the general area where he had deposited a dead body only four days earlier. He was suddenly filled with fear, and try as he might, he couldn't get his hands to stop shaking.

Bud went silent while the others argued back and forth. He tried to pick up any information as to just how close the two had come. It was hard to tell since they had come from the route 35 side of the woods and Bud had gone in from the railroad tracks, but it sounded like it had been a close call.

"You believe us don't you Bud?" Johnny said for the third time. His wide grin showed a mouthful of yellow teeth.

Finding himself back in the conversation, Bud tried to act as normal as possible. "I don't know. I mean, I'm sure you guys must have seen something, but bigfoots only live out in the northwest or someplace."

"Well I'm here to tell you that they don't live only in the northwest!" Johnny was almost screaming. He pounded his index finger on the bar and yelled, "We saw one running through the woods right here in County Line. Make no mistake about it, when somebody else tells you the same story or one gets hit by a truck out on route 35, you just remember you heard it here first. Hell if the flashlight hadn't died we would've brought him back on the back of my truck."

"How far into the woods did you chase him?" Bud said, hoping it wouldn't sound too suspicious. He had one hand in his jacket pocket and the other gripped his beer so tightly his knuckles were turning white.

"About halfway through to the tracks we -- "

"Shit." The muffled word came from behind the door to the office. Jimmy T had tired of the bickering and gone in there, closing the door behind him. Everyone looked curiously in that direction.

Jimmy T came out and stood in the doorway, his stocky frame moving weakly. The bar was silent except for the steady hum of the smoke filter. The conversation had been so intense that nobody noticed when the jukebox ran out of tunes. Even Johnny clammed up when he saw the look in Jimmy T's eyes.

From the office behind Jimmy T they could hear an unintelligible voice on a police scanner. Then another voice. Then the first voice again.

He finally spoke, barely above a whisper. "The police say Phil Waters has found a dead body out in Johnson's woods."

Nobody said a word. Nobody could even move, much less think of anything to say. People just didn't turn up dead bodies in County Line, and with the recent disappearance of George Lewis, everybody seemed to know that one missing person plus one dead body added up to the same guy. All the talk about George winning the lottery or coming to some other favorable end now seemed as empty as a lawn chair in January.

Bud's insides felt like somebody was whipping up a Margarita and had the blender on high. He couldn't believe it had only taken four days for someone to find George's body. His bottom lip shook uncontrollably and his throat tightened, making it difficult to breath. Bud glanced around the room and was morbidly pleased to see that everyone else looked pretty much the same as he did.

After a bit of soul searching, everybody looked to Jimmy T again. Since he was the one who'd broken the news, they thought maybe he had something more to add. It occurred to Bud that Jimmy T and George were the same age, had known each other since grade school. Although the two weren't exactly bosom buddies, Bud figured it was still a long time to know somebody.

Jimmy T just held his hands out and said, "That's all I heard. They're sending a patrol car out there to check it out." He made his way to the end of the bar opposite Bud and sat down with his head in his hands. Tanya delivered a bottle of beer, then poured him a shot of bourbon.

Jimmy T glared at the shot for a moment. As he reached for it he said, "Get anybody else who wants one too."

Bud had a shot of tequila and wondered if it would stay down. After a while it settled in his stomach. He sat there quietly, like the rest of the group. He assumed that speculation and rumors would be plentiful soon enough, but for the time being everybody just stared at the bottom of their beer. Even Tanya popped the top on a bottle. Bud couldn't remember the last time he'd seen that.

The fact that Bud had known of George's death previously and had already done a healthy amount of brooding allowed him to recover more quickly than the rest of them. Even though he knew he was responsible in some way, he'd spent most of his time during the past four days dealing with it.

After he realized the police weren't going to come and arrest him right on the spot, he calmed down quickly. In fact, Bud found that in no time he was right back to his normal state of mind, at least as normal as it had been the past few days. He drained his beer and looked around the room again. The gloomy atmosphere made him uncomfortable and he decided to leave.

Tanya was about to open another beer for him.

"No thanks," Bud said. "I guess I'd better be going."

She put the beer back in the cooler and without so much as a word came over and hugged Bud from across the bar. He felt himself tingle as her big breasts pressed into his chest and he caught the scent of her perfume. Somehow, however, he didn't think that was what she had in mind.

"Take care of yourself," he said in his most sorrowful tone. Tanya just smiled and turned away. The rest of the bar took time out from their bottle staring long enough to nod at Bud as he zipped up his jacket and walked out the door.

Outside in his truck, he noticed how nice it was after the two days of rain. He didn't think he would have much luck sleeping so he rolled down the window and decided to go for a drive.

*****

"What the hell were you doing way out here in the middle of the night anyway?" Tommy said. He and Phil were walking towards the spot where George's body lay.

"Well, I -- " Phil stammered.

Tommy stopped for a second and examined him. Phil realized the magnitude of what it was they were doing out there and concluded that since he was the first one on the scene he was probably going to be considered a suspect. There was no sense in trying to make up a story.

"I was running through to the tracks where Sally was tied up," he finally said.

Tommy almost spoke, looked puzzled, gave his head an exaggerated tilt, and then asked, "Sally?"

“My horse.”

If Tommy was any less perplexed, it didn't show. So Phil added, "I was pulling a prank over on route 35. I was dressed up as a bigfoot."

Understanding spread across Tommy's face. He let out a short huff and said, "So that was you, huh?"

Phil looked both proud and sheepish at the same time. He ducked his head, looked out the top of his eyes and asked, "You heard about it already?"

"No, not this time, but didn't you do the same stunt a while back over in Wyoming County?"

"Yeah, that was me too. I was beginning to wonder if anybody had seen that one."

"It was reported by some old lady from Orangeville," Tommy said. "We all heard about it but everybody figured either she was nuts or it was a hoax so the Sheriff asked us not to make a big deal out of it." He laughed again. "Man in a million years I never would have suspected you. I mean, you're just too clean cut. We are going to have to ask you if you can back this up though, you know, officially. Did anybody see you?"

"Yeah, Johnny Davis and another guy chased me all the way out here before I finally lost them." Phil thought about the rifle but decided not to mention it.

"You hit the jackpot there. The news will likely be all over town before closing time. He's probably down at Jed's or the Nickel right now telling stories." Tommy shook his head. "Leave it to Johnny Davis to chase a freaking bigfoot into its own woods."

"Yeah, well -- " Phil faded. He realized that in the grand scheme of things his little stunt wasn't going to mean much. He pointed in the direction of George and they started walking again. After a few steps they caught a whiff of the corps and Phil said, "This is really going suck."

Tommy nodded in agreement. When his big flashlight hit the scene they saw the bushy tail of a red fox escaping into the darkness. They approached to within about ten feet and stood there, thankful that the wind had shifted.

Finally, after they both muttered something to themselves, Tommy got on his portable radio. "One-thirty-one to Genesee."

"Go ahead one-thirty-one."

"We have confirmation on the human remains. You'd better wake up the investigator on call."

"Ten-four, one-thirty-one, twenty-three thirty-nine."

"Damn," he said. "Twenty to twelve already."

Phil wondered what his hurry was but he didn't ask.

"Okay Phil," Tommy said. "I'm going to need you to come down to the station and give us a statement, but first I need you to show me exactly where you stepped, and which way you came in from."

Phil was looking a little green. He wondered how Tommy could seem so unaffected, but he supposed that due to occasional traffic accidents he was probably more accustomed to dealing with the dead. He managed to point out the direction he came in from, and the log he'd hidden behind.

Tommy put the flashlight on the scene again. Phil had gotten pretty close. "Did you touch anything?"

"Fuck no!" It was Phil's turn to look at Tommy like he was nuts.

"I have to ask," Tommy said.

"Yeah, I know," Phil said, but he wondered why Tommy had to spring it on him like a trap.

Tommy looked the area over some more. The flashlight beam rested on a spot where the ground and leaves were a different color, off to the side, over by the log. He studied it for a moment before asking, "What's that?"

Phil looked up blankly and said, "That's where I puked my guts out."

*****

Bud noticed what a beautiful night it was while driving along on Cascade Rd. The moon lit up the rolling horizon so well he thought if he turned his headlights off he'd still be able to drive home easily.

He had resigned himself to the fact that he was innocent in the death of George Lewis. Maybe not innocent as far as the law was concerned, but not guilty by reason of a higher power, or insanity or something. Or maybe both. At any rate, Bud decided that George's demise was no fault of his own. He reminded himself that George killed his wife and raped that young girl. He wondered for the hundredth time if it was true.

You bet it's true, he heard loud and clear even above the stereo.

"Jasper, my man," Bud said out loud. "I thought you died and went to heaven." He laughed at his own joke and turned the radio down.

Very funny Bud. I see you did a lousy job of hiding the body of our first engagement.

"Yeah, well, actually I thought I did a pretty good job." The cheeriness faded from his voice. "Who knew Phil was going to be out in those woods tonight? But hey, as you always point out, that's not your problem."

Quite true. I'm glad to see that you're getting used to my presence.

Suddenly Bud feared they were going to go out to dinner again and said, "You're not here to -- "

No, Bud, I just dropped by to say hello. I also wanted to see how you are holding up, some of the people I meet turn into driveling slobs in no time. We won't have to feed for a few days yet, I'll let you know -- and perhaps I'll throw some more of my generosity your way in the meantime.

That made Bud think of Toni. "Hey Jasper, are you sure that girl doesn't remember anything about our little get together?"

I told you that already. You don't remember sucking any blood out of George Lewis' neck do you?

Bud thought Jasper sounded a slightly annoyed at his question, but he proceeded anyway. "Well no but -- " He had meant to bring up the fact that he remembered everything before and after, but he was cut off sharply.

I said no. Do you doubt me?

Bud thought about the hammer slamming him in the back of the head and decided an argument was a bad idea.

Good thinking, Jasper said. *It's nice to know that I don't have to discipline you all the time, you know that takes up energy, and the more I use, the more often I have to feed.*

Bud couldn't think of a reply so he drove in silence.

As I said, I just stopped in to see how you were holding up. I'll be back in a while so we can dine together. And when you least expect it, maybe I'll show up in disguise.

"You mean you're going to show up in a woman's body again?" Bud said. He knew there wouldn't be an answer, however, he'd felt Jasper leave before he finished his sentence. A healthy feeling washed over him again, it happened every time Jasper left. Bud had come to think of it as a "Jasper hangover."

He drove in silence for a ways, thinking about what Jasper had said.

He turned right on Exchange, put in a pinch of chewing tobacco, and turned the radio back up. As he came into the village of Attica the healthy feeling quickly turned dreadful. Jasper had made it clear he was coming back. Bud wondered how many people they'd have to kill before he could live in peace.

As he passed Dunbar Rd. the lights of the prison turned night into day and Bud gazed at the towering walls. A full thirty feet high, they dwarfed the cars in the parking lot below. The walls were the color of a muddy creek and paralleled the road for over a quarter mile before turning and running away out of sight. Ominous looking guard towers jutted up every hundred yards or so, and at each corner. There were no chain link fences or razor wire as with so many modern facilities. No places for the inmates to look around at the outside world, just thousands of feet of dispassionate, impenetrable concrete.

As Bud drove by he looked at the big block letters:

ATTICA CORRECTIONAL FACILITY

He kept going, trying not to think of what it would be like to live behind those massive walls. It wasn't easy. Bud knew several guards who worked there, and most of the stories he'd heard over the years were not very nice.

About the time he got to Main St. he realized that although it hadn't happened yet, it was just a matter of time before somebody was put to death under New York's reinstated death penalty law.

Although he didn't want to, Bud had to wonder what that would be like.

CHAPTER 16

"Six-fourteen, and no sign of Bud Rogers yet. You no good dirty rotten bastard."

Tim Castillo was fit to be tied, Thursday morning was starting off on a bad note. He ran his fingers through his short, light brown hair. He had a scar that ran from his right ear to his chin that remained white even though the rest of his round face was beet red.

Tim was alone in the loading room of Aardvark Concrete. The bright lights, white walls and modern office equipment starkly contrasted the rustic look of the old steel silos and wooden frame that made up the rest of the plant.

He looked out from the second story window at the area where the mixer drivers parked their vehicles, then he looked across the gravel yard to where they parked their trucks in a row at the end of each day. There were two trucks still there: number one, the old International M model that was usually only used for a spare, and number fourteen, a much newer one that Bud normally drove.

"You could have at least called, you little shit." Tim spoke out loud, as though there was a room full of people listening. He always talked out loud, whether there was an audience or not. He pretty much said whatever he felt too, even when Chris was around. He and Chris were the same age and despite Tim's incessant complaining the two were great friends.

Tim knew he did a damned good job, especially considering

that he usually didn't have much help. Every day, even on Saturday in the summer, Tim showed up before anybody else, got the concrete plant ready to go, loaded the trucks, ordered material, answered the phone, took orders and made decisions.

He sat in his swivel chair, wondering if Bud was just going to be late or if he was not going to show up at all when the phone rang. Tim looked at it and said, "That better be you, you little prick."

He picked up the receiver and in a smooth, friendly voice said, "Good morning, Aardvark Concrete."

He squinted as the voice identified itself as John Olikowski.

"Good morning, John."

"Yes Tim," John said. He had a heavy Polish accent. "Are all my trucks on the way? We're putting the floor in the new cow barn today, and we don't want any delays, you know?"

Tim wanted to light into him and explain that even though Aardvark did their best for every customer every day, sometimes delays were unavoidable, but that would have been unprofessional. He always saved his outbursts for Chris and the drivers rather than unloading on the customers.

Instead he said, "You got it John, one hundred and sixty cubic yards, delivered in eight yard loads, fifteen minutes apart." He wondered briefly if he would go to hell for lying, but what the heck, it was too early in the day to deal with an irate customer. At least he had the first five loads out and on the road, it would be a good hour before John realized he'd been screwed. Maybe Bud would show up in the next few minutes and then the sixth load would only be a little late. Tim didn't see any reason to get John all excited before he actually had to.

He rolled his eyes and nodded condescendingly as he listened to John spout out the same old rhetoric, and finally ended with, "Ten-four Mr. Olikowski, that first truck should be there any minute." And then, "Yes sir, that's what we're here for." He finally hung up.

He looked up at Chris, who was just coming in the door dressed in brown, denim coveralls. Chris usually ran the loader and kept the plant full of sand and stones on busy days. If they got way behind he would fire up old number one and haul a load or two himself, leaving Tim alone to do everything.

Chris had come up the stairs from inside the plant and wasn't aware that Bud was missing. "How's it going?" he asked.

"It's a quarter after six in the morning and John Olikowski's already driving me nuts, and your fucking brother hasn't shown up for work."

Chris stood up straight, surprised. "Did he call?"

"Not yet. Maybe you better go fire up a truck, John's going to be buying a lot of concrete this summer and I don't want to piss him off any more than usual."

"Yeah, good idea," Chris said. "Try giving Bud a call. When he answers, give him an earful for me, would you?"

"You don't have to worry about that, I can't wait until the little prick picks up the phone."

Chris nodded and marched out the door.

The phone rang. "Good morning, Aardvark Concrete," Tim said, all soft and friendly.

*****

Waiting for Investigator Griswell to get out of bed and meet Tommy by the edge of the woods, introducing him to Phil, and then showing him the body had taken most of the night. With the sun starting to rise, Tommy hoped that Toni hadn't heard the news yet. It wasn't that he was wild about breaking it to her himself, but he figured it would be best for her to hear it from him.

He opened the door to her apartment and looked across the small room. She was sleeping on the sofa. For a moment he thought about letting her sleep, but he realized she'd be very upset if he didn't tell her right away. He cleared his throat and gave the door a little extra slam as he closed it.

Toni woke up slowly. She pulled herself up and looked over the back of the couch. Her eyes blinked constantly as they adjusted to the light.

"Hi," was all Tommy could muster. He knew it wasn't going to be easy, but he was pretty sure something would come out of his mouth when the time came. He walked toward her slowly, trying to find a way to tell her that one of the people in her life that she was closest to was found laying deep in the woods with no clothes on, mostly eaten by wild animals.

When he got near enough, he took her hand and stammered. "I've got something . . . I have to tell you."

Toni regarded him, eyes widening, waking up fast. She must have realized how much trouble he was having and said, "Why don't you come over here and sit down, and then tell me what it is."

Tommy walked around the end of the couch, still holding Toni's hand, and sat down, cradling her head in his lap. He looked past her, stared at his feet, and forced himself to talk. "Earlier this evening, Phil Waters found a body in the woods off route 35." He was going to add that it was probably George's, but the way Toni's hand tightened on his own told him he didn't need to.

Tommy wasn't sure what would happen next. He was afraid to look Toni in the eyes for fear he might send her into hysterics. Eventually he snuck a peek and realized she had her eyes closed. If it wasn't for the ever tightening grip on his hand she might have been sleeping. Finally, perhaps sensing his gaze, she opened her eyes. Tommy saw one tear appear in a corner as she said, "I was afraid you might say something like that."

He was confused. He'd expected much more of a reaction. Toni was very fond of George, and certainly everything he'd learned about her so far had prepared him for a much bigger scene.

Toni, although upset, just stared at him. Tommy reached down with his other hand and stroked her hair. He kept looking into her eyes, trying to figure her out. He felt like he should say more, but he couldn't think of anything.

At last, probably sensing his confusion, Toni said, "I know

he's dead. I've known it for a couple of days now. I've heard all the talk. I've heard all the rumors. I also knew George better than anybody else. There's no way on earth he would have just taken off without taking care of his business first. I've been sure he was dead almost since he disappeared."

Tommy didn't know what to say, but she continued, "I also appreciate your concern. If you're wondering why I'm not crying, it's because I'm all cried out. I've been crying off and on for three days now. I don't think I have much more cry left in me."

As if to prove her wrong, a few tears appeared and ran down the sides of her face.

Tommy finally managed to say, "I'm sorry, Toni." He was still a little taken. "I'm so sorry. I wish there was something I could do."

"There is," she said softly. Her eyes looked out into space.

Tommy raised his eyebrows, questioning. He squeezed her hand.

Toni's voice was flat and steady as she said, "You can find the bastard who did it and hang his ass."

*****

The first thing Bud noticed was how bad his head hurt. Then he realized that his brother Chris was standing over him. Bud was sitting in the living room chair with his feet propped up on a footstool. His right arm cradled an almost empty bottle of whiskey.

"Are you going to go to work this morning?" Chris said. His controlled fury threatened to at erupt any second. "Or are you going to sleep your life away?"

Bud glanced at the antique clock on the fireplace mantle. He couldn't believe it was already past nine o'clock. He knew he must have slept through several attempted phone calls. He stood up, almost fell over, caught his balance and rubbed his eyes. He noticed truck number fourteen out in the driveway. That meant they were behind and that Chris had to help out as a driver.

"Oh shit," Bud said. The light hurt his eyes and he rubbed them. He hadn't realized how much he'd drunk during the night while trying to get to sleep. He knew he'd let Chris down.

During the warm months there was almost no acceptable excuse for a mixer driver not to show up for work. Since the business slowed down so dramatically during the winter, it was commonly understood that if a person couldn't work long, irregular hours during the spring and summer, he had no business driving a concrete mixer for a living.

Not bothering to call was even worse. If a person did have a good excuse, he should at least call somebody and let them know he wasn't coming in.

Bud had overslept because he was drunk, and that was bad. On top of that, he didn't think he would be able to explain that there was an outside force driving him to it. He had to act like it was the result of his own uncaring irresponsibility. He wished he could explain about Jasper and how drinking was the only way he could get to sleep at night.

Bud stumbled towards the door and blubbered, "I'm sorry Chris, I can't believe this. I'm sorry." He bent over to put one of his work shoes on, lost his balance and crashed to the floor in a heap. He couldn't bring himself to look at his brother. He just sat on the floor fumbling with his shoe.

Chris stepped over him on his way out, then stopped at the doorway. He reached down and pulled Bud's head back by his hair so he could look at him and said, "Never mind. We're so far behind now that all our customers are thoroughly pissed. Besides, my insurance agent would cancel me on the spot if he saw you driving one of my trucks in your condition."

Chris let go of Bud's head and walked out. Bud struggled to get his shoe on. "Wait." He tried to get Chris to wait, he'd let him down in a big way and was eager to make it right somehow.

He struggled with his shoe some more, looked up and saw that Chris was almost back to his truck. "Wait. Damn it, Chris, wait up." Finally he gave up on the shoe. He got back to his feet and tripped his way out to the front porch in just his socks. He could tell by Chris' swagger that he was still upset. There was nothing to do but watch as he drove away.

Bud slumped over the railing. He couldn't ever remember feeling so low. He made a silent vow never to let it happen again. He closed his eyes and wished in his heart that the business with Jasper had never started.

CHAPTER 17

On Saturday afternoon the early May temperature rose to almost eighty degrees. The sky was the color of the ocean in a Bahamas commercial, freckled with a smattering of puffy clouds.

A service was being held for George Lewis. George had left behind no family, but his tour in Vietnam had left a lasting impression on him, so he'd made up a will in preparation of his inevitable passing.

Part of that will stated that he should be cremated and have his ashes placed along with his wife's in the antique vase he'd bought for her on their honeymoon. Once there, all of County Line was to be openly invited to attend a brief service, then encouraged to go and have a beer or two in his name.

To help facilitate this, George had arranged for a five hundred dollar tab to be set up at both the Silver Nickel and Jed's Tavern. The only stipulation was that anyone seen pouting, crying or dressed uncomfortably was not to be served. "Remember all the good times," was George's message to his host of friends. "And don't be sad."

The funeral director had simply set the antique vase where the caskets usually sat, and, with no family or designated friends to seat, he invited everyone in on a first come first serve basis. The room was full. The room across the hall was full. The hallway and entrance were full, and for the first time in over forty years of funerals, a pair of loudspeakers had to be wired up so the folks out on the lawn could hear the service.

Toni was among the outsiders. Since Tommy was on duty and she didn't want to go alone, she had arranged to ride there together with Patty Sinclair. Toni had told her about a hundred times to be ready on time because it was sure to be crowded, but they were among the last to show.

Patty had run off with some friends and left Toni standing by herself on the front lawn amid the throng of mourners beneath two giant maple trees. Keeping mindful of George's instructions, Toni wore a pair of cutoff shorts and a navy blue, pullover shirt. Her hair was tied back with a purple bow that matched her favorite sneakers.

The funeral home was a large, white building situated next to a Baptist church on the short, rural stretch of route 98 between Picton and Attica. It had an ancient cemetery behind it with rows of gigantic hemlock trees providing plenty of shade for those resting there. There was a large dairy farm on either side with hundreds of black and white cows in their pastures, but the County Line residents were used to their emanating fragrances and paid them no mind.

Looking around, Toni didn't mind being out on the lawn. It seemed like all the people she knew were outside too, and the weather was beautiful.

She thought about how stuffy it must be inside, and for some reason it made her laugh out loud. She stopped immediately and looked around, feeling guilty for laughing at a funeral. Then she realized that there was actually quite a bit of laughter going on. *Well why not,* she thought. *It's how George wanted it. Besides, if I don't laugh I won't get any free beer.*

She turned and looked at all the cars lined up on both sides of the road. She wondered how many people were showing up just to get a few cold ones free of charge. Then she realized that there weren't too many people in County Line that hadn't known, liked, and respected George.

She tried to take it all in: there was Chris Rogers, who had declared his concrete company closed for the day so all his employees could attend. Most of his customers were there as well. Almost everyone was wearing shorts and sneakers. Phil Waters was there, typically dressed in a western shirt, boots and jeans. Toni wondered if he was skipping a rodeo just to attend.

Jimmy T, his gray hair flowing in the breeze, held his wife's hand. Her medium-length, blonde hair was braided into a pony tail with a chartreuse feather on the end that may or may not have had a roach clip connected. They were both dressed in shorts and tie-dyed tee shirts as though George's funeral was a sixties love festival.

There was old Agnes Scofield, telling anyone who would listen what a great student George had been in the sixth grade. Her silver hair was done up in a bun and she wore a yellow, flowered sun dress.

Investigator Ronald T. Griswell and Tommy were in an unmarked car just down the road recording all the license plate numbers. Toni waved but Tommy seemed not to see her.

Then Toni noticed Bud Rogers walking toward her. It had been just over a week, and Toni had managed to avoid Bud so far. When he looked at her, she expected to see a man who was eager to talk to her. What she saw instead was a man who looked like he had been scared to death. She wasn't sure what she expected Bud to say, but his look had her puzzled. Then she imagined how the story must have looked from his point of view and understood his confusion.

Finally, as if on cue, they both said, "Hi." Then they stared at one another. *This is getting ridiculous,* Toni thought. The silence was unnerving, she'd never felt so uncomfortable.

At last she said, "How've you been, Bud?"

"Oh, pretty good I guess, all things considered."

Toni didn't think Bud looked well at all, but she kept it to herself. "Look," she said. "This probably isn't the time or the place, and I apologize for leaving you hanging, but I -- "

* * * * *

"Don't," Bud said. He realized right away that Jasper had thrown him a bone. Toni may not have remembered everything, but she certainly knew what had happened. *Jasper's a liar,* he thought. He flinched instinctively, but nothing happened.

Toni was looking at him, both questioning and pleading. Bud tried to imagine how she must have felt and immediately understood why she didn't stick around.

"I don't know if you'll believe me," he finally began. "But I probably understand it more than you do, and it's all right. What I mean is, I won't worry about it if you don't. Okay?" He hoped like hell he was saying the right thing.

She looked a little puzzled, but after what seemed like an eternity she said, "Okay, I guess. This is very weird. There was something strange, I just don't know -- "

Bud put his hands on Toni's shoulders and looked her right in the eyes. "I know, I feel the same way. So lets be friends because no matter what happened, I don't think either of us wanted to hurt anybody, right?"

"Right," she said, and they both seemed a little more at ease. Then she said, "And I'm sorry about your lawn."

As the absurdity of it all set in, they both laughed.

"No problem. It'll grow back." Bud stuck out his hand. They shook hands briefly, then turned away. He was glad it was over, and he hoped to God they wouldn't run into each other any time soon.

CHAPTER 18

The tab at Jed's provided by George Lewis was long gone. The remaining crowd was made up of regulars who'd been there for most of the day. Some of them, in fact, were getting downright rambunctious, no doubt the result of a full afternoon and early evening of beer drinking. There had already been one fight over who had the next game on the pool table. Johnny Davis had won, beating up his brother Mick of all people.

Mick had finally left, but only after grabbing the six ball and whipping it in Johnny's general direction. It had missed Johnny's head, glanced off the corner of the jukebox and then gone out through a window. After Johnny chased Mick out of the parking lot a search party was organized. The six ball finally turned up under a blue van and play had continued, with Johnny winning four games in a row, beating Bud in the last one.

Bud had gone straight from the funeral home to Jed's. He realized, as the sun started to go down that he hadn't been home to feed his pigs.

He put his jacket on and worked his way toward the door. He thought about his hungry pigs and pictured them lined up in their pen waiting for him to come home. Bud had always secretly felt that his pigs were cute as a button and the thought had him smiling to himself as he walked out. Just before he reached the door, Jimmy T grabbed his jacket sleeve.

"What's so funny?"

Bud spun around and said, "Oh nothing. I was just remembering something from when George was my Little League coach."

"Yeah, there's a lot of that going around today. Let me buy you a beer, one last one for George."

"No thanks," Bud said. "I'd better get out of here, it's been a long day."

"Yeah I hear that. I'm sure going to miss him," Jimmy T said seriously. As Bud moved towards the door again, he added, "Is the pigeon flying next week?"

That was the ridiculous secret code that Jimmy T always used to ask if Phil was going to Canada. Bud always thought it was kind of corny but he supposed it got the job done.

"I'll have to let you know," he lied again. He had already talked to Phil and had all the particulars, but since the arrival of Jasper the not so friendly ghost, he wasn't sure if he still wanted to play.

"Well don't wait too long, it takes time to set things up you know." Jimmy T told him that every week.

"I'll get back to you." Bud slapped Jimmy T on the back and went out the door.

After stopping at the Attica Deli to get his Saturday supply of crackers, pepperoni and beer, Bud drove home. He parked his truck, left the snacks on the porch, and went out to the barn to feed the dozen pigs.

The small barn was over one hundred years old. The rough hewn beams were as solid as the day they'd been placed, although not as square with each other due to a century of settling under the foundation. The roof was in good shape and the unfinished boards on the walls had long ago turned a dull gray from years of dehydration.

As he turned on the lights, the pigs gave a chorus of squeals from their pen to his right, reminding Bud that it was at least two hours past their supper time.

"Yeah, yeah, yeah," he said. "I hear you hollering. You just better shut your fat snouts or I'll run every one of you porkers to the market Monday morning." The pigs stood in a line in front of their galvanized feed trough, just as Bud had envisioned them earlier. Their cute little noses pointed at him and he wondered if he'd actually be able to market them for slaughter when the time came.

Directly opposite the front door of the barn was a wider door into which Bud had backed an old John Deere tractor halfway inside, leaving the exhaust pointing outdoors. An old tree limb shredder was hooked to the power take-off on the back of the tractor. There was a large storage bin to the left that harbored a truckload of dried corn. Bud liked to buy cheaper, whole ears of corn and run them through the shredder before feeding them to the pigs. It had worked well, Bud noticed. It seemed like every time he went out to the barn he could literally see how much they'd grown. In fact he decided they were big enough to start calling them hogs instead of pigs.

He stuck his arm out straight in their direction, moved it horizontally from pace to place like a king with a sword and said, "I dub thee duly noted, full-fledged hogs of County Line."

Bud got much more of a chuckle than the newly promoted hogs, so he turned his attention to their supper once again.

Behind the shredder was an old wooden wagon with shallow sides that Bud used to catch the flying chunks of corn. He fired up the tractor and sang at the top of his lungs while he fed ear after ear into the shredder's hungry mouth.

After turning the tractor off he rolled the wagon across the rough, hardwood floor and shoveled the corn into the pig's trough. With the noise of the tractor and shredder gone Bud listened to their slurps and grunts while he checked the float in the water tank to make sure it was operating properly.

"Good night, you little ham-asses," Bud said as he headed for the door. Just before he got there he heard:

Good evening Bud.

He looked around the room in a futile attempt to tell himself it wasn't who he thought it was. When he didn't see anybody he said, "Hi Jasper."

It's nice to see you taking care of your responsibilities, Bud. Even if you did make the poor guys wait a little tonight.

Bud had hoped to spend a quiet evening watching TV. The arrival of Jasper told him that it probably wasn't going to happen. "Did you come here to lecture me on the importance of caring for pets?" he asked. He actually hoped that was the case.

No, Bud. I came to talk to you about what you plan to do about that Waters boy when he travels to Canada next week. Haven't I taught you anything about doing unto others yet? Are you still planning to endanger him just to gain a few thousand dollars?

"No, but it's not that easy. Jimmy T comes across as a pretty good guy, but if I tell him the deal's off he's liable to go ballistic."

Well Bud, I just want you to think about it.

"Oh I will, Jasper, I will. Ever since you showed up I think about everything, all of the time. In fact, thanks to you I have to drink half a bottle of whiskey just to get to sleep at night."

Jasper said something but Bud wasn't listening. He was looking at an old broken shovel handle in the corner. He wondered if he stabbed it through his heart while Jasper was inside him if Jasper would die. As soon as that thought hit him, so did the pointed hammer inside his head . . . hard.

The pain slammed Bud's head harder than ever before. He couldn't utter the briefest cry, he just collapsed on the floor.

For a few minutes he just lay there, unable to move. Then, suddenly, he was up and moving against his will. His body ran over to the corner of the barn, grabbed the crude wooden stake, and put it up to his chest in a suicidal, samurai fashion. The point dug into his flesh and Bud thought for a moment that it was going to go right through him and that would be it. Instead, the force lightened up enough so he could hold it back. It wasn't easy, but if he struggled he could manage.

There Bud. Do you like the idea of a bunch of splinters jabbing through your heart? Do you like it? Well, do you?

"No. No, Jasper," he said, still struggling. "Come on, the thought just popped in there, I couldn't help it. Come on, I didn't mean I would actually try it." Bud's skull still throbbed but he was concentrating so hard on holding the shovel handle back he barely noticed.

Well just in case you have any more thoughts like that, keep in mind that in the time it takes for that thing to break the skin, penetrate your ribcage and reach your heart, I could be sailing in the Galapagos.

Bud was wondering if he was going to be able to hold out much longer. Ribcage penetration seemed imminent.

"Come on, Jasper. I said I didn't mean it. Come on, you're going kill me."

In the blink of an eye, the force being applied to the shovel handle was gone. Bud almost fell over frontwards as his arms thrust outward. He was relieved, however. Then Jasper surprised him.

Sorry, Bud. I don't usually resort to violence. It was wrong of me. It's just that you were thinking of wiping out my existence and I can't stand for that. I'll make it up to you, I promise.

"Well, yeah. No hard feelings okay?" Bud was still surprised, but thankful for Jasper's instant turnabout. He said, "Why don't you come in for a beer."

I'd love to, Bud, but I'm afraid I don't drink anymore.

Bud was reminded of the old joke where a skeleton walks into a bar and orders a beer and a mop. That made them both laugh. Then Jasper said, *Really Bud, I just stopped to remind you that I disapprove of your involvement in that Waters boy operation. I'm not going to tell you what to do, but I want you to think about it and remember why I selected you in the first place. Also, I promise that I'll make up for my loss of temper.*

"Yeah well, whatever. You know, you're the boss." Bud wasn't sure what was going to happen, or what Jasper meant by making it up. Then he thought about Toni and added, "Hey Jasper, I don't know what you're thinking, but I wish you'd leave Toni Birch out of it, she's a good girl and doesn't deserve to be involved in any of this."

As you wish, Bud, Jasper said, sounding quite good-natured. *But nonetheless, I will make it up to you.*

"Well, all right. Who am I to argue?"

There was laughter - evil sounding laughter this time - and then Jasper was gone. Bud, feeling healthy except for the lingering ache in the back of his skull and the torn flesh on his chest, went into the house to watch some TV.

*****

Tommy's shift was over at eleven o'clock. He drove home, glad to have the next two days off.

When he came into his house, Toni met him with a kiss and a big hug.

Patty Sinclair was just leaving. Tommy watched as she put on her denim jacket and a cute, round hat. He was always amazed at how much she looked like Toni, except that Patty was probably the only woman in County Line who was smaller than Toni.

The two had gone to Tommy's house with a couple of other friends after the funeral. Toni's apartment was so small she didn't really have the room, but she'd wanted to have some friends with her. Being alone after George's funeral was not something she wanted to do.

"Good night Patty," Tommy said as he let her out the door. "Drive safely, okay?"

"Ten-four, sergeant." She giggled as she walked past him.

"It's not sergeant yet," he said. Tommy wondered if she'd had one to many wine coolers. He watched her walk to her car and decided she was okay.

His thoughts returned to Toni as he felt her tugging on his arm. He let her drag him to the couch where he sat down. Toni tripped over his feet, then landed on him in a heap. Silly laughter spilled out of her as she tried to right herself. Tommy knew then who the one with too many wine coolers was.

"Hi honey," she said. "How was your day?"

Tommy sensed that she really didn't give a hoot. He was relieved, since he didn't think it would be a good time to discuss it.

"It was okay."

They remained silent while Toni adjusted herself to a more comfortable position. Tommy thought back on his day. He'd spent the early part of his shift recording license plate numbers with Ron Griswell, and the rest of the day going over computer printouts.

Tommy wasn't actually part of the investigation, but he lived in County Line and knew most of the people there. The investigator had wanted his opinions on several of the people who were at the funeral service. Tommy hadn't been given all the details as far as autopsy reports, lab results and things of that nature, but he knew enough to be sure of one thing -- George Lewis had been murdered.

He looked down at Toni. She looked so natural cuddled up under his arm. An image of the two of them together years later forced it's way into his mind. He snorted.

Toni looked up at him. "What?"

"Nothing." Tommy decided he'd better get off the subject of raising a family, even if it was only in his own mind. "I've got the next two days off," he said. "What would you like to do?"

Toni put one arm around him. Her warm breath huffed in his ear as she said, "Tomorrow I want to spend relaxing, maybe watch the Winston Cup race. I think they're at Sears Point." She smiled devilishly and added, "Maybe cook some chicken on the grill."

Tommy thought about how different Toni was from Lisa. His mind wandered back to the scene on his porch. It seemed like it had happened months ago. He laughed and gave Toni a squeeze.

She squeezed back. Then she said, with a hint of sadness, "And on Monday I guess I'd better go out and find a job."

Tommy reflected on the empty tables and chairs at the Picton Diner. He wished there was something he could do about it. He took Toni's hand and held it to his lips. "I could drive you around. We'll make a day of it?"

She grabbed his nose, wiggled it back and forth and said, "I'd like that."

*****

Bud lay wide awake in his bed. It was after three in the morning and he wondered if sleep would eventually come or if he should just get back up. He heard the sound of a vehicle coming into his driveway. He hoped it was somebody else who couldn't sleep. Maybe somebody wanted to share a beer.

As he listened to the engine shut off and the door slam, Bud was suddenly reminded of what had happened with Toni Birch just over a week before, and of Jasper's promise to make things up to him.

He threw his hands over his face, as if that would stop anything from happening. He heard footsteps coming down the hall. "No," he said out loud. He wondered who it was and remembered Jasper's promise not to include Toni. He wondered if Jasper had lied again.

His bedroom door opened. In walked a woman with a large bust and a flowing mane of red hair. It was Tanya. Bud watched as she started unbuttoning her blouse. He'd envisioned something similar many times in his fantasies over the years, but somehow he knew that with Jasper involved this wouldn't be good for him.

He decided to try and stop things before they went any further. He got up and stood face to face. Tanya continued to undress, ignoring him. He grabbed her by the arms and shook her. "Tanya."

He knew it wasn't just her, but he had to try. "Tanya," he said again, but he knew it was pointless. Jasper was in control, and one thing Bud had learned was to give Jasper what he wanted.

He felt his loins come to life and his ability to argue dwindled. Tanya peeled off her underwear and stood facing Bud, naked except for a gold chain around her neck. An invisible veil of perfume surrounded her that Bud found increasingly exciting. He tried to look her in the eyes. His own eyes only wanted to drop to those fantastic mounds that had pressed into him from across the bar a few days earlier. He forced himself to look into her eyes, but they had a hypnotic effect that no mortal could resist. He put a hand on each one of Tanya's breasts, she let out a sound that made Bud think of a wild animal.

Something inside him made one last, desperate attempt to put an end to it all. He put his hands back on her shoulders and shook her. "Tanya," he said once again. But even he knew that this time his heart wasn't in it.

Her reply was to take his underwear off. Then she pushed him back onto his bed with the force of ten women. If there was any doubt left, it all disappeared when, just like the time before with Toni, Tanya took him with her full lips. Bud was resigned to the fact that he was helpless so he decided to enjoy himself, but it occurred to him that Jasper wasn't much for variety.

He didn't know if Jasper could read his thoughts while he was inside somebody else or not, but just then Tanya's body spun around a hundred and eighty degrees. Suddenly, he was face to face with a mound of pink flesh. He was so surprised he just looked at it for a moment until it pressed against his face like a magnet.

As if to tell him he wasn't getting the job done, Tanya pressed even further down on his face. Bud opened his mouth and went to work, simultaneously enjoying the work being done on him.

The redhead did most of the work at both ends. Bud was amazed at the intensity with which her lips massaged him. At the same time her sex was all over his face threatening to smother him.

After a while Bud exploded and Tanya peeled herself off his face. After some heavy petting and caressing of her large breasts and nipples, Bud found himself in the saddle, pumping away. The redhead growled like a wild African lion, her fingernails raked his back and her hips thrusted wildly, matching his own frantic rhythm. Several times Bud thought he was going to climax, but each time he looked into her hypnotic eyes he was filled with a new source of energy and lust.

Around and around they went, to the edge of ecstasy and back into their rhythm. So close, then back in control. Bud closed his eyes and saw points of white light as he kept thrusting, sliding in and out.

Finally, the redhead roared. She wrapped her legs around Bud and squeezed so tight he thought something might break. Then he came with a shudder and a loud moan, anticipation finally giving way to deliverance. He felt energy from every nerve pulse it's way through him into the hot flesh below.

Bud rolled over onto his back, panting like a dog on a hot summer day. "Holy shit," he said. He looked over at the redhead for some kind of response, but she was already climbing out of bed and starting to dress. He looked at her eyes, they were no longer the hypnotic orbs he'd seen before, they were like normal eyes.

Not quite normal, he realized. They were still Jasper's eyes.

He looked at her, made a thumb's up gesture and said, "You the man." The redhead gave no response. She simply continued to dress herself. Bud watched closely. He figured it would be his last chance to see Tanya's raw, unencumbered, feline curves.

When she finished she opened the bedroom door, looked at Bud and said in a grating voice that seemed to come straight from the pits of hell, "Sweet dreams, I'll be thinking of you." Then she walked out.

He lay there, trying to separate the feelings of fear that tangled with the complacent feeling he always got after having sex. Fear was winning.

After a few minutes he got up and said out loud, "Fuck it. There's absolutely nothing I can do about it. I am a pawn. I am totally helpless against this entity. I refuse to worry about it anymore. Whatever happens, happens."

Then he went into the kitchen and opened a bottle of beer.

CHAPTER 19

Bud dragged himself out of bed on Sunday morning after only two hours of sleep. His brother Chris was having a family/employee get-together that afternoon. Bud thought it was funny that Chris always referred to them as family/employee get-togethers. The only family Chris had, besides his wife, was Bud. Since Bud was an employee he always wondered why Chris didn't just call it a company party.

With the memory of a bunch of beer and some whiskey reminding him that he was only human, Bud treated himself to breakfast in Batavia. After that he drove around until it was time to go to the party, watching everything turn green and singing along with the radio at full volume.

He found himself leaning on the railing of a balcony that ran around the back of Chris' house.The sun shined in his eyes and Bud squinted as he watched a rabbit run along the creek bank at the far end of the lawn about a hundred feet away. He garnered up a mouthful of tobacco juice and watched the stream of caramel-colored spit as it fell to the ground, while hanging together like a raw egg. It deposited itself in the weedless, perfectly mowed grass that made up Chris's finely trimmed back yard. It seemed to Bud that everything Chris touched turned to gold.

He wondered if he'd gotten involved with Jimmy T's smuggling business because he wanted to keep up with his brother. But mostly he wondered how he was going to get out of it. As he lamented his fate his thoughts wandered on to Phil Waters, and then to Jimmy T and Jasper. If only he could go back in time and get rid of all the problems that had cropped up.

He heard the French doors open behind him. The voices of his coworkers filtered out from inside. Bud was so down he didn't even bother to see who was coming out to join him.

Chris slapped him on the back and said, "What are you doing out here, pouting?"

Bud thought that if Chris knew what he'd been through during the week he'd have given him a medal for being able to walk and talk in complete sentences, instead of just blubbering incoherently, which was what he felt like doing most of the time.

"No, just thinking," he said.

"You've been doing a lot of thinking lately. You're starting to scare me."

Bud's reply was to send another stream of egg-spit into the finely trimmed back yard. The rabbit disappeared into a patch of wild raspberries.

Chris looked at Bud closely and asked, "Is there something I can help you with?"

Bud was hanging onto stability by a thread. He could certainly use some help, so he considered his brother's question. Unfortunately, he didn't think Chris would believe one word of his story. Nor did he think there was any way Chris could help. And the last thing Bud wanted was to get anybody else involved. He thought of how ridiculous he would sound if he laid it all out, then burst into a fit of laughter. He couldn't help it. Bud's emotions were just as wracked as the rest of his mind and body.

Finally, after watching Bud laugh until beer came out his nose, Chris asked, "Is it girl trouble?"

Bud calmed down and wiped the beer from his face with the back of his hand. He thought of Toni and Tanya and said, "To tell the truth, I haven't had any trouble getting the girls at all lately."

Chris just stared at him, giving him time to spill his guts.

If only he could.

"Seriously," Bud finally said, "I've been invaded by a demon who uses my body for all sorts of evil deeds. But don't worry because he says it's only temporary."

Chris shook his head and said, "Come on inside, we're going to start the poker game, and I love taking money from little wise-asses like you."

Just knowing somebody still cared had Bud feeling better. He dug the wad of tobacco out fom between his cheek and gum, watched as it landed in the picture-perfect back yard, rinsed his mouth out with a splash of beer and went inside to play poker.

The balcony was connected to a splendid upstairs game room complete with a pool table, dart board, stereo, pinball machine and a green, felt covered card table.

Across the room from the French doors was a stairway and a railing that looked down into the living room. Bud could hear laughter from the employees wives and girlfriends as they played a board game downstairs.

On the wall to their right was every award, plaque and trophy Chris had ever won. In a glass case on the opposite wall was an arrangement of Chris' favorite antique farm toys which he'd been collecting since his teens.

The poker table was set in the corner with a beer light hanging directly overhead. It was surrounded by stuffed deer heads and various articles of ancient weaponry. As Bud sat down with his brother and coworkers, he thought about how handy it would be to have a guy like Jasper around during a poker game.

Unfortunately, Jasper was never around when Bud needed him.

CHAPTER 20

"I hate this," Toni said.

Tommy shrugged his shoulders. "You want to take a break?"

"No. I've got to find a job or I'll be living in the street." Toni got in the passenger side of Tommy's car and closed the door. She let out a sigh and looked at the floor.

They had covered most of the department stores in Batavia. Toni filled out applications at each one but none had given her much regard. After that they started on the restaurants and diners. With her experience as a waitress and cook there was a little more interest, but still nobody had offered a job starting immediately. Toni was frustrated, she'd been working for George since high school and hadn't had to go job hunting since.

"Where to?" Tommy said.

Toni covered her face with her hands. She was on the verge of crying and didn't want Tommy to see it.

"I don't know," she said. The last word came out long and slow. Toni couldn't help it, she was still trying to accept the fact that George wasn't going to be around to help her any more. She was scared and she was crying in front of Tommy and she felt like a fool.

Tommy put a hand gently on her thigh and said, "It's okay. Everything's going to be fine. We've only been at it for half a day. When one of these guys needs a waitress he's going to call you.

And when he does he's going to see how awesome you are and then you'll be full time."

"Yeah, great." Toni knew she was whining, but she couldn't help it. "The only experience I have is working in a small town diner. Who's going to want to hire me?"

"Hey, don't sell yourself short. You're a great person and people love to be around you. And you play a mean guitar besides, that's something most people think of as special."

"Wonderful. How about giving me a ride to Los Angeles so I can make it big."

"Okay."

The tone in Tommy's voice sounded so sincere she almost believed he would. She looked over at him. He was smiling and he looked like he was ready to drop his career as a cop and take off with her to southern California. She felt so silly she had to laugh. She took his hand in hers and let out another sigh.

"Why don't we get some lunch and then go to Warsaw," Tommy said. "There's plenty of restaurants over there that probably need a waitress. It's in the opposite direction from here, but you wouldn't have to drive much farther from your place."

"Okay," Toni said. "I've got some leftover pizza in my fridge, we can stop and eat it on the way." She was feeling better, Tommy had that effect on her.

As they drove south on route 98 Toni suddenly said, "Taurus."

"What?" Tommy turned his head, questioning.

"When's your birthday?"

"April 29th, you just missed it. So yes, that makes me a Taurus. Why?"

"I knew it. Strong, emotionally stable. Always a cornerstone and a perfect match for an emotional Cancer like me. You and I are going to get along just fine."

"Okay," Tommy said. "I'll bite, when's your birthday?"

"July 13th."

"It figures."

"What figures?"

"That I'm going to have to buy you a birthday present in less than two months while you get to wait almost a year."

Toni thought Tommy had misunderstood her. Wanting to set things straight she squeezed his hand and said, "No. No, that's not what I was getting at. I just meant -- "

As she looked over, she noticed Tommy was smiling. She smacked him on the arm and buried her eyes in her free hand, laughing at herself.

They drove the rest of the way in silence. When they got to her apartment Toni noticed the message light flashing on the answering machine. Charles Lansing, of Lansing and Lansing law offices in Warsaw had left a message requesting that Toni call him. There were some articles of George Lewis' will that remained to be executed.

She called the office, but Mr. Lansing was gone for lunch. Toni looked at her watch, it was twelve-thirty. She explained that she was going to be in Warsaw at about one o'clock. The secretary told her that would be fine. Mr. Lansing should be back by then and he was anxious to see her.

Toni hung up the phone. Tommy had already taken the pizza out of the refrigerator and was chewing on a piece. She grabbed the box off the kitchen table and headed for the door. "Come on," she said.

Tommy looked at her with wide eyes, still chewing. Before he could speak Toni had him by the arm and was pulling him out the door. "I'll explain on the way."

They got back into Tommy's car and drove to Warsaw. Toni told him there was something about George's will that had to do with her.

"I heard the message," Tommy said. "But what's it all about."

"I don't know. The secretary couldn't say, but we're going to meet Mr. Lansing at one o'clock."

They drove in silence for a ways, gently rolling along with the landscape as they watched the farmers work their fields. After a while Tommy said, "You know, Toni, if you don't want me there for this, I'll understand."

Toni said, "I do want you there, Tommy. In fact, I'm grateful that you're with me. I wouldn't want to do this alone."

"Okay." After a few minutes he said, "Any ideas?"

"I can't imagine. George didn't have any family. I'm surprised he had a will."

"Hmm," Tommy said. "I guess we'll find out soon enough."

They found the office of Lansing and Lansing on the first floor of an old brick building on Main Street and went inside. Charles Lansing greeted them at his office door and invited them in. It was a spacious room with dark paneling and even darker, polished woodwork. The walls were covered with shelves, each one full of law books. A large window looked out onto the street.

They sat in soft leather chairs in front of a large oak desk. On the wall behind the desk was a framed diploma from Syracuse University, several pictures of a young Charles Lansing with various people whom neither Toni nor Tommy recognized, and a thirty-five pound King salmon mounted on a wood and brass plaque.

Mr. Lansing was a big, friendly looking man with a full head of gray hair and a nicely trimmed, matching beard. He wore a conservative, navy blue suit with a white shirt and striped tie. Toni understood why George had picked him to be his lawyer. He sat down behind his desk in a comfortable looking leather chair, then smiled and said, "So, I guess you know why I've called you here."

Toni gave him a blank stare. She shook her head and said, "No."

Lansing's eyes popped open and he sat up straight. "Really? Well, it seems that in the eyes of George Lewis you were one special young lady."

Toni was growing anxious. She knew George had thought highly of her, but he'd felt that way about a lot of people. Wishing Mr. Lansing would get to the point, she leaned forward and said, "Yeah?"

Mr. Lansing was obviously surprised to find that Toni was in the dark. At last he cleared his throat and said, "The diner, it's all yours."

Toni couldn't believe her ears. "Huh? What? Are you serious?"

"Indeed," Lansing said. He held up a piece of paper and explained that George's house and some money were to go to Chester Halltree, George's long-time tenant. He was a mildly retarded man and Toni was glad for him.

Then Mr. Lansing read from the paper, " -- and the Picton Diner, along with all it's contents and the money in the bank under it's name shall go entirely to Toni A. Birch." There was more, but Toni was making such a racket that he let his voice trail off.

She stood up and hugged Tommy. Wailing sobs and tears of joy gushed forth. "Oh my God," she cried. "I can't believe it. I can't believe it." She hugged and cried and hugged some more. Nothing like it had ever happened to her. Toni didn't know how she should act. She was still grieving for George, but she was so happy she was beside herself. She hugged Mr. Lansing and cried all over Tommy. Mr. Lansing gave her some tissues and she promptly turned them to mush.

After a while Toni calmed down enough for Mr. Lansing to explain some legal details. He closed by saying, "But if all goes well, you should be able to open sometime next week." He picked up an envelope and added, "There's also this letter for you."

Toni took the envelope and wondered if she was supposed to read it right there or wait. Mr. Lansing shrugged that it didn't matter.

She unsealed the envelope and read about how George was so happy when she'd turned her life around. He explained that he wanted Toni to continue her dream as a musician and the diner could provide her with enough security to do so if she ran it well, as he knew she could. He talked about responsibility and how he was sure Toni had what it took to be successful.

The letter was dated a year earlier. Toni couldn't believe that George thought so highly of her. She had constantly tried to please him, but she'd always felt like she came up short. As she read the letter Toni realized that George was like the father she never had. She regretted that she probably never expressed her love for him as much as she should have.

After another round of tears and hugs she thanked Mr. Lansing and made arrangements for some legal work which he said he would explain later. Toni and Tommy headed for the door but stopped when Mr. Lansing said, "Oh dear, I almost forgot. How careless of me."

From behind his large desk Charles Lansing produced an old, dusty guitar case. "This was in George's attic, and it's for you also."

Toni didn't think she could take much more good news, but she opened up the guitar case anyway. Inside she found a beautiful, vintage Martin HD-28 six-string. It was the most splendid instrument she had ever seen. She couldn't imagine what it was worth, although she knew it was well over a thousand dollars. What she understood completely was that there was a reason it was worth so much. If people thought she sounded good before, they'd better get ready to have their socks knocked off.

"Oh my," was all Toni could say. She hugged Tommy like he was going out of style. She was overwhelmed with emotions and they poured out of her like champagne on New Year's eve.

They thanked Mr. Lansing again and walked out. Toni wouldn't let Tommy carry the guitar, she insisted that he let her do it. When they reached the car they realized that Toni no longer had to look for a job.

"Well?" Tommy said.

Let's find a music store and get some new strings. You won't believe the magic this thing will make."

Tommy drove around town looking for a music store. They were both sure there was one in Warsaw someplace, but neither of them spent enough time there to be that familiar. It was a nice enough day so they kept driving, enjoying the rustic buildings and historic atmosphere.

After a bit Tommy looked over and saw that Toni was crying

again. "Now what?" he said.

"I'm never going to be able to thank George. I never thanked him enough before. He was so good to me. If it hadn't been for George I'd be a worthless slug, and probably a drug addict too. I just can't believe I'm never going to see him again. I'm sorry Tommy. I must be a sight."

Tommy smiled and said, "You're a sight all right, but I wouldn't have you any other way."

CHAPTER 21

Tuesday evening at just after eight o'clock, Bud finally finished delivering concrete for the day. He didn't mind the work, as long as he kept busy he could make it through the day without thinking too much.

Every time Bud started thinking, he started dwelling on Jasper. As he drove home his thoughts were inevitably drawn toward that familiar direction. He wondered how long it would be before Jasper came back. He wished the fiend would just go away and forget the whole thing, but of course that wasn't likely.

Even though Bud was physically exhausted, he knew he'd still have trouble sleeping. He thought about going to Jed's for a few beers, but he didn't want to run into Jimmy T or Tanya. He also knew he should go home and feed his hogs, but he couldn't stand the thought of being home and not being able to sleep. He decided to go to the Silver Nickel.

The Silver Nickel was a much newer building than Jed's with freshly painted walls on the inside that gave it a brighter, more modern appearance. The bar itself was more traditional, made of polished brass and oak and running the length of one wall. There was a regulation pool table, but instead of a jukebox there was a full stereo system behind the bar with a rack of CD's.

The same group of people frequented both the Nickel and Jed's so Bud didn't have to worry about being out of place. When he arrived the bar was entertaining about a dozen County Line regulars. All of them, just like Bud, had stopped in for their own reasons after work. Bud sat at the end of the bar and ordered a beer. He watched Mindy's behind as she bent down to get it out of the cooler, her jeans looked as though they'd been painted on. He wondered who was going to stick around and help her clean up the bar now that George was gone.

He eyed her as she brought his beer. Her short, black hair curled up behind her ears. She wore a pink cutoff sweatshirt that set off her dark, liquid eyes. Bud tossed some loose bills in front of her.

"Thanks," she said, and smiled.

Mindy didn't appear to have just lost a loved one. Bud almost gave her an expression of his sympathy just to see how she would react. He swallowed his words at the last second, reminding himself how foolish that would be considering nobody was supposed to know how close she and George had been. He decided to let Mindy walk away without saying anything.

As Bud looked over to see how many sets of quarters were stacked up on the pool table, Johnny Davis scooted up next to him and said, "Hey, did you hear about the two inmates that came up missing at the afternoon count?"

Bud hadn't heard, but he wasn't overly surprised. The prison ran a dairy farm and certain prisoners whom the state thought they could trust were allowed to go outside and work. It was a good program, but occasionally an inmate or two would just walk off when nobody was looking, especially in the spring when the bitter cold of winter was no longer a factor.

"Farm workers?" Bud said.

"Yeah, I guess so. I just heard about it on the six o'clock news. They showed their pictures and gave the same old precautions: lock your doors, don't let anybody in that you don't know, all that shit. Like anybody who lives around here is going to let two guys wearing prison greens into their house anyway."

"Well you can't be too careful," Bud said, but Johnny was already walking towards the men's room. He shook his head and looked into the bottom of his beer bottle. He imagined the swarm of cops that was bound to be crawling over County Line for the next day or two. He decided it would be a good night to go home early. After working fourteen hours his body was so tired he thought perhaps he could get some real sleep for a change.

As he drove home he wondered how he was going to explain to Jimmy T that he wanted out of the smuggling operation. Bud didn't think that would be easy. He didn't want to be involved in the first place, but Jimmy T hadn't left him much choice. It was already Tuesday and Phil would be leaving on Friday. Bud was still without a solution and running out of time.

He counted out the number of things he had to worry about: Jasper, Jimmy T, and the police investigating George Lewis' murder for starters. He also had to deal with what they'd done to Toni Birch and Tanya Lambert, not to mention the dangerously small amount of sleep he'd been getting which threatened to cost him his job, brother or no brother.

Occasionally Bud even found time to worry about whether or not Phil Waters would eventually get caught and how he'd be able to deal with that. It occurred to Bud that when it came to being a big time criminal he didn't have what it takes, but there he was traveling down that very road with his foot to the floor.

After a while Bud laughed. He'd found himself laughing a lot recently. It was either that or lose control altogether. During a break between songs on the radio he said out loud, "No wonder I can't sleep. With the number of things I've got to worry about, there aren't enough hours in the day."

He'd been talking to himself a lot lately too.

After he got home and fed the hogs, Bud took a long, hot shower. He made a cold-cut sandwich and forced himself to eat it, then grabbed a bottle of whiskey and sat down in the overstuffed chair in the living room. Going to bed had become a waste of time since he would just toss and turn until finally getting back up.

He usually wound up with the TV on, his feet up, and his hand around a whiskey glass. It had come to the point where he'd simply moved his alarm clock out onto the coffee table because he didn't want to miss any more work days.

One thing Bud noticed lately, when he did get to sleep, was that he had some very weird, vivid dreams. Some time after the late news he found himself in the middle of one of those dreams.

He wasn't sure if it was before or after he woke up that he heard:

Are you enjoying yourself, Bud?

He looked around, then wondered why he always did that. He knew that whenever he heard a voice in his head it wasn't anybody he could see. It was only quarter to two, Bud had plenty of time to get back to sleep before he had to go to work. He was a bundle of nerves, afraid that Jasper had returned. But he was sure that if only he had dreamed it, he could get back to sleep.

I asked you a question, Bud.

So much for getting back to sleep.

"Jasper, what a pleasant surprise," Bud said. He thought about that old *Twilight Zone* episode, the one where the kid had special powers and everybody had to do what he wanted or else -- and always think happy thoughts. Dealing with Jasper was a lot like that.

Yes, I've seen that episode. That Rod Serling had quite an imagination, didn't he?

"Either that or a friend from the spirit world," Bud replied. "What brings you into this neck of the woods, old timer?" He knew perfectly well what Jasper was there for. The only real question was whose neck it would be.

It's Time. Are you ready?

Bud considered the question. "I don't suppose -- " He couldn't think of anything to finish with that he didn't already know the answer to, so he started laughing. He laughed when he started to change into his camouflage clothes and he laughed when Jasper told him not to bother. He laughed while he put on his jacket and shoes, and he laughed all the way out to his truck.

Before he started driving, Bud quit laughing long enough to wipe the tears from his eyes.

*****

The mind has a way of dealing with sensory overloads. Bud felt like his mind had shifted into neutral -- he barely remembered the last half-hour or so. He found himself driving along the railroad tracks, not too far from where he'd stopped George Lewis' car and dragged him into the woods. That reminded him that the whole area was crawling with cops. He reached up to turn his headlights off, but Jasper said:

What are you doing?

I'm turning off the lights. There's a police cruiser behind every rock tonight, or haven't you heard of the recently AWOL inmates?"

Of course I've heard about them, that's what we're doing out here. Just do as I tell you, I've selected the perfect spot.

Bud felt relieved that the victim was going to be a stranger rather than somebody he knew. "Shouldn't I turn off my lights, though?" he said. "I mean, I wouldn't expect these guys to come running. How are we supposed to sneak up on them?"

Look, they're out here hoping to catch a train, when they see us coming along the tracks they're going to have to hide. If our timing is right, they should be near a culvert that runs under the tracks with nothing but hay fields on either side. The only hiding place will be in the culvert. We'll drive by and then surprise them on foot. If all goes well, we may even get both of them.

"What were they in for anyway?" Bud figured since they came from the prison they must be murderers or rapists or something.

Jasper corrected him. *Actually Bud, they're not from the prison with the big walls, they're from the Wyoming Correctional Facility. You know, the medium security place behind the main prison?*

"Yeah." Bud was discouraged at missing his chance to meet a couple of hard-timers and kicking some ass. "Still," he said. "They must be some bad dudes, huh?"

One was in for manslaughter, for killing his wife and her lover in a fit of rage. The other has been convicted for armed robbery twice, but those aren't the only reasons for which I chose them. They have each committed much more heinous crimes for which they have never been tried. Kidnapping helpless children, raping and murdering them, and selling children just to name a few.

"Well that's more like it." Bud thought for a moment about his own crimes against humanity. He supposed it was wrong to endanger Phil Waters like he did, but Phil wasn't ever going to get caught, and Bud maintained that it was still a lot less extreme than raping and selling children.

He expected Jasper to reply to his thoughts. Instead he got:

Pull off here, Bud. We should be able to catch them in the culvert now.

Bud pulled off, out of the parallel tire tracks that made up the path along the railroad. It occurred to him that if he could drive along the tracks the police could too, and it was just a matter of time before they did. He pulled back into the roadway again and headed for a tractor crossing that was just ahead.

Bud, what are you doing? Please don't tell me you're going to be difficult.

"Come on Jasper, you know what I'm doing. I can't afford to let anybody see me out here. What good would it do either of us if I get caught?"

It doesn't matter to me if you get caught.

Bud had figured that since the beginning, but hearing Jasper say it stung him and he said, "What does that mean? Sometimes you make me wonder. I mean, you single me out from over five-billion people on this planet, and then tell me you don't care if I get caught. What gives?"

It's part of my strategy. I'm only around you for little bits at a time. If I expect you to be careful when I'm not with you, I've got to keep you off balance.

"Oh I'm off balance all right." Bud wondered if Jasper was Joking. "And maybe it doesn't matter to you, but if I get put into a solitary cell on death row I won't be able to help you rid the world of rapists and murderers. Not to mention what the electric chair would do for our relationship."

Bud knew the electric chair hadn't been used in years, but a lethal injection would have the same result and he didn't think Jasper would bother to argue the point right then. They were already to the crossing anyway and Bud was turning off into a hayfield. "Just let me park over this little hill," he said while turning off the headlights.

For whatever reason, maybe because Jasper thought he finally had himself a partner, the little guy with the hammer stayed put. *Just hurry it up then will you?*

"You got it." Bud pulled over the small hill, just out of sight of the tracks. He turned off the engine and got out in a hurry, not wanting to push his luck. He ran back towards the culvert he'd crossed. When he got to within about seventy-five yards, he slowed to a walk.

It had been more than a week since the last time. Bud noticed that the moon didn't give off nearly as much light as when it had been full. He supposed the darkness was on their side this time. He crouched down and crept along the railroad bed, getting closer and closer. When he reached the end of the culvert he felt Jasper embody him a little more, and his fangs started to grow. Bud spun around the corner, ready to strike, but there was nothing to see. He wondered briefly if they were on Jasper's version of a snipe hunt, but straightened up when Jasper said:

Your little parking episode cost us a few seconds, and they've already started climbing back up on the other side. Now move!

Bud moved forward, but Jasper must have decided to take over because he blacked out.

*****

Bud looked down at the dead body. They were back on top of the railroad bed, a small, Latino looking guy lay crumpled up at his feet. Only one body, Bud noticed. He looked around, wondering where the other guy was.

He got away, Jasper said. *Your little parking fiasco screwed up our plans. But I suppose you had good intentions, so I'll let you slide.*

Bud wondered how things would have been different if they had surprised them in the culvert, but then decided it was pointless to argue seeing as how he had no recollection of anything anyway. He looked back down at the corpse. There was a little blood smudged around the wound. "Hey Jasper," he said. "You're slippin' up."

We were interrupted for a moment. It broke my concentration. I want to thank you though, Bud. I haven't had a meal like that for quite some time. I'll be leaving you again, but don't worry, I'll be back to check on you.

Bud wanted to ask what he meant by being interrupted, but Jasper was already gone. He felt the Jasper hangover bathe him from the inside out. It surprised him that the spirit had let him off so easily for his disobedience, especially considering they'd only managed to get one of the two intended victims.

After Bud regained consciousness Jasper had seemed rather complacent, as though he was enjoying a cigarette after a good round of sex. He supposed the human life force that Jasper was so fond of extracting acted as a sort of diaphanous narcotic, and that Jasper was nothing more than a supernatural, subatomic junkie.

Bud looked around and wondered what he was going to do with the body this time. A rumbling from the east helped make up his mind. He looked down the tracks, catching the first glimpse of an approaching train's headlight. The light grew more intense as the locomotive came around a long bend. Bud looked at the body and wondered if he had time to get it out of sight before being spotted. It seemed unlikely.

He looked up at the light again. It was getting brighter and brighter, closer and closer. He realized that when he could actually see the headlight, the guy behind it would be able to see him. Bud didn't want that. He decided if he left immediately he'd be able to clear the little hill he was parked behind before the train guy could see him. Then he figured that once the train guy spotted a lifeless body along the tracks and notified the authorities, he'd have about two minutes to get out of there.

Bud turned and ran to his truck, looking back at the last minute to see how close the train had come. He thought he was still safe. Leaving along the tracks was not an option anymore because that's the way the cops would be coming in. He started the truck, shoved it into four-wheel drive, and drove straight ahead. He hoped he still knew the tractor paths as well as he thought, and he wished the moon was brighter so he could see better without the headlights.

When he came to a T, Bud stopped for a moment to make sure he turned the right way. He looked in the mirror out of habit, half expecting to see a set of flashing red lights. He noticed that Jasper had left a few drops of blood at the corners of his mouth.

"Oh Jesus," he said. "Jasper, you dirty bastard." He winced, but there was nothing. Part of him wanted to just keep going, to get away from the scene, but something deeper told him to take the time to tidy up. He grabbed a couple napkins from the glove compartment and cleaned himself up. Then he put them in his pocket, figuring to burn his clothes again anyway.

He turned and bounced his way through the labyrinth of trails, using the moon in the southern sky to keep his bearings, and finally came out on route 35. Bud no sooner turned his headlights on than he could see the lights of a vehicle coming the other way. He accelerated to an innocent looking sixty miles per hour and drove west as though he'd been on the road for hours. The oncoming car rose over the hill and Bud was almost blinded by the host of flashing lights shining in his eyes. They were moving fast, however, and didn't bother him for long. He checked his mirror several times but the cop never even slowed down.

Bud figured that since he was heading west, he would just keep going until he got to Alden. It was a much bigger town than County Line and nobody knew him there. He wanted to hit the all night car wash. His truck was covered with dirt from the fields and he didn't want to leave any sign that he'd been anywhere near the murder scene. He figured he had enough time to wash the truck, get home, burn his clothes and still make it to work without being late.

He checked his mirror again for flashing lights and took a closer look to make sure he got all the blood. A thought popped into his mind. *"I haven't had a meal like that for quite some time,"* Jasper had said. Bud wondered what that was supposed to mean. Maybe their victim was a hemophiliac. He thought back to his younger, partying days -- shot-gunning beers, doing funnels, all that stuff. He formed a mental picture of himself/Jasper popping the guys Jugular vein and suddenly finding that the guy was pressurized, like a shook-up can of beer.

The thought of them chugging blood for all they were worth -- trying not to spill any so none of the other vampires could call them a pussy -- had Bud laughing so hard he could barely breath. He became a true believer that a person could die from laughing.

He drove on, checking the mirror and the corners of his mouth again and again. While still laughing at his vision of a vampire frat party, another thought occurred to him. Just another one of those little things to help keep him awake at night.

Bud wondered if either of their victims were HIV positive or had any other diseases he could catch from drinking their blood. There wasn't anything he could do except hope the metamorphosis Jasper had spoken of would take care of such things. Rather than dwell on it he rolled down the window and serenaded the passing countryside at full volume.

CHAPTER 22

Tommy was laying in bed with Toni. She kept asking questions about George. He really couldn't blame her, but there were certain things he wasn't supposed to talk about. He told her that, since he was the only member of the sheriff's department who lived in County Line, they had asked for his help in finding the killer. Toni wasn't satisfied. She wanted to know all there was to know.

Tommy danced around the subject, but he was running out of room and Toni kept after him. He'd spent most of his evening shift getting familiar with the evidence that had been collected so far. Starting the next morning he was to report on a temporary day shift assignment, working closely with Investigator Ronald Griswell. It was also why he'd been allowed to go home and let someone else take his place in the search for the escaped inmates.

"They want me to help because they're convinced it was someone local," Tommy said. "And I know most of the people who live around here."

"How do they know it was someone local?"

Tommy was on his back, staring at the ceiling, but Toni was up on one elbow and he could feel her eyes. He wasn't going to get away without an answer.

"Well, it's like this. The last place George was seen alive was at the Silver Nickel."

"Everybody knows that," Toni said. "He was there until

closing time."

Tommy pursed his lips and scowled at her. "Yeah, everybody who was there thinks they were the last to see him. But get this, you know Mindy?"

"Of course I know Mindy." Toni shook his arm impatiently.

"Well after George left, he parked his car up in the woods behind the bar. Once the bar cleared out, he returned to help Mindy finish cleaning up -- and some other stuff."

"What other stuff?"

"Stuff like sex on the pool table."

Toni slapped his bare chest and said, "Oh bullshit. Come on, Tommy, don't screw around with me."

"I'm serious. And they've been doing it a couple times a week for about three months now."

He had to give Toni a minute as they kept back and forth before she finally believed him. Eventually she said, "So what's that mean, except that George left the Nickel a little later than everybody thinks?"

"Well, we've been able to determine where he parked his car that night, even though that's not where we found it. Mindy showed Gris the spot."

"Gris?"

"You know, Ron Griswell, the guy I'm working with now. One night Mindy and George wanted to do it under the stars, and since George had just bought a new car, they decided to inaugurate it's trunk lid."

Tommy paused there, waiting to see if he was going to get slapped again. Toni just shook him a little, waiting for more. Then, just before he spoke she said, "And how do you know all this?"

Tommy took Toni's hand in his and wondered how much trouble he was be getting into as he said, "Mindy had heard all the bar flies saying how they were the last to see George alive, so she came in and told us her story. She said it was a secret, but if it would help, she didn't want to withhold anything."

"Go on."

"Well, here's the deal. The last place George was seen was walking out of the Nickel, even though it was later than everybody thinks. His body was found out in the woods over a mile from where he'd parked, and his car was found in his driveway. The cause of death, by the way, was loss of blood. But nobody knows exactly how the blood was lost."

Tommy hoped it wasn't too much for her. Toni rubbed his chest, waiting for more.

"Anyway, soil samples from the place in the woods showed absolutely no blood, so there's no way he was killed there. But there was no blood found anywhere near where his car was parked either, or anywhere in or around his house. We believe that even though we don't know where he died, somebody must have killed George, dragged his body into the woods and ditched his clothes, for whatever reason."

"That's not a heck of a lot to go on," Toni said. "Is there anything more?"

Tommy hesitated. He'd already said way too much, but he decided if he was in for a penny he might as well be in for the whole pound.

"Yeah, there's more. Near the place where he parked his car we found a wad of chewing tobacco sitting on one of those fungus things that grows sideways off trees. It had been raining, but they can do remarkable things with chemicals these days. Now, that could have been left by anybody, you know, a farmer riding by on a tractor or something. But as far as anybody knows, George didn't chew tobacco. Did he?"

"No. Yuck, no."

"I didn't think so. So check this out. On the driver's side window of George's car there were some drops of brown, sticky stuff. What do you suppose they turned out to be?"

"Tobacco juice?"

"Yeah. And guess what, it's a perfect match."

They were silent for a bit. Finally Tommy said it out loud. "Somebody was near the spot where George parked his car and spit out a wad of tobacco. That same somebody also spit some tobacco juice from the driver's side of George's car while it was moving. Also, fibers found on the seat of George's car came from a camouflage fabric that's manufactured right in Batavia, and as far as we can tell, George never owned any camo clothes."

Toni nodded in agreement.

"So," Tommy said. "Somebody who owns camouflage clothes and chews tobacco either killed George or knows who did."

Toni was quiet for a minute. Then she said, "How do you know all that? You mean you guys can tell where different clothes are made?"

"No we can't, but the people at the forensics labs and the FBI can tell all sorts of things you wouldn't believe. If you find a footprint they can tell you who made the shoe and where, even if it's some rare European brand."

"All manufactured fibers, like nylon and polyester, are microscopically different from one another. Just like bullets fired from the same gun leave behind distinguishing characteristics unique to that gun, synthetic fibers have intrinsic characteristics associated with the machinery that produces them."

"When we told the forensic lab we suspected someone local, they took samples from the clothing factory in Batavia to see if they could match them up with the ones found in George's car. Sometimes they get lucky that way and it saves countless hours of searching. They might even be able to tell us what brand of tobacco we found after some more tests. The FBI has information on just about everything."

"So that's why you think it was someone local," Toni said.

"Yeah, all that and the fact that whoever was driving the car knew enough to park it in George's driveway, either before he killed him or after."

"So what all do we -- do you know for sure?"

"We know that somebody was at a place in the woods that only George and Mindy knew about. That same somebody was in George's driver's seat, driving. He or she wound up leaving George's car in George's driveway and was wearing camouflage clothing that is manufactured right in Batavia."

Neither of them said a word for a few minutes.

Tommy finally spoke. "You know, I've just told you a lot of things that I shouldn't have, and if you repeat any of it, I'm going to be in a lot of trouble, not to mention that it might hinder the investigation."

"Who do you think I am?" Toni said as she smacked his chest. "I'm not going to say anything to anybody."

"I know. But it's a lot harder to keep things to yourself when you're the only one who knows something. Like the part about George and Mindy getting it on for instance, and how George really left later on that night. When people get to talking and you know they're wrong, you just have to bite your tongue and let them talk. It's not easy."

Toni gave him an exaggerated frown. "Well you should at least be allowed to talk to your girlfriend about it. How can they expect you to keep all that bottled up inside?"

Tommy looked at her seriously, thinking about what he had to say. "You know, there's actually a very good reason."

"Like what?"

"Well, since you've inherited a considerable amount of property and cash, you've been placed very high on the suspect list." Tommy hoped she wouldn't overreact.

Toni started laughing. "If you guys want to think that I would, or could drag George's great big body all that way out into the woods after killing him, all the while chewing tobacco, spitting out the window and carrying on in my camouflage outfit like some sort of Green Beret, then be my guest. There's only one thing that's really going to bother me."

"What's that?"

"Playing pool at the Nickel is never going to be the same."

CHAPTER 23

Toni jumped about a foot when the phone rang. She wasn't sleeping, just laying in bed, but it startled her anyway. She looked at Tommy to see if he was going to answer it. There was no reason for anyone to call her at his house at quarter to six in the morning.

Tommy kept snoring lightly, oblivious to the ringing even though it was only two feet from his head. Toni pushed him once but there was no response. Finally she reached over and grabbed the receiver.

"Hello?"

She heard somebody talking, but not to her. It sounded like a busy man in a crowded room. At last, realizing that somebody must have answered, a friendly voice spoke into the phone:

"Chandler, get your ass into the office right now. We've got us another one, and there's some weird shit you've just got to see. Better yet, meet me right at the medical examiner's office as soon as you can."

Toni waited for the man to take a break, then spoke directly into the receiver, "One moment please."

"Oh, I'm sorry," the voice laughed. "Wake that pretty boy up, would you?"

Toni poked Tommy in the ribs and he came alive instantly, as though he was awake the whole time. Hardly amused, she handed him the phone.

She buried her head under the pillow, but still heard most

of Tommy's short conversation. He said, "No shit" a couple times but mostly it was just "Okay" and "Yeah."

After Tommy hung up Toni tried to ignore him, feigning sleep, but he drove her crazy by not speaking. Finally she gave in. "Well, who is it this time?"

Tommy didn't say anything right away and Toni felt a brief moment of anger. Then he said, "One of the escaped inmates."

She didn't know what to say. Not liking the silence, she finally asked, "Do they think it's the same person?"

Tommy, apparently not too well informed himself, said, "I don't really know. All Gris said was that there was some really weird shit going on. I guess it could be the same person, until we find out differently."

It occurred to Toni that Tommy was doing more lately than writing speeding tickets and running regular patrols. She knew that could be dangerous too, of course, but this time he was definitely going after somebody who had already killed. It gave her chills.

She stared at Tommy to make sure he knew she was serious. Then she said, "Tommy be careful, okay?"

"Don't worry, Hon. The sheriff always gets his man."

"I mean it." She spoke through clenched teeth and a stiff jaw. Then she softened and said, "Whoever you're looking for has already killed. Don't think for a minute that he would hesitate to kill you just because you have a cute smile."

Tommy jumped back on the bed and wrapped her in his arms. "You mean you don't want anything to happen to me because of my lovely smile?"

Toni felt then that perhaps she was overreacting, but she wasn't about to apologize. "No, that's not it at all. It's just that -- " She carried on, looking away and pouting with her bottom lip curled out. When she figured he was hooked, she looked back at him and said, "It's just that you're my only alibi, so I can't afford to let anything happen to you."

Toni laughed and pushed him away.

Tommy, knowing he'd been had, overpowered her and gave

her a big, sloppy kiss. "You just keep this bed warm. I'm not going to be gone forever, so when I come back you just better watch out."

*****

The truck was hopelessly stuck in the mud. It was just one of the things you had to deal with in the concrete redi-mix industry.

John Olikowski was jumping up and down, screaming his head off about how his ten thousand dollar floor was going to be ruined if they didn't get the truck unstuck and start pouring right away. He was a lean, elderly man with a wrinkled face and two slits for eyes that rooted him into a perpetual squint. Sixty years of farming had produced a pair of large, rough, muscular hands that habitually opened and closed into fists whenever he got excited, which was often.

Bud wanted to tell John what he thought about the whole mess, but John was the customer, and you have to be nice to the customer. Still, it was fun to go over it in his head. *Listen you grumpy old bastard, if you would have just kept unloading the trucks from the driveway with wheelbarrows you wouldn't have this problem. But no, you have to make me try to drive through three feet of mud just to save a few minutes of unloading time. Well guess what Johnny, you're fucked!*

Bud was pretty sure the truck was going to get stuck even before he tried going around the building. But the customer is always right, however, and John had thrown a fit the minute Bud suggested he might not make it.

There wasn't any sense in arguing, they'd been down that road before. After getting John to sign the waiver -- a special section of fine print on the delivery ticket that basically says once the customer signs for it the concrete is his and he will pay for it regardless of what happens thereafter, including getting stuck in the mud -- Bud had started trying to drive his truck around to the back side of the new cow barn.

It was wonderful. John had pointed out a rough path that he said the tractors would go down without sinking in too deep. Bud had tried one last time to talk him out of it. He pointed out that the tractors probably weighed around ten thousand pounds each, whereas the truck and it's cargo came in at just under fifty thousand. John would have none of it, so Bud went ahead and got stuck. And there he sat, still behind the wheel, sunk in up to the axles, wheels spinning hopelessly while John jumped up and down like a leprechaun on speed.

It was Bud's first load that morning and the circumstances would normally foretell the onset of a bad day.

But this was the new Bud.

Sometime during the previous night, after he'd just missed the police and spent the night dealing with Jasper's latest victim, Bud vowed not to allow any consequences resulting from Jasper's subjugation to antagonize him. He told himself he was powerless, and therefore helpless to do anything about it.

The new Bud didn't care about anything or anyone but himself anymore. Deep down he knew that was exactly the attitude that had mired him so deeply in his present quandary. But the recent exposure to unnatural events, coupled with an increasingly portentous lack of sleep had resulted in Bud's instinct for self-preservation taking command.

Though he would have liked to, Bud couldn't undo any of his former deeds. He resolved to play whatever hand was dealt to him as well as he could. He was still without a solution for dealing with Jimmy T and the Phil Waters predicament, but he told himself he'd take care of the situation as it evolved, and resigned himself to accept any incriminations without losing his mind.

The new Bud went about his daily routine smiling, acting happy, and taking great pleasure in watching other people go goofy. John was putting on quite a show, and Bud was ecstatic.

"Dispatch to Fourteen," came over the radio.

Bud wondered if Tim Castillo didn't have anything else to do but call him every thirty seconds. "Go ahead, dispatch."

"How's it coming out there?" Tim said. Bud had been stuck for over forty minutes. Tim continued to load the rest of the trucks behind him, and the laborers were still unloading from the driveway, but at a much slower pace since some of John's help had stayed with them in order to get Bud's truck unstuck. Bud could imagine Tim sitting in his chair, the phone ringing off the hook with people screaming as Aardvark Concrete got further and further behind in it's daily schedule.

Poor Tim, he thought. He keyed the mike and said, "Not much better I'm afraid, but we still might be able to unload it. I'll let you know."

"Ten-four."

Bud laughed at the tone of his voice. It sounded tired and Bud wondered if Tim had been up chasing escaped convicts all night like he was.

That made him laugh even louder until John stuck his head in the window and screamed, "What the fuck is so funny?" John had a loud, grinding voice that caught Bud off guard. "I spend thousands of dollars with your company every year. Now when I got trouble you just sit there and laugh."

Bud knew John was right. You shouldn't treat a customer that way, even if he deserves it. He got out and looked at the truck. The green cab with the hot pink drum always made Bud think of something from outer space. He'd told Chris he was nuts when he wanted to paint the trucks pink, but Chris was right as usual. People seemed to love the colors. Everywhere Bud drove he would see children pointing at his truck. He'd honk the horn and the they would smile.

The truck was so deep in the mud it reminded Bud of a fishing bobber, all alone on top of the water. Mud from the wheels had splattered on the drum and just about covered the green aardvark as it went around and around.

They tried several times to pull it out with John's tractor, but all it would do was spin the wheels. They finally had to give up or risk having two vehicles stuck.

John had parked the tractor off to the side and walked over

to where Bud stood by the mixer. "You call a tow truck?" John said. "Huh? You call a tow truck or you just going to stand around while my concrete gets hard in your truck?"

One could add water and keep mixing a load of concrete, but that only prolonged the inevitable. Sooner or later the concrete was going to set up hard as a rock, and it didn't care if it was still inside the truck or not. Bud understood John's frustration and was starting to get concerned himself.

"No, not yet. We -- "

"What the Fuck?" John was shaking from head to toe. His hands pulsed like a pair of furiously beating hearts. "What the hell you been doing?"

"Just wait a minute." Bud was letting John get to him. He reminded himself that he was the new Bud Rogers and smiled. "It's going take a king-sized tow truck, which will cost you a fortune to get this thing out, and they'll probably make us unload it first anyway. Why don't you get that tractor over there with the bucket on the front?" Bud pointed to a different tractor sitting next to the barn. "We can unload the concrete a little at a time into the bucket and drive it up to the barn. Once the truck is empty, we should be able to pull it out if we use both tractors. It'll take some time, but I don't think we have much choice, and it'll be cheaper than calling a tow-truck."

Without another word to Bud, John stomped towards the green tractor with the hydraulic bucket on the front, barking orders to anybody within earshot.

Bud decided to add some water to the load in order to keep it from getting too stiff while he waited to unload it. As he wound up the engine, opened the water valve and spun the drum, he saw his brother Chris walking towards him. Chris had fired up good old number one and brought a load out to help cover for the loss of Bud's truck in the rotation.

Bud wondered if Chris was going to make him switch trucks -- let Bud run old number one while Chris stayed and dealt with John. One look at Chris told him he didn't have to worry. Chris was the one person who didn't mind driving the old M model. It was, after all, the truck that had started it all. Bud remembered more than once seeing Chris driving down the road in that old thing, rusted fenders flapping in the breeze, leaning a little to one side, looking like something out of a *Mad Max* movie. Chris would go by waving and honking the horn like there was no tomorrow, grinning from ear to ear.

"Damn. You got her in good this time," Chris yelled above the roar of the mixer. He was smiling. It's not that he was happy, but getting trucks stuck was a fact of concrete life and Chris had learned to accept it long ago. Besides, he had Tim Castillo to do his worrying for him.

"Yeah, well, you know John," Bud said. "I just couldn't talk him out of it."

"Yeah, I hear that. You just can't reason with some people." Chris studied his brother and said, "You look happier lately, although you don't look like you've been sleeping much."

"Well, there's a new Bud Rogers now, and he's not going to let anything bother him."

"Good," Chris yelled in his ear. "Happy is the only way to be." He punched Bud on the arm. Then, seeing that John was headed their way, he shouted, "I've got to run, somebody has to pick up your slack!"

Bud watched as Chris ran off towards the old rust-bucket, then he heard some hollering behind him. He turned around and saw John, tractor bucket under the chute, waiting for some concrete and screaming, "Let's go. Come on, let's go. Come on!"

"Yep," Bud said to himself. "That's right, happy is the only way to be."

*****

After Tommy left, Toni couldn't sleep. She went back to her apartment and spent the morning getting used to the feel of George's old guitar. It sounded wonderful. She wished there was somebody else there to play it for her so she could listen to it from the front. The worst place to listen to a guitar is from behind it. Still, she was impressed.

As she sat there, cross-legged on the couch, Toni let her mind swim through the jumble of emotions she'd been feeling recently. She thought about Tommy and George. Bud Rogers sneaked into her mind occasionally and sent a chill down her spine.

As she sat there letting her mind wander, she absent-mindedly strummed a variety of chords. She'd been hoping to write a new song but struggling. Knowing that she couldn't force a new song out, she turned her attention to the chords she'd been strumming. She realized she was playing the same four over and over. She played them again, with a little feeling. Suddenly the first lines of a song Toni had written years before popped into her head.

"That's it," she said. "Yahoo!" It was one of the many songs she'd written even before she was very good on the guitar. She had tried several times over the years to put it to music, but she never seemed to get it right.

Toni set the guitar on the couch and got up. It had been years since she'd written the words and she didn't want to lose the melody. She ran over to a desk in the corner of her one-room apartment and grabbed her notebook. On the way she stubbed her toe on the coffee table and let out a howl.

Undaunted, she ran back out to the couch and grabbed the guitar. With a little more work had the chord changes and chorus down. She scribbled the chords above the words in the book and decided to give it a try. She started in slowly, always having to remind herself not to play too fast.

When Toni finished, she was pleased. She sat on the couch and giggled like a schoolgirl. She hit a couple more chords, then a thought occurred to her. It would be great to use that guitar at Jed's on Friday, but she'd have to get an electronic pickup installed.

She decided to call the music store and ask if they could do it in time. As she reached for the phone, Toni thought about how happy she was despite her grieving. She loved to make music.

*****

Tommy entered the medical examiner's office in the basement of Batavia's Municipal Hospital. He wondered if he was dressed okay. Of course he knew the corpse wouldn't mind, but Gris had told him not to bother wearing his deputy's uniform. That didn't really bother him, but the investigators always wore suits with ties. The fact was, Tommy only owned one suit, and it just didn't seem right. As far as he was concerned, suits were just for weddings and funerals. He'd decided to dress in blue jeans and a flannel shirt rather than wear the same suit to work every day. Besides, he figured if they expected him to catch somebody from County Line they shouldn't expect him to parade around in clothes that were outside his normal character.

Gris was a tall, friendly looking man who had been with the sheriff's department forever. He had a strip of white hair that started behind his ears and went around the back of his head, leaving the top as bald as a baby's bottom. His face had wrinkled handsomely over the years with big, sad eyes and strong jowls that reminded Tommy of a faithful watchdog.

Gris smiled, slapped him on the back and handed him a Styrofoam cup of black coffee. Tommy found it hard to believe Gris had been up for most of the night.

"The victim's name is Mateo Martinez," Gris said. "Recently on unauthorized leave from the Wyoming Correctional Facility. You're right on time, we're just getting to the good stuff."

Tommy took the coffee and nodded thanks. He'd never witnessed an autopsy before, although he'd heard about them. He wondered exactly what Gris meant by good stuff.

They walked down a shimmering, well lit hallway and entered a spotless, stainless steel filled room just in time to see the medical examiner scoop the dead man's brain out of his skull. The air smelled sharply of antiseptic, but there was a softer, sickly sweet smell underneath. Tommy wondered why he had to be a part of this particular exercise, but figured there must be a reason. Getting the facts straight from the doctor certainly wouldn't hurt either. He'd heard more than one story of how an investigation was hindered because somebody mis-typed something on a report.

"Hey Doc," Gris said. "What do you have there, a handful of cauliflower?"

The doctor was standing at the head of the naked corpse, still holding the brain. He looked at Tommy for a moment, then back down at the organ in his hands. He let out a short laugh and deposited the brain in a stainless steel pan. Tommy surprised himself by not feeling the least bit queasy. He'd prepared for the ordeal by telling himself it was an everyday occurrence and that he should be able to handle it. So far it was working.

Gris put his hand on Tommy's shoulder and said, "Doc, this is Tommy Chandler, one of Genesee County's finest young deputies. Tommy Chandler, meet Doc Blake."

The doctor nodded curtly. Tommy looked at his rubber gloves, thought about brain, and decided a curt nod would be fine. At Gris' grand introduction he wondered again if he was dressed okay, but neither Gris nor the doctor gave him a second look.

"Why don't you bring us up to date, Doc?" Gris suggested. Tommy had an idea that Gris was already up to date.

The doctor looked at Tommy. He was a short, wraith of a man with skinny lips and thin gray hair. He had on a surgical outfit -- white, like everything else in the room that wasn't stainless steel -- with the mask tied around his neck but hanging down on his chest like a bib. He wore a pair of round, wire rimmed glasses that sat so far down on the end of his pointed nose that Tommy expected them to fall any second.

The doctor spoke in a squeaky voice. "Basically, there's not a whole lot to say. Let's see, the cause of death is from loss of blood."

Tommy looked at Gris who nodded that he caught the connection.

"There is absolutely no sign of a struggle," the doctor continued. "I mean nothing. There are just a few minor bruises on the body, but nothing more than you would expect to find on any farm worker. Nothing under the fingernails but some dirt."

Tommy didn't know what to expect, so he looked at Gris who said, "Show him the wounds, Doc."

For the first time, Tommy wondered just how the loss of blood was executed. And since there was no struggle, he was curious as to precisely what kind of wounds there were.

"You'll have to come around to the other side." The doctor waved him over.

Tommy walked around the end of the table. The doctor stepped back so he could get to the opposite side of the body. As he passed the head with the top sawed off, he couldn't resist looking to see what the inside looked like with the brain missing. He was a little disappointed, there really wasn't much to see except a smooth, pale lining and a cavity the size of a brain..

Tommy looked up and saw that Gris had busted him. He smiled a knowing smile. Tommy looked back down at the corpse but still didn't see any wounds. He wasn't really looking, he was staring at the abdomen, amused at how it had been laid open by the doctor's scalpel.

"If you look here -- " Doc Blake pointed to the corpse's neck. "You'll see a pair of fresh puncture wounds where the blood exited the body."

Tommy looked and, sure enough, there were two little holes in the neck. Bullet holes came to mind first, but they would have been damned small bullets. He looked up questioningly at the two men, then realized what he had just seen. He looked back at the two holes, leaning forward to get closer. His mind was momentarily jumbled, but one thought kept pushing to the front. They looked for all the world like the marks a vampire would leave if it had sucked the blood from the man's neck.

Tommy kept pushing that thought away. There had to be a more acceptable rationale.

Finally, he looked up at the two men again, hoping for some

clarification. He only got a shrug from Gris. The doctor was even less help. At last Tommy said, "There must be some explanation, right?"

"I'm sure there is," Gris said, no longer smiling. "At least, I hope to hell there is."

Tommy looked at Doc Blake. "What do you think made these wounds Doc -- I mean Doctor Blake?"

"I don't know," the doctor squeaked. "All I can say is that they were made by separate objects, although very similar. Each one was pointed, mostly round, and was at least three quarters of an inch long."

That wasn't exactly what Tommy wanted to hear.

CHAPTER 24

Bud was just plain tired. He'd slept very little the previous night, and that had been interrupted by Jasper. The rest of the night was a mad scramble to avoid the cops, wash his truck, burn his clothes, shoes and so on. Then to top it all off, Bud had started his day by getting stuck in John Olikowski's barnyard. The rest of the day hadn't been a whole lot better even for the new Bud, and the good weather had made for long hours.

The sun was just going down when Bud pulled into his driveway. He looked at his house, took a deep breath, then closed his eyes and rested his head on the steering wheel. The events of the past week and a half boiled to the surface of his mind.

Instantly he caught himself. He snapped his head up, looked at himself in the mirror and said, "Bullshit. I'm not going to worry about something I have no control over. The new Bud Rogers is always happy, because happy is the only way to be."

With his affirmation in place, he went out to the barn to feed his hogs. Thoughts of Jasper would seep into his conscious mind and Bud would dismiss them just as quickly. He whistled as he walked. He sang songs to himself. He did anything and everything except think about Jasper, George and the dead inmate.

After a hot shower he grabbed a beer out of the refrigerator, made a sandwich out of some cold-cuts and propped his feet up on his favorite foot stool. He set his alarm for six in the morning and grabbed the remote.

As he surfed through the channels Bud thought about how good it was to have *(a vampire in your head)* cable TV. It was simply wonderful to have *(a few dead bodies)* about forty channels to choose from. Such modern technology at the touch of a button.

Bud set his beer aside and laid his head back, absolutely amazed at how tired he was and looking forward to a good night's sleep. Then he heard a car coming up his driveway. *Oh great,* he thought. *Who can this be?* He did his best to ignore it, and it was so long before anybody came in that Bud was almost asleep again. The sound of his front door opening brought him back to consciousness.

He looked up to see Jimmy T standing over him. He was dressed in a denim shirt and a leather hat. Bud suddenly remembered about Phil and the weekend and all the things he was supposed to keep Jimmy T up on.

"Hey Fuckbubble," Jimmy T said. He wasn't happy.

Bud straightened up and acted like he had everything under control.

"You're slippin' up," Jimmy T said. "I'm glad I ran into Phil Waters myself and found out he's going north this weekend. When were you going to tell me? Do you know how long it takes to get that shit packaged and ready to go?"

"I meant to tell you." Bud scrambled for an excuse. "I've been busier than hell lately, you know?"

"What I know is that we have an important transaction about to take place, and you almost fucked it up."

Bud didn't know what to say. With all the events of the last two days he'd completely forgotten about Phil. He gave Jimmy T a helpless shrug.

"The shit's already in your truck," Jimmy T said. He held his hands out. "Think you can remember to deliver it?"

Before Bud could answer, Jimmy T turned and headed out. He was almost outside when Bud thought about Jasper. This time the thought didn't go away. Jasper didn't want Bud to help Jimmy T anymore and what Jasper wanted, Jasper got. Bud didn't have a clue what he was going to say, but he knew he had to try.

"Wait," he said. Jimmy T stopped and turned, but said nothing.

"Come on in and have a beer." Bud didn't know what else to say so he tried to buy some time.

"No thanks." Jimmy T started away again.

"Wait, it's important." Bud almost hoped Jimmy T would keep walking. "I've got to talk to you."

Jimmy T came back inside. He softened a little. "Okay, I'll have one quick one."

He grabbed a beer out of Bud's kitchen, sat down on the couch and said, "What?"

Bud still didn't know where to begin. At last he said, "I don't think I want to, you know, do this anymore," he stammered. Whatever softening Bud thought he'd seen from Jimmy T was gone.

"Are you crazy?" Jimmy T's eyes grew incredibly wide. "You can't just drop out, you're in the big league now. You can't just up and quit, it's not like you're having a bad night at the bingo hall."

"I'm sorry, I just can't do it anymore. I have my reasons."

Jimmy T slammed his beer down on the coffee table, spilling a little on Bud's alarm clock. He got up and straddled Bud's legs. Then he bent down so their faces were just inches apart. "I don't think you understand," he said. He was holding himself back, but he looked ready to beat Bud to a pulp. "I don't give a flying fuck about your reasons, whatever they are. Do you know what happens to people who don't come through on a deal? We've got to get that shit to Port Hope, Ontario, or there's going be hell to pay. Understand?"

Bud thought of Jasper. He didn't think Jimmy T had any idea what it meant to pay hell.

"I understand you're upset," Bud said. "I just can't. That's all there is to it. I can't do it anymore."

"I'm upset? You think I'm upset?" Jimmy T had his nose almost touching Bud's and was on the verge of screaming. His ears were fiery red. Bud could feel little bits of spittle hitting his face, but he didn't think he was in any position to complain.

He tried again. "Look, I know -- "

"You don't know Jack shit! You think it's me you have to worry about? Listen asswipe, I don't know who you think you're dealing with here, but they've got big balls and no sense humor. I'm the last guy on the list of people you have to worry about, although I am on the list."

"You don't understand. I -- "

"I don't give a fuck what kind of excuse you think you've got. Trust me, it's not good enough." Jimmy T was obstinate. "There's only one excuse that's acceptable, and that's if you think the cops are onto us, and if they are you damned well better have said something before now."

Bud thought for an instant that naming the police might be the perfect excuse, but the gleam in Jimmy T's eyes told him that had better not be the case. He was surprised at finding out about a higher authority. He didn't know Jimmy T had people to answer to, but it didn't matter, he still had Jasper to worry about. Finally he said, "Look, I know you're pissed off, but it's -- "

Jimmy T grabbed two handfuls of Bud's shirt and lifted him off the chair. "Listen to me. I'm not fucking around when I say you can't quit. It's not a matter of us finding a different plan. We've already promised this stuff on the other side. People are already taking orders, and if it doesn't show things are really going to suck for me, and that means they're going to suck even worse for you. Do you understand?"

Bud's mind swam in circles. Jimmy T still had him by the shirt and Bud wished there was some way he could make him understand what he was up against. "I don't know how to make you understand. I just can't -- "

Bud found himself flying backwards over the chair. He landed on his left shoulder. A jolt of pain shot down his arm and side, but he barely noticed it after Jimmy T planted his work shoe in his ribs.

Suddenly Bud found it difficult to breath. He swallowed tiny gulps of air and struggled to raise his head while keeping an eye on Jimmy T's feet.

After a few seconds, when his breath returned, he looked up. Jimmy T was standing there looking sorry for him. Bud struggled to his feet. He hoped his ribs weren't broken.

Jimmy T looked away and rubbed his hands up and down on his face. His ears had softened to a shade of light pink. Finally he turned and said, "Look, Bud. I'm sorry, but you have to believe me when I say that that was nothing compared to what could happen. I know you think you have some excuse, but it isn't going to be enough. I'm even going to double your payment, maybe that'll help."

"It isn't the money," Bud said, although a little upset at how easy that seemed. "I just can't do it anymore."

Jimmy T slammed Bud up against the wall. Bud felt his shoulder and ribs throb. He struggled to breath again as Jimmy T's hand closed around his windpipe.

"Bud, we can't even debate this." Jimmy T was spoke slowly, looking directly into Bud's eyes. "Just imagine two guys named Biff and Steverino showing up in the middle of the night. Can you imagine how it would feel to have all the bones in your legs broken one at a time?"

For the first time Bud realized maybe Jimmy T could match Jasper's offer.

"Try to imagine that. How many do you think you could take before you passed out from the pain? Wouldn't it be great to wake up with a bucket of cold water in your face just so you could feel each bone break?"

Bud couldn't say anything, he could barely breath.

"I don't think I'd like that to happen to me either. Tell me you'll deliver the goods. I can't take no for an answer, and you can't give no for an answer."

Bud didn't think Jimmy T would leave until he agreed. He tried to say okay, but he couldn't. Finally he just nodded his head.

Jimmy T relaxed his grip, then he let go altogether and stepped back. He looked down at Bud holding his ribs. "I'm sorry, Bud. It's just got to be this way. Once you get to the big time you can never go back. Maybe we can work something out for the future, but this time you've got to come through or really bad things are going happen, understand?"

Bud nodded again, still fighting for his breath. Jimmy T walked over to the coffee table, grabbed his beer and headed out to his car. As he left he said, "Thanks for the beer."

Bud slunk his way back to the chair. He had to struggle to get his feet up, but he finally managed. A stinger of pain shot up his arm as he reached for his beer. He took a long swallow, then said out loud, "Well Jasper, wherever you are, I tried."

For one horrible moment Bud was afraid Jasper would answer him. He didn't think he could handle Jasper right then. When he realized he was alone he took another swallow of beer and said, out loud again, "Yup, it sure is great. The new Bud Rogers is here at last." Then after a minute or two, while rubbing his ribs he added, "Happy, it's the only way to be."

* * * * *

Toni found it easier to get Tommy to talk the second time around. She wanted to know all the details so she pestered him for a few minutes until he gave in.

"Well Toni, it's like this," Tommy finally said. "We have two bodies killed about a week and a half apart. We don't know for sure if it's the same perpetrator, but it seems likely. The cause of death was loss of blood in each case. We're treating it as the same person until we find out otherwise. We figure there's a good chance the killer was at George's funeral so we've got a list of everybody who was there. And of course we think it was someone local. We're trying to get a profile of him based on the other evidence that we have."

"What about the inmate?" Toni asked.

"To be honest, we don't really have much more from him than we had before, except that the body was fresher. There was absolutely no sign of a struggle, and he bled to death."

"Well, what made him bleed to death? I mean, was there a

gunshot wound or something?"

Tommy suddenly became evasive. Toni shook him until he finally said, "There was just a small puncture wound, about the size of a pencil."

"Where?"

"On the neck, just below the ear."

"Sounds like we've got a vampire in County Line," Toni said playfully. She expected Tommy to laugh, but he just closed his eyes.

"Yeah," he said at last. He smiled too, but Toni didn't think it looked very sincere. She decided not to push it.

"What about the blood?" she said. "Was there any at the scene? You said George's body didn't have any blood around it so you figure he was killed someplace else."

"No. There was no blood at the scene."

"So we know that in both cases the body was moved, although the railroad bed seems like a pretty lousy place to try to hide one."

They stayed silent for a while. Then Tommy squeezed her hand and said, "Toni?"

She looked at him. He looked dead serious and he was squeezing the life out of her hand. "Yeah," she said

"There's some very strange things going on, I think. I mean it's bad enough that people are getting killed, but some of the evidence seems to contradict itself, or rather, it just doesn't fit. What I mean is, there's a lot that's happened that we don't understand yet, so promise me you'll be careful. Don't trust anybody. Remember, we probably both know the person who killed George, and I can't think of anybody offhand that I would suspect. That means it's going to come as a surprise, so watch out."

Toni considered that for a minute. It was kind of eerie in that perspective, but also very true. "I promise," she said.

"And since you're a part of this investigation now, you've got to promise to tell me about anything out of the ordinary. Anything. If you see somebody doing something peculiar, don't just dismiss it. You've got to tell me, it may be enough to save somebody's life."

Toni was about to answer when she thought of her frightening episode with Bud Rogers. *Sorry Tommy, but there's no way I'm telling you about that. I don't even know exactly what happened myself.* "I promise," she said again.

Tommy must have sensed her hesitation. "Are you sure?"

"Yeah, I'm sure." She couldn't bring herself to tell Tommy about what had happened with Bud. She told herself it was all right, that it didn't have anything to do with the murders.

"I promise."

CHAPTER 25

Tommy came home at about four-thirty on Thursday afternoon. He laid a stack of papers on the kitchen table. He wondered where Toni was, the two had practically moved in together. Then he saw her note saying she went to Batavia to pick up her guitar at the music store and that she'd be home around six-thirty with some Chinese food.

He took a long, hot shower, put on some sweat pants and a sweatshirt, then grabbed his stack of papers and sat on the couch. Each sheet of paper was a computer printout of a different person who had attended George Lewis' funeral. They were categorized according to their various association with George, and in some cases with the inmate Mateo Martinez, but those were few.

Tommy took all the ones that were women and set them aside. It's not that they were all presumed innocent, but the only evidence they had pointed to a strong, tobacco chewing killer, and Tommy didn't know of any women in County Line who chewed tobacco. He knew it might turn out that the killer was hired by a woman, but the only way to know was to find the killer first.

They were convinced the killer was a local resident, and of course that meant he probably knew George personally. It was for that reason, plus the fact that they didn't have anywhere else to look, that everybody who was at the funeral had to be checked out. The list consisted of two hundred forty-one people. Of those, thirty-six were children. Of the remaining two hundred five, one hundred seven were women.

Setting those aside, Tommy sat with ninety-eight loose pages in front of him. Since he lived in County Line it was his job to evaluate each individual in four different categories, at least as well as he could. County Line was a small town, but even Tommy didn't know everybody personally.

Personality, physical ability to carry out the crime, likelihood of owning camouflaged clothing, and probability of chewing tobacco on a regular basis were the four categories. Tommy was supposed to rate each person on a scale from one to five in each category, after which, the people with the highest scores would be investigated first.

He decided to do physical ability first. He didn't see any sense in wasting time on a person who couldn't possibly have done it. He went through the pile and looked for people he knew couldn't have dragged George's body a half-mile into the woods. Those people, for their various reasons, were graded with a one. Tommy counted them up. There were twenty one. He put them on top of the stack with the women. He thought about how many women on the list could have done the job. He figured there were several, but dismissed them after remembering there weren't any tobacco chewing women in County Line that he knew of.

A little quick math told him he had seventy-seven pages left in front of him. He went back through, grading the rest. Strong young men like Johnny Davis received a five, while others received lesser numbers. Tommy tried to be fair, but he kept coming across names of people he was sure weren't killers. He had to keep reminding himself there was a separate category for personality.

As he moved on to the camouflage category, he wondered if there wasn't a better way. Without much choice, however, he kept on, doing his best to give a grade on what he knew. Guys like Phil Waters, Bud Rogers, and the Davis boys, all of whom Tommy could remember seeing in person wearing camouflage during the hunting seasons, were again given a five.

He reminded himself that it was mostly bowhunters and turkey hunters that wore camouflage. Most of the people who hunted deer with guns wore orange. The ones that Tommy knew hunted, but didn't know for sure if they owned camouflage were given a four, and so on. This time he didn't remove any of the names. There were a few people he couldn't picture ever wearing camouflage, but if the crime was premeditated there was always a chance.

Since he didn't have a clue as to whether or not most of them chewed tobacco, he moved on to the personality section. This was the most difficult. Tommy didn't think he could give anybody a five. It was still hard to believe that anybody from County Line could do such a thing.

He whisked through, giving most people either a three or a four, not really believing anybody on the list was the killer. *Or a vampire,* part of him said. He pushed that thought away, telling himself there was a more logical explanation. After some quick addition, purposefully looking just at the numbers and not the names, he rearranged the pages with the lowest scores on top.

"Well, here goes," he said out loud. He went through the list quickly the first time, looking only for people whom he knew for sure weren't tobacco users. There weren't many that he was sure about, but there were a few. There were six, in fact. Tommy gave them all a one and placed them on the pile of unlikely suspects.

Although he knew it was foolish, he felt a bit of relief. One of the six names had been his. It was just a precaution, but Gris had insisted that Tommy include himself among the list of suspects. He'd been getting high marks until then.

He went through the list again, giving out mostly three different answers: five for definite, two for probably not, and the third was to leave it blank because he just didn't know. He took the ones with the blanks and set them aside, figuring they would just have to be checked out. For the time being he would concentrate on what they had. That way, if they found the killer, they wouldn't be wasting time on any of the less likely subjects.

Out of the seventy-one pages left, there were forty-two that made it into the "don't know" pile. Tommy took the remaining twenty-nine pages and stacked them, again ignoring the names, with the highest numbers on top. He was surprised to find that they were basically divided up into two groups. He took the ones who had scored low because he was pretty sure they didn't chew and temporarily set them aside also. He was left with a stack of thirteen names. They had scored four or five for physical ability, four or five for camouflaged clothing, five for Tommy being sure they were tobacco users, and either a three or four for their personality.

He looked at the names and tried to convince himself that one of them was the killer. It wasn't easy. He was also surprised to find that he knew most of them quite well. There was Phil Waters, Johnny Davis, Bud and Chris Rogers. All were guys that Tommy had known since grade school.

He was so absorbed he didn't hear the door open when Toni came in with her new guitar in one hand and a bag of Chinese food in the other.

"What are you doing?" she said.

Tommy jumped, looked up from the stack of papers and said, "I'm trying to decide which one of my friends is a killer."

*****

Bud sat with his feet up. He'd gone to the Silver Nickel after work and dwelled on his problems until closing time. Since declaring himself the new Bud Rogers he'd been looking forward to getting some real sleep, but after Jimmy T's arrival the night before it was impossible. He'd driven home from the Nickel, even though he shouldn't have. The pain in his ribs and shoulder was gone, but only because his senses were thoroughly impaired.

With a beer in one hand and a bottle of whiskey in the other, Bud babbled to no one in particular about what a bunch of no good sons-of-bitches Jasper and Jimmy T were.

"Jasper!" he yelled. "Where the fuck are you boy? Come on out and play you piece of shit." He'd been cursing for over an hour with no recourse so the fear of Jasper's hammer was mostly gone. As if to test him, however, Bud kept right on talking. "Jasper, come on. I need your help. Biff and Steverino are coming to town and you and me are going to kick some ass."

He quieted down for a minute, first taking a slug of whiskey, then washing it down with a splash of beer. Giving up on Jasper, he thought about Biff and Steverino and yelled, "Fuck those assholes."

That caused a fit of laughter, after which he said, "And fuck Jimmy T, too. Yeah, fuck Jimmy T. I'll show you, you old burned out hippie. I'll fix you and your thugs right up. Then maybe you'll learn not to mess with Bud Rogers and his good friend Jasper Shimmy-ack."

He took another swig of whiskey, noticed the bottle was empty, and threw it against the brick fireplace. It smashed and the pieces fell on top of those from several beer bottles. The loud crash brought him out of his hysteria, but he was still plenty drunk. He shook his head and drained his beer.

Bud still intended to plant the dope for Jimmy T. He didn't think Jasper could do him much worse, but the thought of Jimmy T's thugs working him over scared the hell out of him. He'd find a way to deal with the situation, but he needed time to think. He also needed to get some sleep. His mind was mush from the insomnia and it was impossible for him to reason. He decided he'd send Phil with the packages and hoped he'd be able to find a solution before it was time for the next run.

As he set his clock for six in the morning, Bud thought about how Tim Castillo had whined when he told him he was taking the next day off.

"And fuck Tim Castillo too if he don't like it," he yelled.

Then he laughed and said, "Happy, it's the only way to be."

CHAPTER 26

The Fletcher parking lot shone with the gloomy reflection of rain puddles. Bud sat in his truck wearing sunglasses despite the overcast sky. His hangover was a killer. He frowned as he thought about sliding under Phil's pickup and laying on the wet asphalt.

He looked around to see if he was alone, then he grabbed the two packages of coke that Jimmy T had left in his truck. Bud wondered what Jasper would do since he hadn't taken his advice on quitting the smuggling scheme. He didn't know how he could get out of it. Jimmy T had made it clear what would happen if he didn't come through. With Jasper it was still a gray area as to what would happen, although Bud didn't think it could get any worse.

A thought crossed his mind just then and Bud realized there was probably only one way he could get out of the smuggling business. It probably wasn't what Jasper had in mind, but it was all Bud could think of. He put one of the packages back under his seat, then fastened the other to the frame of Phil's truck.

With that done, he drove out of the parking lot, rolled down the window to get some air despite the rain, and headed down 490 towards County Line with the radio playing softly. His head, ribs and shoulder hurt too much to sing.

Bud felt bad about what he was doing, but he didn't see any other way. He had to stop smuggling drugs to appease Jasper, but Jimmy T would make life even more miserable if he quit. If he'd been thinking clearly he probably would have been able to talk himself out of it, but his congested state of mind forced his self-preservation instinct to override his conscience.

When he got to Batavia, Bud stopped at a gas station on route 33. He went inside, got some change from the clerk and went back outside to the pay phone. As he dialed the number for information he had a sick feeling in his gut that he knew was due to more than just the previous night's overindulgence.

"What city, please?" a grating, female voice said.

"Fort Erie, Ontario."

"I'm sorry sir, we don't have Canadian listings. You'll have to call area code 905-555-1212."

"Fine," Bud said. He slammed the receiver and dug out some more quarters.

He dialed the new number and got a Canadian operator with a friendlier voice. After the same series of questions he finally said, "Yeah, I'd like the number for the Canadian Border Patrol."

"You mean Canadian Customs?"

"I guess so," Bud said. "The people who watch the border for drug smugglers and stuff."

He got the number and made the call, giving Phil's license plate number and saying approximately when Phil would be coming. After he hung up, he got back into his truck and drove home.

Bud felt wretched, but he made himself take the remaining package of cocaine and wrap it in a plastic garbage bag. He took it out behind the barn and buried it in a large pile of pig manure.

When he'd realized what he was going to do he didn't see any sense in losing both packages. He thought maybe he could buy his way to freedom or something with the remaining package. Bud wasn't sure what he was doing or why, his head was like a block of concrete with seaweed for brains.

He went inside and flopped on the couch, hoping to get some sleep and sort things out later.

CHAPTER 27

"Wait a minute," Toni called. She took her guitar out of its case.

Tommy was headed out the door with the stack of computer printouts in his hand. He held them up and said, "Come on, honey. I have to get to the office, Gris wants to get going on our investigations."

"This'll only take a minute. I want to play it tonight, but I need an honest opinion."

She sat on the coffee table and began to play. Tommy started to object, but Toni scowled at him. He finally decided she was worth it and sat down on the arm of the couch.

Toni sang the song she'd put to music two days before. She had been practicing and figured it was as good as it was going to get. Tommy listened, a little impatiently at first. As the song went on, though, he relaxed and listened closer. By the time Toni finished he looked thoroughly impressed.

She looked up at him.

Tommy smiled and said, "It's a great song, they're going to love it. Who'd you write it for anyway? It sounds like you got dumped."

"Yeah, well, I did."

"Dave Taggert," he said with a knowing smile. "He's the only guy I know who's dumb enough to dump a girl like you."

"Thanks, I think."

Tommy laughed, then leaned forward and kissed her. "And

it's definitely his loss." He turned and headed for the door. "I'll probably have to work late tonight, but I'll be sure to swing by Jed's afterwards. I love to hear you sing."

He smiled and walked out. Toni watched him through the window until he was down the driveway and out of sight.

*****

The Canadian border was approaching fast. Phil turned the volume down on the stereo. As he moved another spot closer to the inspection booth, he looked down at his music collection. He had about sixty tapes, every one loaded with classic rock.

He was thinking about how much success he'd had in previous rodeos in Port Hope as he moved ahead to the booth. He'd finished first once and third twice in his last three trips there.

Then he thought about the time the year before when all the bulls had broken out of their pen on Saturday night. Everybody took off from the dance, grabbed a horse and rounded them up in the dark. Chasing bulls through people's back yards at night, it was a wonder nobody got strangled by a clothesline or something.

Going for the championship was worthwhile in Phil's eyes, but it was spontaneous events like that, and the comaraderie that sprang from it, which he loved so much about the rodeo scene. It was the kind of stuff you could tell your grandchildren about someday. The memories had him smiling as he approached the booth, and that was good. Phil always figured that sitting in one of those inspection booths all day could take its toll on a person, so he always did his best not to antagonize any of the inspectors.

"What's your citizenship?" the young woman said. She had short, brown hair and a slight lisp. Phil had never seen her before. He wondered if she was new.

"United States," Phil said.

"What is the purpose of your trip?"

"I'm going to a rodeo in Port Hope."

She was staring at something inside her booth which Phil couldn't see. He knew they had computers in there but he'd never seen anyone spend so much time looking at one.

Finally she looked up at Phil again. Then she turned her head towards the main building that was just beyond the booths. She looked back and said, "What are you bringing into Canada with you, besides your clothes and personal items?"

"Just a case of beer and a carton of cigarettes for a friend." The woman kept looking towards the building and Phil was getting anxious. It had been more than two years since he'd had his truck searched and he wasn't looking forward to that kind of delay.

The inspectress pointed to a row of parking spaces near the customs building and said, "Pull over on the other side of that blue van, please."

Phil was upset, but not concerned. He figured it was just his luck to run into a new girl. There was no sense in arguing, so he nodded and said, "Okay."

He pulled in front of the white, one-story building, parked alongside the blue van and shut the truck off. He remembered the last time he'd had his truck searched. They'd just let their dog sniff around the outside, put him up in the back so he could sniff around some more, and then sent Phil on his way. He'd heard stories, however, of people who had their bags searched and their vehicles taken apart. He hoped nothing like that would happen this time.

Two uniformed men approached. One was tall and lean, the other was short and stocky. The stocky one led a German Shepherd on a leash. The two men were complete opposites except that they both had identical, bushy mustaches. Phil formed a picture of them each wearing a pair of those phony glasses with the big plastic noses. He couldn't help but laugh.

He got out of the truck and stood at the place on the sidewalk where the officers indicated. Without a word the tall one stood next to Phil while the short one led the dog to the rear bumper of his pickup. Phil watched as the dog methodically sniffed his way around the truck's wheel wells and underside.

Their silence was unnerving. "What's his name?" Phil said to the guy next to him.

"Duke," the officer replied.

Phil laughed. "That's original."

The officer just looked at the dog.

Phil thought about saying something funny like, "I meant the *dog's* name." But then Duke, on the passenger side by the door, simply sat down and licked his chops. The short officer looked at the one next to Phil who motioned and said, "Would you please come over here and place your hands on the hood."

Phil was wondering what was going on, but he did what the officer asked. He was shocked when the man grabbed his right arm and pulled it behind his back. Before he could even respond he felt what could only be a handcuff closing with a metallic clink.

"What the -- what's going on? Is this how you welcome everybody to your country?" Phil was feeling more than a little indignant. Without answering the officer grabbed his other arm and connected it behind his back.

"Aw come on. You guys have to be kidding me." Phil didn't understand what was going on, but he was pretty sure they weren't kidding.

When the short officer with the dog saw that Phil was cuffed, he dropped down out of sight. After a few seconds Phil heard his muffled, accented voice say, "Bingo!"

"What the fuck does he mean by Bingo?" Phil craned his neck, trying to look at the officer behind him. The tall man held his arms and prevented him from turning. "What's going on. Come on you guys, I'm not a trouble maker. What's going on?"

He still didn't know why he'd been handcuffed, but he was getting worried and the guy behind him wasn't offering any explanations.

A minute later the officer with the dog slid out from under Phil's truck and set the plastic wrapped package on the hood. He smiled and said, "Got you, eh?"

*****

Toni was almost done with her first set, wondering and worrying where Tommy was. She'd just finished singing a song called *Filter* by a couple friends of hers who called themselves the *Stray Dogs,* and the place was rocking. She wanted Tommy to be there when she played her new song, but the crowd was in a great mood so she decided right then was the best time to try it.

"I'm going to play a new song for you now," Toni said.

The throng shouted and whistled to the point where Toni almost thought they were being facetious.

"Actually, it's not really all that new," she said above the roar. "I just finally got the music right for it. This one's called -- "

Toni was mortified. She hadn't realized until that very moment that the song didn't have a name.

"Um . . . " she stammered. "I must confess that until this very moment, it never occurred to me to give this song a name. For now I'll call it "The Ballad of Jed's Tavern."

By their enthusiastic reaction, Toni knew the name would stick.

After reminding herself not to start out too fast, she played the tune and was happy that the crowd seemed to like it. She no sooner finished when Tommy came in the door.

"Thanks," she said. "I hope you liked it." A round of applause told her they did. "I've got to take a little break now."

She made her way over to where Tommy was getting a beer. She touched him lightly on the back and said, "Hi, I've missed you."

Tommy turned and said, "Sorry I didn't get here sooner." He looked tired.

"Where've you been?"

"I suppose you've heard that Phil Waters got busted at the Canadian border, right?"

Toni's eyes widened. "Yeah, I did. But who can believe it?"

He nodded in agreement. "It surprised me too. But they found almost four and a half pounds of coke strapped to the frame of his pickup truck."

Toni didn't know what to say. She shook her head.

"So anyway, seeing as how we've been trying to investigate just about everybody in this town, especially anybody who seems to be acting strangely, we decided we wanted to talk to Phil. Unfortunately the Canadian government, after letting us wait around for four hours, decided that Monday would be soon enough."

"It sounds like you've had a lousy day. Have a couple beers and relax."

Tommy laughed and said, "Yeah, that sounds like a plan, but looking around here, I'll probably have to leave soon."

"Why?" Toni tilted her head and looked hurt.

"There's certain people I want to observe over the weekend, and none of them are here."

"Are you supposed to be a cop twenty-four hours a day?" There was a bit of tension building. Toni regretted it, she hadn't meant to start an argument.

"No, but it was expected of me when I took this assignment that I would do certain things. I'm supposed to act like I've got the next two days off and see if I can find anything out. I'm the only cop who doesn't look out of place around here, and I'd sure like to catch whoever killed George. Wouldn't you?"

Toni couldn't argue with that. "Yeah," she said at last. "But I'll be glad when it's over and you go back to writing speeding tickets for a living."

"Oh thanks." Tommy laughed. "I guess one beer wouldn't hurt."

Toni hugged him and the tension was gone.

CHAPTER 28

Bud was trying to decide. He wanted to go to Jed's and see Toni Birch play and sing. He didn't want to see Jimmy T, however. The Silver Nickel seemed like the logical choice.

As he drove down route 98 he thought of Phil Waters. Having a hangover coupled with complete exhaustion, Bud had managed to get some real sleep after he got home that morning, and like everything else he'd been involved with recently, after he woke up it seemed distant, like a dream.

Bud couldn't believe what he'd done, but he told himself it was in the interest of self-preservation. It was the only way he could think of to get out of the smuggling business. He felt bad for Phil, though. He wondered if an anonymous letter exonerating Phil and implicating Jimmy T would be of any use. He decided to give it some thought.

When he saw route 238 approaching, he knew it was decision time. He was right on top of the intersection when he finally made up his mind.

"What I want to do is go to Jed's and see Toni Birch," he said. "I guess that's what I'll do. I can't hide from Jimmy T forever, and the new Bud fears no man. Jimmy T can kiss my ass."

Bud drove straight down route 98 until he got to Jed's. He found a spot near the back of the lot and backed his truck in. He turned off the lights and engine. He was about to head inside when he saw Tommy Chandler coming out the door. Bud was glad he hadn't started in yet, Tommy wasn't a bad guy, but he was a cop and Bud didn't feel like talking to the cops.

He wondered if there was any chance Tommy was leaving because he'd had a fight with Toni.

"Like that's going to make any difference as far as you're concerned," he said to himself. He noticed he'd been doing that a lot. He waited for Tommy to leave, then went inside.

Bud scanned the bar, hoping to see Jimmy T before Jimmy T saw him. He was surprised when he didn't see him at all. Toni was on stage and the rest of the bar seemed normal, except for being a little busier than usual.

As he made his way towards the bar, Bud suddenly wondered if seeing Tanya for the first time was going to be like seeing Toni was. He didn't think so. Then he reminded himself that he was the new Bud, and he didn't care.

When he got to the bar, he looked Tanya right in the eyes, challenging her. She looked back at him and finally said, "Well, you want a beer or something else."

Bud nodded that a beer would be fine. He eyed Tanya as she turned around. His mind drifted back to the previous Saturday night and he smiled to himself.

When she came back he asked, "Where's Jimmy T?" Bud wanted to face him off and get it over with.

Tanya shrugged and said, "Nobody knows, not even his wife."

Bud took his beer and watched Tanya as she walked away. He turned and looked at Toni on the stage and wondered if anybody else in the place had had the two of them. Then realized that just left him feeling guilty.

Just then Lisa Bahn sidled up beside him. "Hey sailor, how about a shot of tequila."

Bud was surprised. Lisa hardly ever said more than two words to him. He looked her over. Mostly he looked into her eyes, trying to figure out if his friend Jasper was in on it.

The answer was no. Lisa Bahn, Tommy Chandler's ex-girlfriend, was doing this of her own free will. Bud didn't mean to stare, but Lisa had a knockout body and she wore a skintight, short-sleeved shirt that highlighted every curve. Eventually Bud got around to saying, "Right on, I was thinking the same thing myself." They turned to face the bar and waited for Tanya to work her way back to them.

Bud caught Lisa's reflection in the mirror behind the bar and stared some more. She caught him looking but didn't seem to mind.

When Tanya reached them Lisa said, "Two tequila shots with the works."

Tanya came back with two shots, a salt shaker and two lemon wedges on a napkin. Bud watched as Lisa paid for them. Then she grabbed a lemon wedge, smiled at him and said, "Body shot?"

Bud couldn't believe his ears. Lisa must have taken his blank stare as a yes. She brushed her long, dark hair back over her shoulder. Then she took the lemon wedge and rubbed some of the juice on her neck. She shook a little salt on the same place, smiled and said, "Go nuts."

Bud thought he might do just that. He put the shot in his hand and put his other arm around Lisa's neck, holding her hair out of the way. He leaned forward and sucked the salt off her neck, lingering, enjoying the moment.

Of course her exposed neck made him think of Jasper, but the new Bud didn't let it bother him. He licked Lisa's neck an extra time, just because he wanted too, then backed away and slammed the shot of tequila. He felt the fiery liquid coat his mouth and throat, but Lisa was right there, pushing the lemon wedge between his lips. The reaction was pleasant and Bud grinned from ear to ear.

She handed him the other lemon wedge and said, "My turn."

Bud gave her a devilish grin. He handed the lemon back and turned his head, baring his neck. Lisa smiled and made a production out of applying the lemon and salt. When she took her turn licking Bud's neck he could feel her breasts rubbing against his arm. He breathed deeply when she sucked on his neck for an extra long of time.

He watched as Lisa slammed the shot and tongued her lemon. When she finished she kissed him on the cheek. "Thanks," she said. Then she trotted off towards the far end of the bar where three of her girlfriends stood snickering.

“Thank you,” Bud murmured as he watched her bounce away, wondering what it was all about. He considered following her, but before he'd made up his mind Johnny Davis slapped him on the back.

Bud looked at him. Johnny just looked back, smiling from ear to ear. Bud smiled too. Finally Johnny said, "All right man. What's your secret? I thought she was going to fuck you right there on the bar."

Bud laughed. Before he could think of a reply Johnny said, "Let me buy you one. I feel like I owe it to you just for the show."

Bud looked at the far end of the bar. Lisa was talking to Patty Sinclair. She didn't look as though she would get too far away so Bud shrugged and said, "Okay, but you don't get to lick me."

*****

The crowd was long gone. Toni sat at the bar at two-thirty in the morning talking to Tanya.

"I love these Friday nights when you play," Tanya said. "It reminds me of my younger days, seeing all those kids getting crazy at the start of the weekend. And you're so good."

"Thanks." Toni wasn't sure but she thought she might be blushing. Compliments always made her feel awkward. She sat in silence for a minute, watching Tanya wash the last of the glasses.

After a while, Tanya poured herself a vodka and tonic, then looked at Toni to see if she wanted another beer. Toni was about to decline, but Tanya had a peculiar look about her. She noticed that Tanya had been drinking heavier than usual too.

"Sure," she finally said. "I've got no place to be right away."

As she looked around to make sure the place was deserted,

Toni thought about Tommy. He might be home waiting for her. But then again, with his investigation going on he might not be home at all.

Tanya threw a towel under the bar and came around and sat next to her. Toni looked her over. There definitely seemed to be something wrong, but she didn't know if she should ask about it or just let Tanya work it out.

Tanya decided for her when she said, "Did you ever have something really weird happen to you?"

Toni thought about some of the things that had happened to her in the past few weeks and almost burst out laughing. She wasn't about to tell Tanya of her horrifying experience with Bud. She thought about how she should answer, but before she could come up with anything Tanya added:

"I mean really weird. Like so weird you weren't even sure of what happened? I mean, you think you know what happened, in fact you're sure of it, but you really can't remember?" Tanya looked down at her hands. "I'm sorry, I have no business laying all this on you. I suppose I'm just overreacting."

Toni was astonished at what she was hearing. Tanya couldn't be talking about the same thing. But by the way she looked, so confused, almost pleading for understanding, Toni decided it had to be.

"As a matter-of-fact," she finally said. "I have." They turned toward each other and held hands. "Are we talking about the same thing?"

"I don't know." Tanya looked past her, out into space. "It was like I was under a spell. And then when I came out of it there was a big blank in my memory. I knew what had happened, but I couldn't remember it happening. It's so scary. I can't even talk about it for fear of people thinking I'm a lunatic. I'm sorry, You must think I'm --"

"I don't think any such thing. The same thing happened to me exactly two weeks ago."

Tanya looked at her skeptically. Toni said, "I'm serious. It was like I'd lost all control of my body, and then I blacked out. I've got to tell you, I was scared to death when I woke up in a strange bed."

Tanya squeezed Toni's hands. "You woke up in a bed? Oh my God! I thought I'd had a horrible experience just because I couldn't remember anything. Oh dear. Was anybody there with you?"

"No, thank God. I had to sneak out while he was in the shower. I can't believe it's happened to someone else. I was so afraid I'd done something foolish or was losing my marbles or -- "

"Oh you poor thing," Tanya cut in. "And here I was feeling sorry for myself thinking I'd had the worst experience a person could have. I can't imagine how scared I would have been. I just sort of came to while I was driving down route 98."

Toni snapped her head up. "Route 98? Are we talking about the same person?"

Tanya raised her eyebrows and said, "I don't know. Whose bed did you wake up in."

CHAPTER 29

Tommy woke up to see Toni shaking him.

"Wake up," she said. "Come on, we've got to talk. Come on. Wake up."

"Okay, okay. I'm awake." He glanced at the clock, it was almost three-thirty. "What's up?"

"Remember when you told me to tell you if anybody was acting funny?"

"Yeah."

"I have," Toni said.

Tommy opened his eyes a little wider.

"And Tanya Lambert. She's been acting weird too."

Tommy was sure it was just the grogginess, but he struggled to understand what Toni was talking about. He squinted and said, "I'm trying to see a relationship between you and Tanya. I haven't seen any strange activity from either of you . . . until now that is."

"No, it's not us. We're just the ones who have it in common." Toni was still shaking him as though it would make him understand. "We've both had a very strange experience in the last couple weeks. And the common denominator is Bud Rogers." She sounded as though she'd just solved every riddle known to man.

"Well at least we're getting somewhere," Tommy said. "Why don't you tell me just exactly what it is that Bud Rogers has done, and how you and Tanya happen to know about it?" After a second he added, "And why did it take until now to tell me?"

Toni hesitated. She looked away before saying, "It's going to be difficult for me to make you understand, so why don't I start from the beginning?"

"Good idea."

She filled Tommy in on what she'd been through the night before she met him in the park, and how she had a blank spot in her memory. She went to great lengths to explain that she was totally helpless. Tommy was skeptical, but when she added the story about a very similar event happening to Tanya, he let up a little.

When Toni was done she said, "So what's it all mean?"

Tommy shrugged and answered, "Beats the hell out of me. I'd have said you were nuts until you pointed out that it happened to somebody else too. Plus everything seems weird around here lately. I don't really know what it has to do with anything, except that I think we should make Bud Rogers our prime suspect and investigate him first, especially considering his high score in the evaluations."

Tommy let himself sink back into bed, expecting Toni to get out of her clothes and join him. She shook him some more and pleaded, "Aren't you going to do something?"

Tommy took a deep breath before saying, "Just what, for Christ's sake, would you like me to do at three-thirty in the morning? Though I can assure you we will be talking about this some more in the future."

Toni knew what Tommy meant by that, and she couldn't blame him. But they both seemed to realize it wasn't the time for it. So she was happy to let it slide for the time being too. "I don't know. There must be something you can do. He could be out killing somebody right now for all we know."

Tommy wanted to go back to sleep and leave it until morning. "I know," he said. "Let's give him a call. If he answers the phone in a grumpy mood we'll know he's home in bed and not out killing anybody."

He'd meant to sound sarcastic, but Toni jumped up and ran

out to find the phone book as if that was exactly what they should do.

She ran back in and plopped herself on the bed. She spread the phone book out on her lap and said, "Do you want to do the honors, or should I?"

Tommy closed his eyes and buried his head in the pillow.

*****

Bud was half-awake in his chair with the TV off. Springtime meant that he had to work on Saturdays and he wondered if he'd get any sleep. Lisa Bahn had seemed more interested in doing tequila shots than anything else so he'd finally left Jed's and gone home.

For the past hour he'd slept off and on. He kept thinking about what he'd done to Phil Waters and what was going to happen because of it. On top of Jimmy T, Jasper and Phil, he had the threat of a couple thugs from New York City weighing on his mind.

All those thoughts revolved in Bud's head like a merry-go-round. His conscious mind jumped on and off as he drifted in and out of sleep. Somewhere along the line he heard a car pulling up the driveway. He wondered who it was, but was so close to sleeping he didn't want to get up and look.

When he thought again of Jimmy T's thugs he came fully awake. Then he pictured Jasper driving up to see him in a hard, cold-steel automobile. That made him laugh.

His laughter faded quickly when he realized that Jasper had done exactly that on more than one occasion. But he doubted Jasper would be bringing Lisa Bahn or anybody else to him any time soon, even though it would serve her right for teasing him all night. Bud didn't think Jasper would be doing him any of his so-called favors for a while.

He got up and turned on the lights. He decided he'd better go to the door and find out who it was before he drove himself crazy.

Halfway across the room he heard the screen door on the outside open up. The front door swung inwards and Bud looked up to see Jimmy T standing there. He was wearing a black leather jacket and holding a baseball bat.

Jimmy T came into the house with both hands on the bat, winding up like Mickey Mantle. Bud backed away, but he figured that would only work for a few seconds and there would be no place to go.

"Jimmy," he said, hands up in front. "Come on, don't kill me. I didn't do anything."

Jimmy T kept coming until Bud was backed up against the fireplace. He stopped there, holding the bat like he meant to do business and said, "Look asshole, I don't know how you managed to get Phil busted, but don't tell me it came as a surprise."

Bud started to object, but Jimmy T cut him off. "Don't even say it. I don't give a fuck. The only reason you're still alive right now is because the news said the Canadians confiscated two kilos of coke. That's one package. I left you with two packages. That's two more kilos the feds don't have their hands on, and you've got two seconds to tell me where they are."

Bud figured he was in trouble no matter what he said. Somebody was going to kill him one way or another. "I can't say anything right now."

Jimmy T swung the bat at Bud's head. Bud ducked just in time and heard the antique clock on the mantle crunch. He sidestepped but that only put him in the corner.

Jimmy T was right on top of him and said, "I don't want to hear one more fucking word out of you unless it's directions to that other package." He pulled the bat back to take another swing.

Bud scrunched down and put his hands up, palms out. "Wait! I can't say anything. I think the cops are onto us." He suddenly remembered what Jimmy T had said the other day about that being the only possible excuse. It didn't exactly put Jimmy T at ease, but at least the bat didn't come crashing down.

"Don't fuck with me." Jimmy T cocked his head and stared at

Bud with one cold eye. "What do you mean the cops are onto us?"

"There's been some things happening that just don't seem right." Bud was able to say that convincingly enough.

"Things like what?" Jimmy T was still holding the bat up over his shoulder, he waited for Bud to answer.

Just then the phone rang. Bud couldn't imagine who would be calling at that particular hour, but he was thankful.

Jimmy T looked at the phone, then back at Bud. He moved aside and let Bud go past him.

Bud picked up the receiver, wondering who it was and what he would say to him or her. He thought maybe it was Lisa calling to tell him she'd changed her mind and wanted to come over. Or maybe it was Jasper calling from the Galapagos.

"Hello?" he said. As soon as he did he heard a click and the line went dead. He looked at the receiver questioningly, then he looked at Jimmy T and shrugged.

Jimmy T grabbed the receiver and put it up to his ear. He must have heard the new dial tone because he handed the receiver back to Bud.

Bud hung up the phone. Jimmy T was still upset, but at least he didn't look ready to kill. He lowered the bat and said, "Why didn't you tell me?"

Bud breathed easier and said, "I wasn't sure. And the other night you scared me so bad I didn't know what to do." He automatically rubbed his tender ribs where Jimmy T had kicked him. "At the last minute yesterday I decided to only plant one package, just in case. I didn't know if it was the right thing or not, but when I came down to Jed's to find you, nobody knew where you were."

Jimmy T stared at Bud for a minute. He looked puzzled.

"I've got the other package buried out behind the barn. In a pile of pig shit." Bud said. He was glad he could say something truthful for a change. "You want me to go get it?"

Jimmy T thought for another minute before answering. "No, you just sit on it for a while. And take good care of it. We've got to find out just exactly what the cops know. It can't be too much or they'd be here already, but until things cool down, you just sit on it. Don't try to move it or get rid of it. Remember, there are still people who will want to kill you if it doesn't turn up, starting with me."

"Yeah, okay. Whatever you say. I hope I didn't screw up too bad, I don't have a lot of experience with this sort of thing, it all used to be so easy before."

Jimmy T looked restless as he made his way to the door. "Just sit on it for a while until we figure out what's up," he said. Then he left.

Bud looked at the clock. It was only quarter to four, but he didn't think he'd get any more sleep. He considered opening a beer, but then thought about driving his truck in just a few hours. He decided to fire up the coffee maker instead.

As he waited for the coffee to brew, he popped a CD into the stereo and tried to wake the neighbors – who lived a quarter mile away - while he sang along at the top of his lungs.

He poured himself the first cup and sipped it, his feet once again propped up on his favorite footstool, and wondered who had rung his phone at such a favorable time. So far the new Bud was pretty lucky.

CHAPTER 30

Toni and Tommy spent most of Saturday sitting around the house. Toni wrote songs and tried them out on Tommy. Tommy offered his opinions and occasionally helped out with the lyrics. He was supposed to be investigating his suspects, but there wasn't a whole lot he could do during the middle of the day. He'd gone to the grocery store in the morning and seen Bud Rogers driving by in his concrete mixer. He didn't figured Bud could cause much trouble while he was working, especially while driving around in a giant pink truck with an anteater on the side.

Tommy decided he'd go out early in the evening and hit the bars to see if there was any talk. It was amazing what some people would say after a few beers, especially if they thought they were just talking to one person and nobody else could hear them. He'd spent enough time in the local taverns to know you could usually overhear a conversation from only a bar stool away.

Toni had called Bud's house two more times during the afternoon and he'd answered both times. She kept Tommy apprised of the situation each time.

Tommy figured it was important to Toni, so he didn't say anything. And it did tell them Bud was home from work but still not out killing anybody. Tommy tried not to think about that too much. It was still hard for him to believe the killer was somebody from County Line.

It was just before dark when Toni picked up the phone and dialed Bud's number again. Tommy acted as though he wasn't interested. It was, after all, a pretty lousy way of doing business. He couldn't help but notice, however, that instead of hanging up immediately Toni just held the phone to her ear.

After a bit she hung up. She looked at Tommy and said, "Bud's gone out."

Tommy tried to think of a way to explain to her that it didn't really mean anything, but then decided it was probably time to head out for the evening anyway. "I'm going to go do a little bar hopping," he said. "Would you care to join me?"

"Of course, we're a team aren't we?"

Tommy wondered how much trouble he'd be in if anybody found out that Toni knew almost as much about the investigation as he did.

"Okay," he finally said. "But you know the rules. You can't say anything to anybody about the things I've told you."

Toni began to counter, but it was just too important and Tommy cut her off. "Nothing, to nobody. Got it?"

"Okay, I understand."

Tommy sensed a little tension between them so he said, "It's a nice night. Why don't you bring your guitar along in case we get invited to a campfire someplace?"

Toni smiled. The tension was gone, just like that.

*****

After work Bud spent the afternoon sleeping. The only interruptions were a couple of those mysterious phone calls. He wondered who might be doing such a thing, but he'd grown accustomed to strange things happening. He'd moved the phone to the coffee table, next to the alarm clock, so each time he got a call he just shrugged, readjusted his feet and went back to sleep.

He woke up feeling refreshed for a change. He fed the hogs, took a shower and decided to go to the Attica Deli and stock up on his Saturday night supplies. On his way out the door Bud heard the phone ring again. He started back to answer it, but then figured he'd just get an earful of nothing so he let it ring.

As Bud headed towards Attica, he thought about the previous two Saturday nights. Each one had involved a visit from Jasper, one of which was followed by a trip out to the back forty to kill George Lewis. He decided to change his routine. He turned right on 238 and headed for the Silver Nickel.

As he drove along, he found himself thinking about guys and girls and having sex. He wondered if Mindy had found anybody new yet. Of course that made him think of George and Jasper.

Bud was determined not to let himself dwell on Jasper all night. He closed his eyes and tried to will the thoughts away. He kept them closed until he felt the truck going off the shoulder of the road. He waited as long as he dared, then he opened his eyes just in time to keep from going in the ditch.

It had an exhilarating effect and Bud found himself laughing hysterically. He laughed and sang along with the radio all the way to the Nickel.

As he pulled into the parking lot, Bud realized that he felt better than he had in weeks. His new Bud declaration and the resolution not to let anything get to him was actually working. He went inside and ordered a shot and a beer.

*****

Tommy and Toni came into the Silver Nickel at just past nine-thirty. They had already hit several other places, including Jed's Tavern. Tommy was surprised that he hadn't seen Bud there, Jed's was his most popular hangout. They'd been in no hurry to leave, however, since most of the bar conversations had centered around either the recent murders or the arrest of Phil Waters at the Canadian border.

One thing was for sure, the town was full of gossip. More than once Tommy found himself engaged in one conversation while trying to listen in on another. Unfortunately, although he learned that most of the people in County Line were badly misinformed, nobody really said anything that stuck in his mind as damning.

Tommy was glad to see Bud in the Nickel, along with a couple others who were on his list. He and Toni decided to split an order of chicken wings. As they sat at one of the tables eating, Tommy noticed that Bud was getting quite drunk. In fact, Bud was holding two beers at once.

They watched the crowd for a while. Toni pointed out a couple of guys who were wearing camouflaged shirts. Tommy figured they were spring turkey hunters who hadn't been home to change. He made a mental note to check their names against his files when he got home.

The two were seated slightly behind Bud, who was at the end of the bar and facing away from them so Tommy could keep an eye on him. He watched as Bud put his lips on one of the beer bottles but didn't tip it up. Tommy suddenly realized that Bud wasn't drinking from both bottles, he was chewing tobacco and spitting into one of them.

Tommy wasn't sure why he was so excited, he'd seen people do that plenty of times, but he decided to try and get a sample. Bud was as high on the suspect list as anybody, the highest even, after the story Toni had told him.

For some reason, possibly because it was uncomfortable sitting in his back pocket, Bud pulled the round tobacco container out and set it on the bar next to his two bottles and spread of loose bills. Tommy had seen people do that many times over the years, but he'd never taken much notice, it hadn't ever seemed important before. He strained his eyes against the dim lights but he couldn't see the label. He wanted to know what kind it was in case the crime lab was able to determine the brand of the sample they'd found near George's parking spot.

He looked at Toni's beer, it was just under half full. "Drain it," he ordered. He pointed to her bottle and chugged what was left of his.

Toni started to protest, but a swift kick under the table

along with a stern look had her slugging down the rest of hers immediately. Tommy grabbed the two empty bottles and made his way towards the bar. It wasn't very crowded and he found a spot right next to Bud.

Mindy came over and grabbed the empties. Tommy indicated that two more would be in order. As he waited he looked at Bud and said, "How's it going?"

"Not bad," Bud said without looking up. "You?"

"Can't complain. You get any turkeys this spring?"

"I don't really have the time any more," Bud said. He finally looked in Tommy's general direction. "The concrete business really heats up around the time the season opens, you know?"

"Yeah, I hear you. And besides, you've got to get up too damn early in the morning if you expect to see anything. I haven't been turkey hunting in four or five years myself."

Tommy sneaked a look at the round, plastic can on the bar. He noted the brand and then wondered how he could get a sample of Bud's spit. It had to be something Bud left behind on his own. In order to be able to force Bud into surrendering a sample Tommy would first have to arrest him or go through some other red tape. He didn't think two dubious stories from Toni and Tanya would constitute reasonable suspicion for two murders.

"Take care," he said. He took the two beers and headed towards Toni.

"You too," Bud answered. He took his two beer bottles and walked towards the pool table.

Tommy rejoined Toni at their table.

"What was that all about?" she said as Tommy handed her a beer.

"I wanted to see what brand he was chewing," was all Tommy told her. He decided not to share his plan to get a spit sample if he could. She'd been harassing Bud enough as it was.

A while later Tommy saw Bud head for the men's room. He noticed that Bud had the spit bottle with him. He waited a minute, then excused himself, hoping to distract Bud into forgetting to bring the bottle back out with him.

When he entered the men's room he was dismayed to find Bud at the sink rinsing the spit out of the beer bottle. Tommy stood and stared at the clean brown glass and shiny blue label.

Bud turned around. He saw Tommy looking at the bottle and said, "Gotta clean 'em out or Mindy gives me holy hell. She threatened to shut me off one night just because I turned in a bottle full of spit. Can't say as I blame her though. Once she drops that bottle down the chute and it goes into the sorting bin in the basement, who knows where the stuff will wind up?"

Tommy faked a laugh and said, "Yeah, no doubt." He hoped he didn't look too disappointed. He turned and headed for the urinal, deciding it was as good a time as any. As he went about his business Tommy noticed in the mirror that just before Bud left he pulled the wad of tobacco out of his mouth and flung it in the general direction of the waste basket.

Tommy was so excited he almost peed on himself. He hurried things along as best he could, then went over by the sink to see if he could find the discarded chew. Just as he'd hoped, the fairly intoxicated Bud had missed the basket. He grabbed a paper towel from the dispenser, gave a quick listen at the door to see if he could hear anybody approaching, then dove under the sink and scooped up his prize.

He no sooner got out from under the sink when he could hear somebody coming towards the door from the other side. He looked at the loosely wrapped object in his hand and, not wanting to explain to anybody who might question him, stuck the whole works haphazardly into his jeans pocket.

When he left the men's room, Tommy didn't see Toni right away. Finally he noticed her at the far end of the bar talking to Mindy. As he worked his way in their direction he hoped she wouldn't slip up and reveal the fact that they'd discussed the case.

CHAPTER 31

"Thanks," Bud said. "I appreciate the ride."

"No problem, take care of yourself." Tommy nodded as Bud climbed out of his car. Then he said, "And if you need a ride back to your truck tomorrow, just give me a call."

"I'll keep you in mind. Thanks again." Bud closed the door on Tommy's car. He hadn't really wanted a lift, but when a cop asks you if you want a ride, off duty or not, you have to figure maybe you shouldn't be driving.

Bud made his way into the house, his senses still tingling from the elegant scent that had drifted up from where Toni sat in the back seat. He sat down and put his feet up without bothering to kick off his sneakers. The digital clock said it was just after two and he was glad he didn't have to work the next day. Despite Bud's afternoon nap he felt like he could sleep forever.

When the car came in the driveway, Bud wasn't the least bit surprised. Nothing surprised him any more. He wondered, without getting excited, who it might be, but the bottom line was that he just didn't care. He'd had just about enough of everything and decided to stay put until whoever it was made himself known.

When the door opened Bud saw the outline of Jimmy T charging in. He'd brought the baseball bat and was out for blood.

Bud threw himself over the coffee table just in time to hear a muffled thud on the chair where his head had been. Then he heard a crash that could only be Jimmy T falling over the coffee table in the semi-darkness. He ran toward the hallway and wondered if he had time to get to his bedroom closet, grab his shotgun and load it before Jimmy T got to him. He looked back, saw that the old hippie was already up and moving and decided the answer was no. Instead he turned right and ran down the hallway to the back door.

The yard behind house was lit up by a light on the barn. Bud looked behind him and was horrified see Jimmy T right there. He'd always figured Jimmy T was the kind of guy who couldn't get out of his own way.

He ducked his head and dove to the left, rolled over and bounced back up on his feet. It bought him a few seconds as Jimmy T regrouped. Bud threw his hands up in front of him and cried, "Wait a minute."

"You little fuck!" Jimmy T said. He wasn't about to wait. "There ain't no cops onto you or me or anybody else you lying little fuck!"

"Wait! What about the dope? If you kill me, you'll never find it."

Jimmy T took a step forward, Bud countered with a step backward.

"I'm not going to kill you," Jimmy T said. "I'm just going to fuck you up. Then you're going to tell me exactly where the dope is and I'm going to leave what's left of you for Biff and the boys."

"No wait."

Jimmy T came after him again. Bud ducked and felt the breeze from the bat over his head. He squirmed his way around Jimmy T and ran for all he was worth towards the door of the barn. He hoped that if he got Jimmy T in there in the dark he might be able to even up his chances. He ran into the door, smashed the latch, and tumbled into the darkness. He cut to the right as soon as he thought he was out of sight, then scrunched down by the hog pen.

He looked at the doorway, Jimmy T had stopped there when he ran out of light. Bud could see his head moving back and forth, searching for him in the darkness. A single ray of light shone in from outside. Most of it was blocked by Jimmy T, but Bud realized horribly that the small amount of light that seeped in was shining right onto the switch on the wall.

As if he'd read Bud's mind, Jimmy T reached over and turned on the lights. It took him a second to find Bud, then he smiled and said, "Say good night, fucker."

Bud looked around. He wondered if he could run fast and hard enough into the side of the building to knock a few of the barn boards off and come up outside again, but dismissed the thought just as quickly. His shoulder hurt just from breaking the door down and his ribs were still tender from when Jimmy T had kicked him. Besides, the barn was old but it was still rock-solid and Bud was afraid he would only manage to save Jimmy T the trouble of breaking something else.

The old wooden wagon that Bud used to move the corn from the shredder to the hog pen was there next to him. He moved around to the backside of it, trying to shield himself from Jimmy T. He didn't know what else to do.

Jimmy T came after him. He had fire in his eyes as he rounded the wagon. Bud was about to curl up into a ball and cover his head for lack of a better plan when he was suddenly inundated with a familiar surge of power.

Jasper was back.

Jimmy T was getting ready to tee off, but Bud stood up straight and challenged him. Their eyes locked and Bud watched as Jimmy T struggled to swing the bat, then lowered it and finally dropped it. He looked on in awe as the old hippie surrendered. A lustful, inviting look replaced the savagery in his eyes. Bud felt his incisors grow into fangs -- and he realized he was enjoying himself immensely.

*****

I thought you could use some help.

Bud looked at the slumped, lifeless form that used to be

Jimmy T. He wasn't sure exactly how he felt about it, but he knew it beat the hell out of what had almost happened.

"Jasper," he said. "How the heck are you?"

Just offhand, Bud, I'd say I'm doing a whole lot better than you are. You seem to have gotten yourself into a heap of trouble.

Bud couldn't believe his ears. There was Jasper, the source of all the bad luck and hard times Bud had ever known, telling him what a fine mess he'd gotten himself into.

Jasper read his thoughts and said, *Really Bud, you know your troubles started when you brought that Waters boy into your life of crime. And while we're on the subject, I must say that I'm very disappointed in you. Didn't I explain that I wanted you to quit doing such things? Just imagine how Mr. Waters must feel, sitting in a jail cell in a foreign country without a clue as to why or how he came to be there. And all his friends, how do you think they feel? Not to mention the poor boy's parents, a finer couple of human beings you'll never meet. Shame on you, Bud.*

Bud knew Jasper was right, but he'd spent the better part of each waking moment worrying and dealing with his own misfortunes. He had, in fact, become quite numb to the whole thing. He decided not to bother trying to explain. Jasper usually knew more about Bud than Bud did anyway.

"I'm glad you stopped in," he said truthfully. "I was just entertaining one of my friends when I was pleasantly surprised to find that I had even more company. It's good to see you, so to speak." Bud had learned that Jasper appreciated a certain amount of humor. Since humor and happiness was Bud's new theme, he didn't see any reason to drag their conversation down. He stood above Jimmy T and laughed.

Yes, I see you had everything under control. I guess you're lucky I stopped in when I did, you two might have had more fun than is healthy.

"Yeah well, you know how it is. Sometimes us darned kids just get so carried away. It's good to have you around to keep us in line, you know?"

You can stop all the flattery. I'm quite certain you know that I must have had my own reasons for doing what I did. And now, as usual after a large meal, I'm going to go take a nap. Try to behave yourself, will you?

"Ten-four good buddy," Bud answered. Then he added, with a serious touch, "And thanks for bailing me out. I mean it. I would've been hurting if you hadn't come along."

Really Bud, adulation doesn't become you. Rest assured, the only reason I helped you eliminate the fiend that lays before you is that he was on my list to begin with.

"Yeah? Well, I want thank you anyway just for stopping in. I'm sure there are a number of places in the world you'd rather be. And if not for you taking the time to be here I'd probably look like a jellyfish in blue jeans by now."

Quite correct on all counts. Now I really must be going. Try to take care of yourself, Bud. Jasper was gone as quickly as he'd appeared.

Bud embraced the Jasper hangover. A river of euphoria poured down his spine and flooded his entire body. Despite everything, he was feeling just fine. In fact, he found himself singing to the hogs as he hoisted Jimmy T's body onto the old wooden wagon.

As he sloughed the limp body off his shoulder, Bud caught a strong whiff of Jimmy T's last gift to the world. He looked down into the open eyes and said, "I told you to give up those deviled eggs. It smells like something crawled inside you and died. I don't know who's worse, you or the hogs." One of the hogs let out a little grunt. It didn't surprise Bud, nothing did.

He rolled the wagon across the floor until it rested at it's usual place on the receiving end of the corn shredder. Bud tried to hoist Jimmy T off the wagon, but then decided there was no sense in working too hard.

As he walked over to the tool room, he wondered if there was a line a person crossed when going from normal to crazy, and if so, how hard it was to cross back. Bud was afraid he'd already gone too far. He grabbed a wood splitting ax from the tool room, looked at the edge to see how sharp it was, and went back to make Jimmy T a little more manageable.

He looked at Jimmy T's head as it hung off the side of the wagon. Something deep inside told him not to do it, that it wasn't too late to save his sanity.

"Bullshit," he said. "It's been too late for a long time." He looked into Jimmy T's eyes one last time, then brought the ax down. It landed with a crunch and a thud.

Jimmy T's neck was slightly wider than the ax blade. Bud looked with wonder as a thin, taught strip of skin held the head from hitting the floor. He watched as it spun slowly back and forth. It was laugh or cry, and laugh he did in a high-pitched, unnatural way while he chopped Jimmy T's arms and legs off.

Piece by piece Bud fed the parts of his former business partner into the shredder. The sound of the body parts going through was muffled compared to the sound the dried corn ears usually made. Bud thought it sounded like a motorcycle running under water.

He laughed his way around the shredder and back to the pile of Jimmy T that was stacked up on the bed of the wagon. He noticed that some of the bones had come through chopped into round pieces and had stacked themselves haphazardly into one corner of the wagon's shallow sideboards. They reminded Bud of poker chips and it occurred to him ironically that the last time he played poker with Jimmy T he'd had his clock cleaned.

He pushed the wagon across the floor to the hog pen. "I'll see your femur," he said to the hogs as they looked up at him curiously. "And raise you two fibulas." That caused another fit of laughter after which he said, "Looks like you guys are going to get a little midnight snack. Chopped liver for those of you who like it, fresh entrails for those who don't."

As Bud scooped the soft parts out of the wagon with a shovel, he worried that the hogs might not eat the bones, and that posed a problem. He couldn't leave any evidence laying around. He thought for a moment, came up with the answer, and finished scraping the soft parts into the feed trough. The hogs snorted and grunted their appreciation as they ate.

When he'd finished, Bud shoveled the rest of the hard pieces, along with the soft pieces that stuck to them -- he wasn't very picky -- into a pair of old burlap bags. Then he pushed the wagon, along with the ax and shovel, out the door and over to an area between the house and barn where he occasionally had campfires on warm nights in the summer. He removed the two burlap bags and set the old wagon on fire. It took off rapidly, but just to make sure everything got burned Bud put the splintered remains of the barn door and an armload of firewood on top.

The fire would be hot, but not nearly hot enough to incinerate the bones. Bud grabbed the two burlap bags containing Jimmy T's leftovers and loaded them into the trunk of Jimmy T's car. Fortunately Jimmy T had left the keys in the ignition so Bud drove out the driveway and headed towards County Line. He went through the village of Attica and continued south on route 98 towards Varysburg.

When Bud had left work on Saturday, Tim Castillo told him he had to start early on Monday. They were going to fill one of the ventilation shafts in an abandoned salt mine in North Java. It would take all day considering that they would have to cover their regular orders too, so Tim wanted each driver to come in early and get in at least two trips to the mine before the regular work started.

Bud thought about the stuff they would use to fill the mine shaft. *Flowable fill* it was called, and although they used concrete mixers to deliver it, it wasn't anything at all like regular concrete. He thought about how flowable fill came out of the truck looking like dark gray pancake batter -- lumps and all. Bud knew there wasn't a person in the world who would notice an extra hundred pounds of lumps mixed in with ten tons of that goup. He was determined not to let anybody find the body this time.

As he drove up the monstrous hill that lay between County Line and the property that belonged to Aardvark Concrete, Bud felt the car fighting a stiff wind that had picked up in the past few hours. It gusted fiercely and he thought about the fire he'd left unattended. He hoped the wind wasn't strong enough to blow the sparks onto the barn. It didn't seem likely and it hadn't ever happened before so he didn't worry for long.

After finally cresting the hill, Bud started down the far side. He laughed as his headlights shined on the railroad bridge near the bottom. On the face of the huge concrete wall that ran almost perpendicular to the road, somebody had at one time spray-painted THE MASK in four-foot letters.

Although it had been there for as long as Bud could remember, it never failed to bring him a chuckle. He'd always wondered who the prankster was. Before learning of George Lewis' affair with Mindy, Bud had always thought that was County Line's only true secret. Nobody ever seemed to know who THE MASK was, or if they did they never told.

Bud drove past the wall and finally turned into the driveway of Aardvark Concrete. He turned his headlights off, but there were several lights that lit the yard anyway. He drove up behind the line of mixers, stopping when he thought the batch plant would hide Jimmy T's car from the road.

He got out and opened the trunk. He looked up at the pink mixer drums and shook his head as he considered the collection of aardvarks lined up in a row. Chris had named it Aardvark Concrete because he wanted to be the first thing listed in the phone book. Bud told him it was a waste of time, but of course Chris had been right.

Bud grabbed the burlap sacks and hoisted them up the ladder that led to the loading hopper at the rear of his truck. He emptied the contents into the mixer drum and climbed back down. He wondered if anybody would smell anything on Monday morning, but figured that since it was already almost Sunday he'd probably be okay. He reminded himself that flowable fill wasn't the best smelling stuff anyway. He threw the sacks back into the trunk, not wanting to take a chance on them coming out wrong and clogging things up on Monday.

He drove Jimmy T's car back to Jed's. It seemed as good a place as any to leave it. He took the two burlap sacks out of the trunk and started walking. It was a couple miles by road from Jed's to where his truck was still at the Nickel, but the railroad tracks ran behind both places and that distance was only about a half mile. Bud used the benefit of the still lingering Jasper hangover to start jogging, and covered the distance in no time.

*****

Bud was wide awake, and Jasper had a sobering effect. He didn't feel drunk like he was earlier so he decided to take a drive and blast some rock and roll. He found himself cruising around by the old loop. He thought about all the good times he'd had up there back in the days when he was just out of high school.

He followed the road around the pond. When he got to the wide spot on the high side he shut off the engine and got out. It was windy but Bud didn't mind. He put in a chew and looked down at the lights of County Line. The breeze blew through him and he enjoyed its freshness.

He looked down at the lights of the prison and wondered if he would wind up there someday. Then he scanned across the fields until he came to his house. He could see the fire in the yard even though it was over a mile away. He snapped to attention when he saw a pair of headlights coming from his driveway. He thought maybe somebody couldn't sleep and had stopped in for a late-night beer, but it was pretty late for that. It occurred to him that it was probably Biff and Steverino, Jimmy T's thugs.

Bud decided not to go home for a while, but as he sat there watching over his house he noticed that the fire seemed to be getting bigger. After another minute he realized his barn was going up in flames. He started up the truck and drove home frantically, barely avoiding the ditch several times.

By the time he pulled into the driveway the fire had already engulfed the whole north side of the building. Bud got out and ran to the house to dial 911. About halfway there he stopped and looked at the barn. There was no way he could save it.

He ran back to the truck, grabbed the two burlap sacks, and

ran across the yard. After getting on the upwind side of the fire he flung the two burlap sacks into the fifteen foot flames. He looked down at himself and tried to think of where he'd been and what he'd touched. "Aw screw it," he said. "Better safe than sorry."

Bud stripped down to his underwear, threw his clothes and sneakers into the fire and then ran across the yard like a streaker from the seventies. He went into the house and dialed 911. After putting some new clothes on he opened a beer and tried to tell himself that he couldn't hear the hogs squealing as they burned inside the barn.

CHAPTER 32

The sun played hide and seek behind a broken pattern of fluffy clouds. Bud sat at the picnic table in his back yard talking to Chris. Chris had shown up with a twelve-pack after hearing about the fire. They spent the afternoon drinking beer and watching the remains of the barn smolder.

Bud's older brother sipped from his beer, nodded at the smoking ashes and said, "You going to build a new one or just take the insurance money?"

Bud had been up all night, but that was nothing new. Still, he hadn't spent much time thinking about it. He'd been too busy getting rid of Jimmy T's body. "I don't know yet," he said. "What do you think?"

"It depends." Chris shrugged his shoulders and chewed his lip. "Were you making any money with the pigs? It would be nice to have another barn, but if you're not going to use it for anything maybe you could use the money for something else."

Bud's mind was somewhere else. He almost asked Chris if he knew any good defense lawyers. He couldn't believe how he'd almost slipped up but the words were formed and ready to come out of his mouth when he caught himself. He choked them back, cleared his throat and said, "Too bad I didn't save the hogs. I was just getting ready to cash them in. You think the insurance will pay extra for them?"

Bud hated having to act like he was interested. A normal person would be concerned with such things. To Bud, the question of whether or not to rebuild the barn was as unimportant as whether his dead hogs could fly. For a moment he considered telling Chris about his real troubles. He wanted to just lay it all out and see if the man with the golden touch could help him. He knew it was hopeless, however, there wasn't a man alive that could help Bud.

"They should," Chris said. "If you had the right coverage." He stood up, punched Bud on the arm and walked towards his car. "I've got to get going. Think about it. Let me know if there's anything I can do."

"Okay. Thanks."

Bud laid his head back on the table. He listened to Chris drive away as he rubbed his eyes. He longed for the refreshing feeling he'd experienced the day before after finally getting some real sleep. It was nice, but it wasn't nearly enough. Bud's body was getting painfully thin and his mind was like a brick wall. He'd already lost the ability to make the simplest of decisions and his emotions changed constantly.

He felt the sun on his face as it slipped out from behind another cloud. Bud took deep breaths and tried not to think about anything. After a few minutes he heard another vehicle coming up the driveway. He listened as it passed the house and continued up the path that led to the barn.

Suddenly he remembered Jimmy T's thugs. He jerked his head up to see if it was them. Johnny Davis was walking across the yard with another twelve-pack. Bud laughed, Chris had left at least six beers behind. Bud had to get up early for work and hadn't expected to spend all day drinking, but he supposed it didn't really matter. As he looked at the remains of his barn he decided he was looking at a carbon copy of his future: a smoking heap of what had once been useful and solid.

"I thought maybe you could use a beer," Johnny said. He tossed a can at Bud.

Bud caught it with one hand and said, "Thanks."

"That was a hell of a weenie roast you had last night. How come I wasn't invited?"

Bud just shook his head.

"So how are you?" Johnny said. "You look like shit."

Bud had to laugh at Johnny's way with words. "I'm still kicking," he said and shrugged. He hated when people asked him how he was doing. It was too painful to think about giving an honest answer.

Johnny looked him over. He kept looking at Bud's sunken eyes. "You really do look like hell. You sick or something?"

"You sound like my brother. I just had this conversation ten minutes ago. The truth is I haven't been sleeping well."

"Smoke a joint. It always works for me."

Bud laughed. He hadn't smoked a joint in years. He'd never smoked much anyway, it just wasn't his buzz. But when he started driving for Chris, state regulations required random drug testing, so he gave it up altogether. The more he thought about the idea, however, the better it sounded. To hell with the drug tests, Bud needed sleep.

"I might just do that," he said. He looked at Johnny and grinned. "You got any?"

"Of course. In fact, I can do you one better. I've got a fresh shipment of top quality Turkish hash."

"Hash?" Bud wasn't into the drug scene, but he hadn't exactly been living in a closet. "I thought that stuff was hard to come by around here."

"Hey," Johnny said as he thumped his chest. "You're talking to the man."

Bud thought it over for several minutes. He didn't care for the idea of using drugs after not touching them for years, but he'd been doing a lot of things he didn't used to do. He tried telling himself that he didn't need it, but the truth was he needed sleep and getting bombed on whiskey always left him with a wicked headache in the morning.

He rubbed his hands over his face, raised his eyebrows and said, "How much?"

"Really?"

Bud nodded and smiled. "For medicinal purposes only."

*****

Toni sat on Tommy's front porch playing her guitar and relaxing. She didn't feel like writing so she just played some of her old favorites. There was something very soothing about playing and singing a song just for the fun of it.

She was in the middle of a song when Tommy came in the driveway. He'd gone into Attica to pick up some chicken for the grill. Chicken on the grill was becoming a race-day tradition with them.

She watched as he carried his purchase toward the house. She didn't want to quit singing, but she didn't want to be rude either. She smiled at Tommy as he came up the steps, but when he didn't keep going inside she stopped playing and questioned him with her eyes.

"Bud Rogers' barn burned to the ground last night," Tommy said. "It's still smoking, but there's nothing left but ashes."

Toni was shocked. She'd made Tommy promise to drive by Bud's house on his way to town just to check up on him, but she hadn't expected to hear anything of that magnitude.

Tommy shrugged and said, "I don't know, but it seems like Bud Rogers' name pops up a lot lately."

"What do you think we should do?"

"I think one of us should play the guitar while the other one starts cooking chicken."

Toni gave him a dirty look. "Don't you think we should keep an eye on him?"

"He's got all sorts of company right now. I saw Johnny Davis' flatbed and a couple other vehicles. I don't think there's a whole lot to watch." After a moment he added, "And besides, if you think about it, none of the things we think he might have done have happened during daylight hours. Not one. So I'm thinking of staying up to watch his place and see if he goes anywhere tonight. You're welcome to join me."

Toni considered objecting. She wanted to do something

right away but of course Tommy was right. She shrugged her shoulders and started playing another song.

CHAPTER 33

Bud was in his familiar position: feet up on the stool, beer on his left, remote control on his right. The only difference was the small chunk of Turkish hash stuck on the end of a pin that had been pushed through a paper plate.

He sat there, thoroughly stoned and thinking how wonderful it was going to feel to get a good night's sleep. He'd had way too many things on his mind recently, but the hash smoke had erased his need to care. That is until he heard:

What's the matter, Bud? Are you down in the dumps?

Bud laughed. He thought of saying something, then just kept laughing. After a while he finally said, "Jasper. Here I was minding my own business, hoping to get a good night's sleep for a change, and along comes my dear, sweet friend Jasper."

But Bud, I've got some news for you. Don't you want to hear it?

Bud couldn't imagine what kind of news Jasper might have that he would want to hear. "Do I have a choice?" he said.

Bud, sometimes I wonder about you. I should think you'd be happy to hear what I have to say.

Bud was silent for a few seconds. After a while he said, "The only thing you could say that would make me happy would be something like, 'Bud, I've decided that I've used you enough. You've paid your dues and I'm taking my business elsewhere. Thanks for all the good times.'"

But Bud, that's just it. I've decided to leave you alone. I may pop in to see you once in a while, but our partnership is dissolved. I'm moving on.

Bud couldn't believe his ears. "Do you mean it?" he said. "Do you really mean it?"

Have I ever lied to you?

He didn't think he wanted to answer honestly, so he said, "No, I don't suppose you have. This is great. I thought you'd be mad at me after what I did to Phil."

I'm disappointed to say the least. But I only set out to teach you a lesson and give you an example of how it feels to have someone screw up your life against your will. How you react to it is entirely up to you. Hopefully you have seen the error of your ways and will try to change. But I could never be mad at you. After all, we've been intimate. I'll always have a place for you in my supernatural heart.

"I don't know what to say. I've spent all my time hating you, but if you're serious about leaving me alone, I'm ecstatic. I don't know what I can do to help Phil, but don't think for a minute that I'll just forget about it." He thought for a minute before continuing. "I wish I could say it's been a pleasure meeting you, but I'm sure you understand. I can say that my life will never be the same."

No, I don't suppose it will, but then I seem to have that effect on people wherever I go. Have you learned anything? Do you plan to change the way you treat people in the future?

Bud considered all the things that had happened since Jasper arrived and said, "Man, I've learned more than a lifetime in the last two weeks. I can't tell you what an eye-opening experience it's been meeting you."

Well then, despite your hint of sarcasm, I do feel that my work here is finished. There were two people in this immediate area that I initially wanted to cleanse from this world. The prison inmate was a bonus. I must say, Bud, you performed wonderfully. Some of the people I meet aren't half as strong as you. It's been a wonderful experience getting to know you.

Bud was overjoyed, not so much by Jasper's heaps of praise as by his promise of departure. There was a large part of him that wanted to be angry and lash out at Jasper and his omnipotent behavior, but he understood the fruitlessness of such actions. Instead of going on about how he really felt, Bud asked, "What can I say? I suppose thanks are in order. Where are you off to now?"

Jasper laughed and said, *It's okay, Bud, I know how you really feel. It would be nothing less than self-absorption for me to expect anything else. To answer your other question, I've found some people in Toronto I'd like to straighten out. Just think, I'll only be a short hop across Lake Ontario from you. Maybe I'll stop in and say hello sometime, but you have my word that I won't use you anymore.*

Bud was smiling from ear to ear. His life had been turned upside down, and now it was suddenly going to be back under his control. Things were going to be different, that was certain, but the idea of looking forward to the next day without having to worry about Jasper showing up was like finding out there was a miracle cure for your terminal disease.

Bud struggled to find the right words.

Don't say anything, Bud. Just remember me.

He didn't think that would be too hard.

And try to take care of yourself. You know you drink too much, and this black stuff you're smoking now is a sure dead-end.

Bud looked at the chunk of hash, then at his bottle of beer. He'd always liked to party as much as the next guy, but Jasper was the reason for his recent overindulgence. He didn't want to mention that, however, things were going too well. He finally said, "Well, you take care of yourself too, you hear?"

I will. There's just one more thing I want to tell you. There are two men who will be coming after you, and they have the worst intentions. Also, I should let you know that the police are a lot closer to finding you out than you think. In fact, I want you to seriously consider a full confession. You're probably going to get caught anyway, the least you could do is vindicate Phil Waters.

Bud wasn't quite as happy all of a sudden. "What do you mean?"

Well, it seems these two men work for a man called --

"No!" Bud cut Jasper off, he didn't want to know who the

thugs worked for. "I mean about the police. I already know about those other guys."

Oh, I see. Well, it seems that a certain police officer has collected a sample of your chewing tobacco and is preparing to send it off to a lab to see if it matches that of the sample you left on the window of George Lewis' car. I don't know what you can do about it, but rest assured that I will be watching, and I don't expect you to take any action against this young fellow. He is a good man doing what is right. I am very serious about this one point. If you think I've made a mess of your life, believe me when I say, "You ain't seen nothing yet." But, that aside, I want to wish you the best of luck. Adios, my friend, if you're ever in Toronto, look me up.

Jasper's laughter faded as he left Bud's body. Bud sat motionless, he was dealing with too many things at once. He was furious with Jasper for ruining his life, but was helpless to do anything about it and that made it seem even worse.

He told himself to let it go and concentrate on more important things. On one hand, he was exhilarated by the notion that Jasper was going to leave him alone. On the other hand, the police -- most likely Tommy Chandler, he was sure of that -- were going to place Bud in George's car around the time he was murdered.

Bud thought back to that fateful night. He was so nervous, he just had to have a chew. He didn't think there was any way anybody would find a connection, hadn't ever even considered it. But he wasn't surprised. As he'd told himself before, there was a whole prison full of killers down on Exchange St. who thought they'd never get caught.

He sat there wondering what to do. He couldn't take out Tommy Chandler. He didn't think he could do that even if Jasper hadn't warned him. Besides, if Tommy had collected a sample, they must have pegged Bud as a suspect already, and taking Tommy out wouldn't change that.

His thoughts shifted to the two thugs. He wondered if he could buy his freedom with the two kilos of coke he still had, but he doubted it. They'd probably just take the dope and kill him anyway.

Then there was the police. Maybe he could make a deal with them, but they'd never buy his story about Jasper, and he doubted they'd trade three murders for two kilos and a pair of thugs.

He let out a long sigh. There didn't seem to be anything he could do. He was still glad to be rid of Jasper, but Jasper had come in handy when Bud found himself in trouble with Jimmy T. He'd never considered what things would be like if Jasper left him to fend for himself.

When he realized he was on his own Bud jumped up and ran into his bedroom. He came back out with a twelve-gauge shotgun, fully loaded with buckshot in case the two thugs came around looking for him. He'd give them the dope if they wanted it, but they'd have to go out into the pig manure and dig it up themselves.

Bud set the shotgun on the coffee table, easily within reach. He wondered why, if Jasper's news was so wonderful, he felt so lousy. He picked up the paper plate with the pin stuck through it. Then he grabbed his lighter and started cooking the chunk of hash that was impaled on the end of it. He needed to get some sleep so he could get his mind working again. He had to come up with a reason why he was in George's car to satisfy the police. He might wind up giving a full confession if he got caught, but he wasn't throwing in the towel just yet. Phil Waters was just going to have to wait.

Once he got the hash burning, Bud covered it with a glass and watched as it filled with swirls of thick, white smoke. As he tipped the glass up and inhaled he tried to remember any other pieces of evidence he might have left behind. He couldn't think of anything. Jimmy T had been mostly eaten and burned, and the rest of him would be buried in the mine shaft first thing in the morning if all went well.

Suddenly he cursed himself for putting Jimmy T's remains in his own mixer. It never occurred to him to put the bones into somebody else's truck.

After a minute he let it go, figuring it wouldn't make much difference anyway. He checked his alarm, thought briefly about his chances of coming out clean, then smoked his brains out.

*****

"You want some more coffee?" Tommy looked over at Toni to see if she was still awake.

"No thanks" she said. "I'm wired."

They had driven by Bud's house to make sure he was home, then parked along the side of the road about a hundred yards away. If Bud went anywhere in the middle of the night they planned on following him, and they didn't really care if he knew it or not.

So far the only thing of interest was a dark sedan that passed by about once every hour. The third time it went by Tommy took down the license plate number in order to run it through the computer when he got to the office.

It was almost five in the morning and Bud had shown no signs of moving. "Do you think we should give it up?" Tommy said. He had to be at work in just a few hours anyway.

"I don't know. The longer we sit here the harder it is to believe that Bud is some sort of killer."

Yeah? Well don't forget the story you told me about you and Tanya. And Bud's name pops up everywhere lately."

"I know," she said. "And now Jimmy T is missing, although even his wife figures he's probably just off someplace on a three day bender. Lord knows he's done that enough times over the years." Toni started to say something more but stopped when she saw a light come on in Bud's house. She pointed to it.

Tommy looked at the house and said, "Looks like somebody's getting up early."

"Too damned early if you ask me. You think he's going to work at this hour?"

"Probably, those guys put in some serious hours when the weather's good."

Toni eyed the clock on the dash and said, "I hope that's where he's going."

They stared at each other for several seconds, not wanting to acknowledge what that statement inferred.

Tommy had a pair of binoculars. He looked through them every couple minutes as they watched the house in silence.

"What if he's not?" Toni finally said.

"What if he's not what?"

"Going to work. What if he's going someplace else?"

Tommy sensed fear in Toni's voice. He lowered the binoculars and looked at her with wide eyes. He almost said something, then stifled it. He looked down at the floor and finally managed to say, "We'll cross that bridge if we come to it."

He hid behind the binoculars again. After several minutes he said, "I don't think we have to worry about it. He's sure not dressed like a criminal." He sounded happier, like a weight had been lifted.

Toni reached for the binoculars. Tommy handed them over and she raised them up to her eyes. She saw Bud climbing into his truck clad in a fluorescent pink, Aardvark Concrete jacket. "Yeah," she said. "I see what you mean. Nobody would go out to kill somebody wearing one of those."

You can see him from a mile away."

They watched as Bud pulled out of his driveway and headed south. Tommy started the car. When Bud was down in a little dip, he turned on the lights on and pulled out to follow.

"Do you think we even need to bother?" Toni said.

Tommy shrugged and said, "We might as well follow him into Attica. If he goes out the south side on ninety-eight we'll know he's headed for work. Then we can stop at the corner store and get another cup of coffee."

"You can get another cup, I've had enough. My stomach's all tied up in a knot." After a moment she added, "And I have to pee."

Tommy looked at Toni and laughed. He poked at her ribs and said, "Tickle, tickle, tickle!"

Toni slapped his arm and giggled. "Knock it off or I'll be

doing it all over your front seat."

Tommy stopped the tickling.

CHAPTER 34

Bud drove through Attica and continued south on route 98. It was early but he felt good after sleeping soundly for seven hours straight. A little slow and heavy, though, he thought. He decided he'd smoked too much hash the night before and made a note to cut himself back.

Bud never saw the deer until it was smashing into the front of his truck. He hit the brakes instinctively. The deer slid up the hood and into the windshield, sending a crack along its entire length. It scrambled off with its feet flying in every direction as it struggled for traction and finally disappeared into the woods.

He pulled over to the side of the road, got out and looked at the front of the truck. The grill was destroyed and the hood buckled. The radiator was smashed into the fan and there was a steady stream of coolant running out onto the road.

"Damn!" he said. "It's going take a while to fix this baby."

The natural thing to do would be to wait for somebody to come along who could call the police. They would fill out a report so Bud could show it to his insurance agent. Then maybe he could get a special tag for the deer. Bud didn't figure it could've gone too far off the road, and there was bound to be plenty of good meat still on it.

With Jimmy T's remains sitting in the back of his concrete mixer, however, Bud decided that if the truck would start again he'd try to make it to work. He knew he'd probably cause further damage by driving, but he could afford the repairs and would feel a lot better once he was sure Jimmy T was gone for good.

He climbed into the seat and tried the ignition, hoping there hadn't been too much electrical damage under the hood. The truck started instantly, Bud put it in drive and headed down the road.

At first he thought he'd make it with no problems. He supposed everybody would wonder what happened, but he'd just tell them the truth: that he'd hit a deer but didn't want to be late for work waiting around for the cops and a tow-truck.

He knew that sounded pretty lame, but he figured it was small potatoes compared to the importance of getting Jimmy T out of the way once and for all. After that the only thing he had to worry about was explaining his spit on George Lewis' window.

He wondered how he would ever do that, but forgot about it as soon as the temperature light on the dashboard came on.

With no coolant, and no fan, the engine in the truck was heating up quickly. After only another mile, Bud could see whatever traces of coolant that remained in the engine were coming out in puffs of steam. "Come on baby!" he said. "Just a couple more miles and I'll buy you a whole new power plant.

He knew if he could just make it to the top of the hill he could coast the nearly two miles to his workplace. He kept his fingers crossed, but the truck was losing power rapidly. He could just see the start of the hill as he came around a bend. Bud pressed his foot further and further to the floor, but the truck was going slower and slower. He looked up at the top of the hill. He didn't think he was going to make it.

He was right. He was no more than a quarter of the way up the hill when the engine died. Bud knew enough about mechanics to know that trying to start it again would be pointless. He knew the engine had heated up so badly that the oil just burned up, forcing the steel parts to expand until they got so tight they would no longer move. The engine in the truck was never going to run again, and Bud was still over two miles from work. It was just about five-thirty and there was nobody else on the road for hitching a ride.

Finally, he got out and started walking, then running. Running uphill was a killer and Bud was definitely out of shape, especially considering all the whiskey and hash smoke he'd ingested lately. After just a few minutes he was walking again.

He walked down the dark road in his bright pink jacket, looking like a firefly in heat.

*****

Toni gave Tommy a kiss as he left for work. It was early but he had plenty to do and decided that less than an hour of sleep wouldn't make much difference.

When he was gone, she filled the tub with piping hot water. She threw in a bunch of bath bubbles and settled in, letting the hot, perfumed water envelop her. She almost fell asleep a couple times, but she wanted to stay up. Part of the reason, she knew, was because she felt guilty seeing Tommy go to work with no sleep, but she also wanted to get over to the diner. She wanted to reopen it that week and had some work to do there.

After a while she turned the hot water tap on again. The diner could wait. It was going on six o'clock and bright rays of sunshine beamed their way through the bathroom window.

She settled back, running her hands over her thighs, then up across her belly. She felt her breasts for a moment and closed her eyes. She tried to relax and let her mind wander. She wasn't surprised to find herself thinking about George and Bud and everything else that had happened recently. Whenever that happened Toni invariably thought about the night she wound up in Bud Rogers' bed. She could never remember what happened, and it was frustrating.

She tried to picture everything in her mind, starting with her conversation with Tanya at the bar. That seemed more important recently, since Tanya had confessed to having a similar experience. Toni could remember herself driving up to the loop, driving down the other side of the hill, and then heading north on 98.

She remembered trying to turn, and trying to move her foot to the brake pedal, but she'd been unable to do either one. She thought about how terrified she was when she felt herself slowing down and turning into Bud's driveway. It was at that point Toni knew she couldn't remember anything that had happened until the next morning. It was also the point at which she usually got scared and quit thinking about it.

This time she forced herself to try and remember. She made herself remember walking towards Bud's house and going up to the front door. It had been like watching a scary movie only worse, she was helpless to stop it, or even to look away.

She lay there in the tub, concentrating on that front door. Her mind impulsively wanted to skip ahead to the next morning when she had awaken and fled. She made herself concentrate on the front door.

Perhaps it was the secure feeling of the hot bath, or maybe the lack of sleep, or maybe both, but suddenly, finally Toni's mind started seeing images. Not everything, but she could see herself at the foot of Bud's bed doing a striptease, and she could see herself looking down on him while she rode him furiously. She didn't remember everything that had happened, but for the first time, Toni remembered the unnatural feeling of whatever it was that had possessed her. It was a dirty, filthy feeling.

She sat up in the tub, her fearful eyes darted back and forth. Despite the hot bubbles and perfumed water, it suddenly felt cold and dirty. She hugged herself and looked around the bathroom, as if the thing she feared might be watching. Toni was scared and altogether certain that whatever it was that she was afraid of, it was beyond anything she could control. She felt like crying.

After a few minutes she realized she was shaking in the squalid water. She got out and dried herself off. Another thought occurred to her as she put on her fluffy bathrobe. She wondered if Bud had been under the same spell, or if he'd been the source of the mystery. Then she realized that it didn't matter. She had to make sure that nothing more happened, and she was sure Bud was the root of the problem. She wanted to get a hold of Tommy but the first thing was to be absolutely certain that Bud had gone into work.

She went into the living room and grabbed the phone directory. She was surprised to find that the number for the concrete company was the first one listed in the whole book.

*****

Tim Castillo was fit to be tied. He'd wanted to get an early start on filling the mine shaft and hoped all the drivers would cooperate. As he pushed the buttons that loaded the truck under the plant, he looked out the dispatch window across the yard. Steve Russer was standing near the back of his mixer trying to tell Tim something with a variety of hand signals.

Tim sent the delivery ticket for the truck he was loading down a PVC chute to the driver. After waiting for the truck to pull away so there would be less noise, he picked up the microphone that was connected to the outdoor PA system and said, "What's the problem, Steve?"

Steve jerked his head in the direction of the truck. He had a long, skinny neck and Tim was always afraid it was going snap like a twig. He often joked that if times were tough, Steve could get a job as a scarecrow.

Steve pointed his index finger horizontally and made a rotating motion. Then he took his other hand and made a slashing motion under his chin.

Tim finally figured it out. "It won't start?"

Steve nodded up and down and smiled. Tim ran his hands through his hair and let out a long sigh. Chris hadn't come in yet so he couldn't vent. He pointed to the truck Bud normally drove and spoke into the mike. "You might as well take number fourteen, it looks like wonder boy isn't coming in again today anyway."

Tim watched Steve follow his Adam's apple over to Bud's mixer and thought about how Mondays always sucked. The phone rang and he stopped just short of ripping its plug out of the wall. Picking up the receiver he said, "Good morning, Aardvark Concrete."

He squinted as he heard John Olikowski's voice. John had one section of floor left to pour in his new barn. They were scheduled to start delivering at nine o'clock.

"Yes, John. What can we do for you?"

"I need three tons of stone delivered in a mixer in order to bring the base under the floor up to grade. You send it up right away?"

Customers often ordered their stone in a mixer. The chute on the back of the truck pivoted and allowed the stones to be placed easily without having to use a wheelbarrow.

Tim couldn't believe it. Three tons of stone would fit on the back of the smallest dump truck, but John wanted him to tie up a mixer which he couldn't spare. He tried to buy some time by asking, "Can you hold off for about an hour?" Chris would be in then and he could run it up in old number one.

"No, no, no. I need it right away." John was excited. "We have to be ready to pour the rest of the floor at nine o'clock. You must send it right now."

Tim wanted to tell John it would be a miracle if he got his concrete at nine o'clock like he was supposed to, but he figured that would set him off even more. He thought about the nonexistent profit to be made by delivering a mere three tons of stone and tried a different angle. "Can you at least take a full fifteen tons so we don't have to send the truck up there almost empty. I'm sure you could stockpile it and use it someplace else at a -- "

"No, no, no. I need three tons of stone right now. Not fifteen, only three." John was getting wound up. Tim gave it one more shot.

"Come on John, give me a break. I'm shorthanded already and we're trying to get the mine shaft filled in today. Can you hold off for a half-hour at least?"

"No, no, no. What's the matter with you? I don't care about

any mine shaft. I buy thousands of dollars worth of concrete from your company every year. Maybe you'd rather have me buy it from that outfit over in Arcade. You're not the only company that sells concrete you know. I'll tell you what, I'll leave it up to you. If you don't give me three tons of stone in a mixer right away I'll start buying my concrete from them today. Okay?"

Tim saw himself reaching his hand through the phone, grabbing John by the neck and squeezing until his eyes popped out. But John had said the magic words. He was a steady customer, whereas the mine shaft was a one-time job. He considered the amount of money at stake and decided the mine shaft would have to wait.

"Okay, John," he said, giving in. "We'll be right there." He hung up before he said anything he'd regret.

Steve was just backing Bud's truck under the plant. Tim pushed the buttons that weighed up three tons of stone. He discharged it into the back of the truck, printed out the ticket and sent it down the chute. He picked up the microphone and said, "I gave you a hot one, Steve. I need you to haul ass and get back here ASAP."

Unlike a load of concrete, a load of stone has no cement dust to rinse off after loading so Steve pulled out from under the plant and headed straight for the road. Tim watched as he pulled away. He hoped either Bud or Chris would show up soon, preferably both. It wasn't even six o'clock yet and they were getting behind. Being a man short would only make things worse.

The phone rang again. Tim used his friendly, sugar coated voice. "Good morning, Aardvark Concrete."

He heard a young woman's voice ask, "Can you tell me if Bud Rogers is working today?"

"Well," he hesitated. He was about to say no when he saw Bud running into the yard from the far side of the road. He let out a sigh and said, "More or less. Can I give him a mes--"

The woman hung up.

Tim looked at the receiver, then cradled it and gazed out across the yard. Bud seemed confused. He'd been heading to where his truck usually parked, then realized it wasn't there. He finally noticed that Steve was driving it and stood there watching as he drove away.

Tim grabbed the microphone and said, "Congratulations loser. You get to drive good old number one today. And if you can manage to move your ass, I could stand to load you as soon as you're able."

CHAPTER 35

Bud was incredulous. As he watched Steve drive away he listened to the sound the mixer drum made as it rotated. Every type of load makes a different sound, and anybody who drove a mixer for a living could tell that Steve wasn't hauling a load of flowable fill. The fact that he drove away without having to wash any cement dust off told Bud it wasn't a load of concrete either. In fact, Bud was certain that Steve Russer had just driven off in his truck, number fourteen, with nothing more than a load of stone.

Worse yet, by listening as the stones rattled inside the drum, Bud concluded it wasn't even a full load. He told himself it would be okay, that wherever Steve was going they would just dump the stones into a hole in the ground and that would be the end of it.

That was just rationalization, however. Deep down Bud knew it was bad. He didn't move until he heard Tim on the PA system again.

"Are you going load up a truck or stand there all day with your thumb up your ass?"

Bud quickly kicked the tires and checked the oil on old number one. He started it up, amazed at how well the old rust bucket ran, and backed it under the plant. He revved the engine and pulled the lever that spun the drum so Tim could load the truck. Then he filled the water tank from a long, flexible hose that hung down above the mixer.

As he waited for the tank to fill, he listened to the sound of water and material going through the hopper and into the back of the truck. He knew even before the ticket came down the chute that he was going to the mine shaft. There was absolutely no sand or stone in his load, which meant he was getting a load of flowable fill. He wished Tim had loaded Steve with the same thing and wondered why he hadn't.

With an overwhelming feeling of alarm, Bud took number one over to the wash-down area and sprayed the excess cement dust off the hopper with his hose. He didn't spend much time on it, old number one wouldn't look much better even if it was clean.

He pulled out onto route 98 and headed north. The job was actually to the south, but there was a posted bridge on 98 that big trucks couldn't drive over. That meant that everybody had to go north, back over the big hill almost all the way to Attica, cut across Dunbar Rd. to Exchange St. and then head south again. *No wonder we're always running behind in this business,* he thought.

The truck grunted and groaned its way towards the big hill. Old number one ran well, but for all the noise the engine made it was gutless compared to the newer models. Bud hated the helpless feeling that accompanied the ineffectual whine of the diesel. He felt like he was trapped in one of those dreams where no matter how hard you try to do something it always seems just out of reach.

Another reason he was uncomfortable was because he just plain had a bad feeling about things.

*****

Chris came up the stairs and into the dispatch office just as Bud was pulling out from under the plant. He had on a pair of overalls because he knew they were busy and was expecting to help out.

Tim didn't even give him a chance to say good morning, he started right in, saying, "Steve's truck won't start and Bud was late again. Bud's driving number one for now. I had to send Steve up to John Olikowski's farm with a lousy fucking three tons of stone." Tim spread his arms, palms up. "I tried to talk to John, but you know how he is."

Chris shrugged his shoulders and said, "So where are we?"

"Bud's only the fourth load headed for the mine shaft. The first truck should be returning from there in about a half-hour so we can start the second round. Steve will likely be tied up for the better part of an hour so we're going to be way behind when it comes time to pour John's cow barn. Hopefully you can get Steve's truck running and take a load, that'll help out a little -- "

Chris held up a hand and hushed him. "I'll go out and get the truck started and get it loaded. But I need you to play salesman."

Tim frowned. His shoulders slumped like a kid who'd just been told he'd have to pay for a broken window. "Come on," he said. "You want me to go up there and talk to that old fart?"

Tim complained about his job constantly, but the fact was he was happy with its familiarity. He knew how to handle any situation that could arise while he was in the dispatch office. He'd gone out to see customers at Chris' request before, but he always felt uncomfortable doing it.

"I know," Chris said. "I wouldn't want to go either. But like you said, the first of the mine trucks won't be back for a while. I can load my own truck, but I really need you to go up and talk to John. He's too valuable a customer to lose." Then he smiled and said, "Come on, it'll only take you a minute to get up there."

Resignation spread across Tim's face. He knew Chris was right and finally said, "Okay." He grabbed his leather jacket and headed for the door.

The phone rang. Before Chris answered it he said to Tim, "Take him a dozen hats and smooth it over."

There was something about concrete customers and hats. You could get away with almost anything as long as you showed up with some hats or tee shirts. Especially pink hats with aardvarks on them.

Tim went down the stairs and got a box of hats from the

storage room. The plant was old and always smelled musty inside. He left the dreary confines of the building and breathed the cool, fresh morning air.

The short drive to John's farm gave Tim time to cool down. John wasn't a bad guy, he was just a little cantankerous, and when he got worked up it had a way of spreading to everyone around him.

The big white farmhouse was surrounded by a conglomeration of buildings – pole-barns, grain bins, corrugated steel structures and concrete bunk crop silos - that radiated out for over a quarter of a mile. Tim pulled into a new driveway at the outer edge of the complex and drove around to the back side of the new building. It was a one-story pole-barn, three hundred feet long and one hundred feet wide. There were carpenters, masons and electricians everywhere busying themselves with their respective trades.

He parked near the large door where Steve was backing his mixer inside, got out and squinted at the sun coming up over the horizon. He could smell the sweetness of the fresh lumber that made up the roof of the barn.

He climbed through an unfinished section of the wall. John was at the end of the building waving Steve back to a spot in the corner where they had yet to pour the floor. John wore tattered old denim clothes that made him look like a pauper, even though Tim knew he was anything but poor. On his feet he wore a pair of knee-high, black rubber boots that were caked with several layers of dried manure.

Tim looked at the recently poured sections of floor. He loved the beauty of virgin concrete, it always gave him a sense of pride knowing that his product looked so indestructible even though it was actually highly vulnerable. Once the cows started living in there the floor would never again have the same polished, unblemished look. Even the dirt tracks left by Steve's truck as it backed into the unfinished corner made Tim want to grab a broom and sweep it clean.

He had more important things to do, however. Because of

the noise of the truck John didn't hear Tim come up behind him. Tim tapped him on the shoulder. John jumped about a foot and spun around. Tim thought he was going to get a tongue lashing but then John spied the box of hats under his arm.

"Hello there," John said over the roar of the mixer. He stuck out his large hand to shake.

Tim shook hands and said, "How you doing John? It's been a while." He noticed that John's eyes never left the box of hats.

"Good, good. Yourself?"

"Fine thanks. I thought I'd stop in and give you a hand spreading these stones." He handed John the hats and said, "These are for you."

John took the box, smiled and nodded thanks. Then he let out an ear-piercing whistle and yelled to all the workers, "Get 'em while they're hot boys!"

The old trick had worked again. Tim looked around as construction workers scrambled from every direction to get their hands on a new hat.

John was going through the box, looking for the pick of the litter, so Tim walked over behind the mixer. He and Steve exchanged knowing glances and smiled. Tim grabbed a rake and waited for Steve to spill the stones out so he could level it off. The only thing better for schmoozing a customer than hats and tee shirts was free labor. Tim wasn't going to do a great deal of work, but the gesture would go a long way toward smoothing things out when he had to tell John they were going to be late with the concrete. He would rake some stones for a while and then approach John apologetically.

John was no fool, and he probably already knew why Tim was there, but he would make Tim go through all the motions just the same. It was an unspoken ritual that each man knew was just a part of doing business in the concrete industry. Suppliers were often late with their deliveries, but when they made an effort to show their customers they did indeed care, it usually made all the difference in the world.

Tim raked the silver-gray stones out evenly. He liked the way that crushed limestone was always perfectly uniform in size, shape and color.

He was thinking along those lines when he noticed something shiny just past the end of his rake. He stepped forward and bent down to pick it up.

Gold! he thought. *I've struck it rich.* Then he realized it was a gold tooth. He wondered how something like that could get into the back of a mixer. He looked around to see if there were any more. He didn't see any, but he did notice several objects that didn't fit in with the solid color of the stones. He picked up a round, white object that looked like a poker chip and studied it.

Steve Russer saw him and said in his powerful, low voice, "Got something?"

Stone bins being as large and exposed as they were, foreign objects were always coming out the backs of mixers. Things like dead pigeons, pieces of steel and strips of rubber from worn out conveyor belts were common.

"I hope it ain't a dead skunk again," Steve said. "Last time my truck stunk for a week."

Tim thought he was looking at a piece of bone. "It looks like a bone from some sort of animal," he said. He no sooner got that out when it hit him. *There's only one animal I know of that has gold teeth!* He let out an involuntary, high pitched scream.

Tim was suddenly aware of the underlying stench that forced its way through the ever present smell of manure. He looked down at the stones he was standing in and felt surrounded by the white pieces of bone. He dropped the rake and ran over to the edge of the new concrete slab, seeking its uniform safety, and jumped onto it as though the devil himself was nipping at his heels.

Steve looked at Tim like he was crazy. His head bobbed on its long neck and his mouth hung wide open as he asked, "What is it?"

Tim's reply was to throw up all over the smooth, virgin concrete.

*****

Old number one was making progress, but without much of a head start, it was pretty slow going up the big hill. Bud was down to low gear, barely moving. He was becoming a nervous wreck. It seemed like the slower he went, the more time he had to dwell on things.

After what seemed like forever, he finally saw the crest of the hill. He crawled along on the shoulder so he wouldn't hold up traffic behind him.

He was just coming to the flat part at the top, hoping to gain some speed for a change, when he heard an edgy, baritone voice on the radio.

"Truck forty-three, I mean, truck fourteen to dispatch."

That was Steve Russer. Bud felt his stomach tighten even more than usual. Rather than speeding up, he crept along at the same pace for a minute in case he was going to be sick.

"Go ahead," Bud heard his brother say. That seemed odd too, he should have heard Tim's voice.

"You want to call the police and have them send somebody up to the Olikowski farm?"

Mixer drivers, because they spent so much time on the road, were always calling in accidents and things. Most times their radios were faster than running to the nearest house. Bud thought maybe Steve was doing something similar. He clung to that one bit of hope anyway.

"Yeah, I'll send them right up," Chris said. "Has there been an accident? Do you need an ambulance or anything?"

"No ambulance." There was some hesitation, then Steve said, "But maybe they should . . . uh . . . send the coroner or something.

There was silence for a while. Bud's heart sank. He was almost sure he'd felt it stop. He stopped the truck on the side of the road.

Steve's voice came alive again. "I think we've got -- " He was struggling. "It looks like some parts of a person in the back of the truck."

There was more silence. Finally Chris said he'd send somebody right up. Bud stared at the steering wheel. His dreadful premonitions had come to a head. His mind whirled with a hundred thoughts at once. He sat on the side of the road, staring without seeing.

He wasn't sure how much time had passed, but finally he came out of his trance and was suddenly sure he had the answer. He grabbed his clipboard and a pen, turned the delivery ticket over and scrawled a note.

He threw the note, stuck to the stainless-steel clipboard, out the window. It landed on the pavement where Bud was sure it would be found. Then he made a three-point turn and pointed old number one back down the hill.

There were no second thoughts. Bud was sure he was doing the right thing, convinced even, although he was surprised to find his eyes gushing rivers of tears. He headed down the long hill, the fully loaded truck picking up speed rapidly. The speedometer was broken and he wondered how fast he was going. Then he realized he was in high gear but the engine was actually holding him back. He shifted into neutral to let the truck coast. Then he zeroed the nose of old number one in on it's target, the flat face of the old Erie Railroad bridge.

Bud aimed the truck right between THE and MASK. The four-foot letters reminded him of the numbers on the deck of an aircraft carrier. He grabbed the radio mike and said, "Good old number one coming in for a landing." His laughter mixed with tears in an eerie combination.

As he neared THE MASK, things seemed to go slower instead of faster. Bud found himself viewing scenes from his entire life as he rolled down the hill. Images from Bud's past burst into view with crystal clarity, only to be replaced by a new one just as quickly. There were no mysteries, no anxiety, no fear of the unknown. Every person Bud had ever met, every thing he'd ever done, was as easy to read as the words on a page.

All his questions were answered, including one that had been upsetting him regularly. Bud finally knew for sure that George Lewis hadn't done the things Jasper had accused him of. George was every bit as good a man as people remembered him to be. Jasper, on the other hand, was an evil, self-serving, wicked, lying entity whose benevolent ravings were nothing more than a smoke screen designed to bewilder his subjects and weaken their resistance.

During the last few seconds, before Bud crashed into the wall of solid concrete, he was slightly more conscious. He realized right up until the end that there was time to chicken out, but he had no desire to do so. He tried to picture the mess of twisted steel and dark gray pancake batter he was going to leave behind, and that made him laugh.

"Bud Rogers, meet 'THE MASK,'" he said just before the nose of the truck collided with the bridge.

As the front of the truck came to a sudden halt, as the frame bent and twisted itself upward, as the mixer drum's anchor bolts snapped, and as the steel drum and ten tons of slop came through the back of the cab, Bud was filled with an unabridged sense of relief.

CHAPTER 36

Tommy came home exhausted. He and Toni shared in a long, passionate hug, after which she started asking questions one right after another. She was unable to pause long enough to wait for any answers. Her disquietude had been building since she'd heard about Bud, and it poured over Tommy like a flood from a collapsed dam.

Tommy let her get it all out, listening quietly. When she settled down a little he produced a piece of paper from his shirt pocket. Since Bud's only apparent crime in Wyoming County was suicide, the sheriff's department had released his note to the officials from Genesee County to help with their investigation.

"Here," he said. "I brought this home for you to see."

Toni sat on the couch and read.

To all,

I am sorry. To help solve the riddle, it was me. I was the one who killed George Lewis, Jimmy T, and the escaped inmate. More specifically, it was the result of my deadly possession by a madman spirit named Jasper Shimmy-ack, but his horrendous deeds were carried out through me, and for that I am eternally sorry. I wish to apologize to Jimmy T's wife Dawn, Toni Birch, Tanya Lambert and anyone else I've harmed. Please believe me, I was powerless to stop.

I also need to clear the air in the case of Phil Waters. Phil Waters is totally innocent. It was I who planted the coke on his pickup. Please don't allow him to be prosecuted for this. He is innocent. As proof I can say that the package was attached to the frame of his truck with two black bungee cords underneath the passenger side door. In addition, there is an identical package buried in the mound of pig shit behind what used to be my barn. This package is identical to the one found on Phil's truck. He's a man who made regular trips across the border and he was being used without his knowledge. Please believe this, as I am about to give my life and have no reason to lie.

I'm sorry Chris, maybe I can do better in the next life.

To everyone, there are forces in this world which we can't explain. Do unto others as you would have them do unto you, and maybe you can avoid becoming as pitiful as myself.

I am sorry. Please sell my house and take the cash from my closet. Split it up between the girls and Phil Waters. I realize this is no consolation, but it is all I have, and I give it willingly.

I am truly sorry.

Jeffrey Rogers

Toni raised her eyebrows and looked up. "Who's Jasper Shimmy-ack?"

Tommy shrugged. "All we can find is a Jasper C-z-y-m-i-a-k, who was born in Buffalo in nineteen forty-nine. He's been listed as Missing In Action in Vietnam for almost twenty years, and has no known family."

Toni looked puzzled. "Could that be the same guy?"

Tommy shrugged again and said, "I don't know. There's a lot we don't know. Like what, exactly, is a deadly possession, or a madman spirit? Is that the Jasper guy? Is he a real person, or was Bud just insane, you know, hearing voices in his head?"

Toni got up, embraced Tommy and asked, "Do you think it's over?"

"Yeah," he finally said. "I guess so."

She remembered the evil force that had embodied her on that terrifying night at Bud's house. She locked her arms behind Tommy and buried her face in his shoulder.

They held each other for several minutes. After a while Toni whispered, "I hope so."

EPILOGUE

Memorial day weekend had left County Line deserted as most of its residents vacationed in the Adirondack mountains or the Finger Lakes region. The Silver Nickel only had a handful of patrons on Saturday evening.

Business at Jed's was slow so Toni had convinced Tanya to close up and meet her at the Nickel. They sat at the bar and talked about whatever came up. Their horrible encounter with Bud had drawn them together and the two were becoming close friends.

Behind them, Tommy played pool with Phil Waters. Phil had been cleared of all charges and released. Tommy had taken it upon himself to make sure Phil got back into the mainstream in order to see that the people of County Line still accepted him. Phil had been through a frightening experience and needed some encouragement to bring him out of his shell.

Behind the bar, Mindy helped Johnny Davis tune in a Toronto TV station that the local cable company didn't carry. Johnny wanted to watch the hockey playoffs so they struggled with an old set of rabbit ears, trying to get a good picture before the game started.

When the station finally came in the volume was too high and the end of a Toronto news broadcast caught everyone's attention. A middle aged woman with dark hair and a plastic smile was recapping the station's top story of the evening. They all turned their heads and kept quiet as the anchorwoman spoke:

"The third fatality in two weeks turned up in downtown Toronto this evening. Officials say the body of John Guy LeClair, of Scarborough, became the third victim in a rash of Yonge St. brutality. While authorities are reluctant to give details about the crimes, they will admit to startling similarities between the bodies of the victims. Many people are suggesting that it's the work of a serial killer."

"A spokesman for the Royal Canadian Mounted Police said an announcement will be made after a conference with local authorities. Residents and visitors are urged to stay away from poorly lit areas, as well as any areas of ill repute. It is generally accepted that all three victims were drug dealers."

After Johnny turned the volume down, Toni turned her attention back to Tanya and said, "Every time I see something like that on TV it always seems to affect me more than it used to. I mean, before, even though stuff like that happened every day, it seemed distant. It never used to happen so close to us. I don't like it, it makes me sick to my stomach."

"Don't talk about being sick," Tanya said. "When I woke up this morning I could hardly make it to the bathroom."

"Maybe you're pregnant." Toni wished she hadn't said that, but it was too late. She'd meant for it to be a joke, but the more she thought about it the more ominous it seemed. She worried about the fact that both of them had felt possessed by something when they had unknowingly had sex with Bud Rogers.

Tanya took it well. She reached out and touched Toni's hand as she said, "Oh honey, don't say that. I've got three monsters at home already."

They looked at each other and laughed.

ABOUT THE AUTHOR

M. K. Danielson

M. K. Danielson is a retired Operating Engineer who was born in Batavia, New York. He has lived most of his life in western New York near the boundary of the Genesee and Wyoming county line. In his retirement he loves to write, play a little music now and then, and also occasionally drive to places he's never been just to see what's on the other side of the hill.

Made in the USA
Thornton, CO
06/17/24 23:17:48

2461583c-45cf-420c-9f54-2d93283e44beR01